MW01230806

To My Boys...

Thank YOU FOR BEING MY DAILY *inspiration.*

MAY YOU *never* STOP WISHING ON *stars.*

AND ALWAYS *remember* THAT

I *love* YOU SO MUCH MORE

THAN TO THE *moon* AND BACK.

Stars

SUPER TO WISH ON,
TWINKLING AGAINST THE DARK SKY,
AMAZING BALLS OF GAS AND LIGHT,
REVEALING THE CONSTELLATIONS,
SHINING SO BRIGHT.

DAVY Z

Prologue

"WHATCHA DOIN'?" I hear a girl's voice and I glance over slightly without looking up at her. She's wearing purple sparkly flip flops and each one of her toenails is painted a different glittery color.

"Building a sand castle. What does it look like?" I wish she would go away and just leave me alone.

Dad is in one of his bad moods again this morning. As soon as I could get out of the house, I did. Ever since baby Matt came home from the hospital, dad has acted like a different person. He's been so mean to everyone.

Matt cried last night and instead of anyone going in to pick him up, my dad just yelled at him. This only made him cry more. Dad hates having his sleep disturbed. I know that I shouldn't have, but I snuck into his room, climbed into his crib, and curled up with him so he would go back to sleep. He's such a nice little baby. I don't know why they won't love on him more.

"Well, it doesn't look like much. Can I help?" she asks.

I stiffen a little. That was kind of mean and I didn't ask for her opinion.

"Why?" I can see her fidgeting with her fingers out of the corner of my eye.

"Because, I want to play with you," she says a little too enthusiastically for me.

"But why?"

"Because we just moved here and I want to be friends. Do you live here?" I can't help but wonder if she means temporarily or permanently. Most of the people who stay in these rental houses use the expressions, 'Move-in day' and 'Move-out day,' so what she just said about moving here can mean different things. That's the problem about living on the beach. No one ever stays. Drew and I make friends all the time, but six days later, they leave.

"Yeah, I live here. Down that dock footpath over there. Did you move here for the week or for good?" I take my bucket and fill it full with more sand.

"For good; we are here to stay. I got to meet my new teacher yesterday."

"Oh. Who's your teacher?"

"Mrs. Paggio." That must mean she's in Drew's grade. One year ahead of me.

"How old are you?" I ask her.

"Eight."

"Cool, me too," I tell her, still busying myself with the sand. "But, I'm only going into the second grade. Where did you move to?"

"A house down that street over there."

I glance as she points to the street next to mine. I guess it would be nice to make a friend who's not leaving, even if that friend is a girl.

"Why do you have those Ninja Turtles out here?"

"Because when I am done with the castle they are going to protect it," I answer, pouring a little water on top of the sand that's in the bucket and packing it down with my hands.

"From who?"

Geez, she asks a lot of questions.

"Enemy invaders, who else?" Doesn't this girl know anything?

"Where's the princess? Every castle has to have a princess." I can't help but laugh. I tip the bucket over to add a tower to the castle and the sand comes out perfectly.

"No they don't. Drew and I have never ever had a princess in any of our castles."

"Who's Drew?"

"My older brother," I say as she squats down next to me and starts digging a moat.

"Oh, I don't have any brothers or sisters. Do you like him?"

What a strange thing to ask, I think to myself. "Yes, I like him very much. He's the best."

"Well, I still think you should have a princess." This girl has to be out of her mind. There's no way I'm having a princess. I finally look over at her and I feel my breath catch in my throat. This girl has reddish colored pigtail braids and she's staring straight at me with the brightest blue eyes. She has a nice smile and light freckles all across her face. She is the prettiest girl I have ever seen.

I smile back at her and look away.

Even though I am only eight, I know that something big just happened. My chest suddenly feels funny and my heart is pounding really fast. Being just friends with her seems almost too simple. She instantly becomes so much more. I decide right then and there, as long as this girl is in my life, I am going to try to make her happy. Always.

"Okay . . . but you and only you get to be the princess," I say looking back at her. Her eyes grow wide and her smile

stretches even bigger.

"What's your name," she asks me?

"Beau, what's yours?"

"Leila."

BEAU

THE HALL IS dark and I run my fingertips down the wall as I
tiptoe toward my bedroom. I know I shouldn't have snuck out,
but I promised Leila that I would meet her, and over the last
six years I have never broken a promise to her.

When I reach my door, I notice it's closed. I don't remember closing the door, and I can't help but to think that he
did this on purpose. He knows I left and wasn't here. This is
his way of letting me know that he knows, and that he's listening for me.

Leila and I had made plans earlier in the day to meet and
ride our bikes down to Bean Point at midnight. In school we
were taught about the Quadrantids, the first meteor shower of
every year. Usually it can be seen near the Big Dipper. It starts
during the last week in December, and it ends sometime in the
middle of January.

Stupid me; forgot to leave the ladder outside of my room.

Moving it during the night to climb back in through my window would have made too much noise, so instead I went in and out of Drew's. He doesn't care that I sneak out; he just worries that I'll get caught.

Slowly, quietly, and very carefully, my shaking hand stills to turn the knob and open my bedroom door. *What if he is on the other side of the door just waiting for me?* Sweat breaks out across my forehead from the anxiety—and the fear of what might come.

Gritting my teeth, I crack the door, peek inside, and see that it's empty. A small sigh of relief escapes me and a drop of sweat rolls down the back of my neck. I don't want him to hear any clicks or squeaks so I push the door open just wide enough to slip by it, moving as slowly as possible.

Once in my room, I gently close the door, throw on my pajamas, and head straight for the closet.

The closet should be the safest place, I think to myself, and I hide behind the shirts hung on the bottom. Trying to get settled, I bump into the hangers and they scrape across the bar. Reality tells me that the noise wasn't loud, but every muscle has locked up, and an uncontrollable panic has taken over.

Did he hear me?

My hands clench into fists, my eyes squeeze shut, breathing is difficult, and every part of me is shaking.

Did I wake him?

My heart is pounding so wildly, it's beating all over my body. I feel it in my chest, in my stomach, in my fingers and toes, and in my ears. It's thumping so hard, it's drowning out the whistling of the white noise that is the night.

I need to calm down . . . I need to escape. Sitting on my hands—I go to that place—that place in my mind where everything that's around me shuts out and drifts away.

Star light, star bright, first star I see tonight, I wish I may, I wish I might, have this wish I wish tonight.

With my lips moving and nothing coming out, I repeat this in my mind over and over until my heart begins to slow.

My wish is always the same, and that's to be with her.

The summer that I met Leila was the summer I fell in love with the stars . . . and with her. Looking back, there's no doubt in my mind that's exactly what was happening, and I enjoyed every minute of it. Night after night, we would gaze up at the stars, yell out the childhood rhyme, and make up as many wishes as we could.

Opening my eyes, light peeks in from the crack of the door. I didn't close it all the way and the moonlight from the window illuminates the room.

Times passes, I'm not sure how much, but it doesn't matter. Fear keeps me tucked back into this corner. Wondering if I should just climb into my bed and go to sleep, I lean forward and peek through the crack of the closet door to look around the room and see if anything looks out of place. I glance toward the window and I'm surprised to see that the night sky is pitch-black. Other than the moon, it's a starless night.

Where are the stars? I need to see the stars!

The stars always make me feel better. Did they disappear? How did they disappear? They were there a little while ago. Bad things always happen on starless nights. Leila and I both commented just a little bit ago on how bright and how many there were.

My heart rate calms a little as I think of Leila. She is my bright star. She always sparkles and shines. I will never again be able to think about the stars and not think about her.

The tree outside of my window sways in the breeze, breaking the streaks of moonlight, causing shadows to be cast around the room.

I follow the light of the moon as it shines into one corner of my room. Sitting there is my mother. When did she get there? Why is she here? Why isn't she moving? My heart begins to race again, and I almost jump up to go to her. Something isn't right. Looking closer, her head is tilted backward a little and her eyes are open but she isn't blinking. Blood is running from her head, down the side of her face, dripping onto her shirt. I continue to stare at her, but she never moves. My whole body is back to shaking. Is she dead?

Something hits the wall out in the hallway and I gasp a little too loudly, while jerking back further into the closet, pulling my legs up and hiding my face in my knees.

He's coming! I know it.

The fear in me now lengthens its grasp, and its fingers slowly begin to slide their way up my legs, over my knees, down to my waist, and straight up my back to my neck. It squeezes and I can't breathe.

I woke him. He's coming for me; of this I am certain. I listen for the creaks in the wood floor, as it would adjust to accommodate his weight.

Time passes. Seconds, minutes, hours, I just don't know. I've lost the ability to think coherently. Focusing on what I might hear, I listen until there are no more creaks and no more sounds.

Instead, I smell the familiar heaviness of smoke. Lifting my head from my knees, I open my eyes and they instantly burn from the cloud that has filled my little closet. Panic fills me and I kick open the closet door, forgetting that I'm supposed to be quiet. Most people have that one thing that fills them with an irrational fear, and aside from my father, for me, it's fire.

The alarm bells in my head are screaming.

The house is on fire! I have to get out of here!

Jumping out of the closet, I gasp at the sight of my room. The flames completely surround my bed and the door. Fear of the fire causes me to freeze. I don't know where to look or what to do. My eyes are darting all around my room and that's when I see her. Leila is sitting in the middle of my bed.

When did she get here? How did she get here? Did she follow me home?

She is staring at me and fidgeting with her fingers, but she isn't moving. Why isn't she moving?

"Leila! You need to get out of here!" I yell at her.

Her eyes are swollen and red. She's been crying and I don't know why.

"Leila?" She isn't responding to me.

What do I do?

The heat from the flames is intensifying and it's like she doesn't even see them. The fire stretches throughout the room, and if I didn't know any better I would think that the walls were moving in on me. It's like they are closer, pushing in on me, wanting to suffocate me.

I don't understand! Something here isn't right.

Instantly, the flames around the bed grow larger and higher. I duck my face into my shoulder to not get burned. They are crackling, hissing, and slicing through the air. The heat from them is so overwhelming, my skin has started to burn and my heart beats erratically. On my arms, blisters are beginning to form, and tears burst from my eyes at the intense pain that they are causing.

In the background I hear a small cry. It's Matt's cry. Looking over to the corner where my mother is, she's no longer there. When did she leave the room? Was I still in the clos-

5

et? How did I not notice her leaving, and why didn't she take me with her? Why isn't she going after Matt? He's only seven. He shouldn't be in his room crying! *Where is everyone?*

I try to move but can't. The sheer terror that is ripping through me has left me completely immobile. My feet are stuck to the floor. I can't lift them no matter how hard I try.

What do I do? I try to come up with a plan on how we can escape, but all I can focus on is that we are going to burn to death. The tears running down my face feel cool next to the fire.

Matt's cries get louder and he starts yelling for someone to help him. I need to go to him, but if I do, what happens to Leila? Suddenly, I realize that I am being made to choose. I have to choose between saving her or him. My tears turn to sobs.

This isn't a punishment or torture. This is a life and death decision, one that will be on my hands and conscience forever.

The sootiness of the smoke has coated my nose and my mouth. I can't catch my breath, breathing becomes hard and shallow, and the dizziness sets in, distorting the room more than it already is.

Images of Matt flash before me on the smoke and play out like old home movies. He's running around on the beach chasing the seagulls, he's lying on the bed listening to me read about Greek mythology, and he's smiling at me when he sees the pair of binoculars that I gave him just as an everyday random gift. Matt never smiles, so that day, my heart swelled at his happiness.

"Beau . . . ," Leila says to me calmly. Through the flames surrounding the bed, my eyes snap and lock onto hers. Tears are now rolling down her face. "Go. Forget me."

"What? I don't want to go, Leila! I could never forget

you. Please! Wrap up in the blanket and get off of the bed. We have to get out of here!" I'm begging and pleading with her but she doesn't move.

From behind me I hear the bedroom door swing open. Relief floods through me because someone is here to save us— and then I hear him laugh.

It's this laugh that has become the focal point of all my nightmares and all my fears. It's evil, sinister, conniving, vengeful, and possessive. It affects every cell in my body. I know that when I hear this laugh, bad things and pain are to come. I think again about the starless night.

"Tsk tsk tsk, Beau. Did you really think that I was going to let you have her? You belong to me and you do what I say. She is a distraction and distractions must be removed and eliminated." I can't look at him, I just can't. Keeping my eyes on Leila, I see him walk through the fire and toward the bed. Why isn't he getting burned? Or is he and he just doesn't care? His purpose is me—that's why he's here.

Matt's cries are now loud and hysterical. He starts screaming from pain, not fear, and I know that the fire has reached him. My heart is slamming so hard in my chest that it hurts and my fingers are tingling.

"Matt..." I whisper out, glancing toward the door. More tears run down my face and my body feels like it is cracking and breaking from grief. I didn't save him. He is burning to death.

My father stops next to the bed, looks over to me and, with a vindictive smirk he says, "He was never wanted and won't be missed. He was a mistake and an unwelcome one at that. Don't you see? This fire was the perfect solution. I can get rid of so many, but don't worry . . . I'm keeping you." The laugh returns and Matt's cries stop.

I'm in such a state of shock that the vision before me moves in slow motion. My father whips out my tennis racket from behind his back, raises it over his head, and forcefully brings it down on Leila.

"NO!"

My hands shoot out in front of me, reaching for her, but my feet still won't move. Over and over, he beats her, and her piercing screams fill every tiny space in my head. I can think of nothing but her screaming and how I have failed her, too.

Dropping to the floor, I cover my ears and squeeze my eyes shut. He's killing her, and I'm not doing anything to stop him. Rocking back and forth, my head finally hits the floor. The heat, the smoke, the terror, the helplessness, the surrender, it has all consumed me.

They're all dying and it's all my fault. I've failed them . . .

"God, please take me too . . ."

BOOM!

Chapter Two

BEAU

A LOUD NOISE coming from the outside startles me awake. I'm on the floor next to the bed, completely tangled up in the sheets. Sitting up, I look around the room. Sweat covers me from head to toe and my eyes are swollen and blurry from tears. My heart is racing erratically. The smell of smoke lingers in my nose. I can still feel his eyes boring into me, and this fear causes my already nauseated stomach to turn over.

Stumbling out of the sheets, I rush to the bathroom and my stomach empties.

Of all the dreams that I have had over the years, this one is the worst. At least twice a month it makes an appearance, leaving me rocked for days. Sitting on the floor next to the toilet, I stretch my arm across the seat and lay my head down.

Listening to the sounds of the night, I try to clear my head of his laughter, the screaming, and Leila saying to forget her. With my eyes squeezed shut, my heart frowns. Leila's letter quickly flashes through my mind. I'll never understand why she thought I could ever forget her.

A garbage truck in the alley drops its dumpster and the noise breaks me from my thoughts. In the distance I can hear the beeping from delivery trucks as they back up to local retailers, and a few car horns blaring throughout the surrounding streets. I welcome the distractions.

Star light, star bright, first star I see tonight, I wish I may, I wish I might, have this wish I wish tonight.

I look up at the window. Shining in are the neon lights from the sign of the jazz bar across the street.

There are no stars.

That's right, I remind myself once again. I'm in my loft in New York City. He's not here. He's in jail and has been for the last fourteen months. Nothing is going to happen to me. There is no fire. I am safe, I am fine, and so are the people that I love.

Getting up off of the floor, I brace myself against the counter as I stare back at the reflection looking at me. I barely recognize myself anymore. Splashing water on my face, I try to rub away the exhaustion that seems to have permanently taken up residence under my eyes. I brush my teeth and look over at the clock; it's four forty-five. There is no way I'm going to be able to go back to sleep. I may as well just get up and get out.

I throw on a pair of gym shorts, a T-shirt, a Salt Life pullover, a pair of flip flops, and a baseball hat. I have plans this morning to get a few sets in with Nate, so I shove a change of clothes into a backpack along with my racket.

Looking across the open space of my loft that makes up the kitchen, dining room, and living room, I see that Matt is still curled up on the bed of the pull-out couch. I'm thankful that this morning's episode didn't wake him—it has in the past.

On the refrigerator there's a dry erase board. I leave him a quick note letting him know that I'll be back for lunch. Grabbing the brown leather-bound notebook off of my desk, along with my wallet, phone, and keys, I quietly sneak out of the loft.

A couple of days ago, I noticed a local coffee shop around the block. Surely it must open at five.

Locking my door, I skip down the five flights of steps to the front door of my brownstone walk-up. Outside, the air is slightly humid and today the mixture in the air is one of fresh bread and chocolate. Drew never understood why I picked this neighborhood to move into, but waking up every day to different delicious smells is just one of the reasons.

Greenwich Village to me feels like home. I know that I probably should live closer to campus, but hey, that's what the subway is for. I love the uniqueness of the stores, the many different foods from around the world, and the eclectic crowd of people that lives and moves through this neighborhood daily.

Leaving my mother in Florida was bittersweet, but for years I have wanted to escape that house, and now that I am here, I miss it. Well, I miss her. I can only imagine how much worse this feeling will be once Matt leaves.

School doesn't start until next month, but I decided to head on up here July first. My brother Drew is planning a birthday party out in the West Hamptons for himself and his girlfriend Ali. I know for a fact that both of them would get their feelings hurt and be hugely disappointed if I didn't come.

Stopping in front of the coffee shop, The Grind, it looks empty but the lights are on. I push through the door and a bell chimes, letting them know that I've walked in. I pick a large leather lounge chair by the front window and sit down. This place reminds me a lot of Aunt Ella's cafe back home, Beach-side Café, but this one definitely fits its location.

Looking around, one wall is covered with signed photographs of famous people who have been in the café, and the other is covered with what I assume are local paintings that are for sale.

Placing my notebook on the little table next to the chair, I lean forward, resting my elbows on my knees. That nightmare has been coming more frequently over the last couple of months and this time it has left me completely drained and more uncomfortable than usual. I should probably talk to someone about them. I know that they aren't normal, but if I do, I know that I'll have to relive so many moments that I'm trying to forget.

Pulling my hat down a little lower, I reach and rub the back of my neck, letting out a deep sigh.

LEILA

EVERY MORNING, AT ten minutes until five, I unlock the door and walk into the café. Most people say that they can't function in the morning until they have had their cup of coffee. For me, I don't feel fully awake until I take in a breath and smell the aroma that makes up this unique and friendly place. It's how I start my day and I love it.

Talk about being at the right place at the right time. One day, early last fall, I was walking home from school when I decided that today was the day for me to stop in and grab a latte. I had been passing by this little café for weeks and really, for no reason at all, I hadn't previously stopped by.

When I pushed through the door, heard the bell above me, and took one look around, I was spellbound.

I love my Aunt Ella's café back down in Florida on the island. It has a quaint charm that can only be found on the beach. The colors are calming, the furniture is shabby, and there is no way to completely remove the sand from the floor. It has its share of current regulars, but mostly it's filled daily with tourists and travelers from all over the world.

This little café here in the city seems to be the opposite. It is a neighborhood café and is most likely filled with more long-time loyal patrons than passersby. The overall décor is dark. It feels inviting and warm. The walls are brick, the tables are wood, and there is a heavy farm table- type countertop bar that runs down one side of the café, across the back, and up the other side. There are high back chairs strategically placed, as well as outlets for electronics.

Across the floor of the café, there are a few tables and then there are large leather lounge chairs set up for individuals or groups of customers. Heavy drapes pool on the floor next to the front windows, and across the back are chalkboard signs that list the menu and daily specials. The walls are stylishly decorated and I knew in that minute, I was in love.

I approached a woman at the counter in the back to order the latte and that's when I overheard her say that someone had just quit and now she would need to find a new opener. Without even thinking twice I said, "I'll do it." She paused mid-sentence, gave me a once-over, and told the person on the other end of the line that she would have to call them back.

"You want to open the café daily? Are you sure?" Her look was filled with skepticism.

"Yes, ma'am."

"Have you even worked in a café before?" I couldn't help the smile that split across my face.

"As a matter of fact I have. My aunt owns a café back in Florida, where I am from. I worked there for years."

"Hmmm. Are you a student?"

"Yes, over at Parson's." I could see the wheels turning in her head.

"The hours are weekdays, four fifty a.m. to ten a.m."

"How about nine thirty-five, so I can get to class on time, and then I can make it up on the weekends, if I'm needed."

She hesitated and gave me another once-over while making her decision. I rocked up on my toes in excitement.

"Well alright then, if it sounds good to you, it sounds good to me. Let's give this a shot." I couldn't believe that I had landed a job, just like that. I ordered the latte, and then spent the next four hours learning all about the café.

This morning, I had just unlocked the doors, started the coffee maker, and gone into the back to pull out some fresh muffins that were made the night before when I heard the bell sound over the door. Most mornings the crowd starts to wander in around five thirty, so I am a little surprised that someone is here so early.

I push through the saloon doors into the café and spot the customer sitting in one of the leather chairs up front by the window. My body reacts before my mind does and I freeze mid-step. My heart crashes into my chest, my hands start sweating, and I am certain that my eyes are playing a trick on me. There is no way that of all the cafés in the city, he would walk into mine. It's just not possible. But there he is, looking almost like I remember him.

Ali, my best friend, must have told him that I work here. I'm going to kill her.

Instead of walking over to greet him, I stare at him. It's been over a year since I've seen him and, all of a sudden, all that time diminishes and it feels like it was just yesterday. I didn't even know that he was here in the city. Ali never told me. I had just assumed that he would be coming up sometime later in July. I feel as if my world has just been thrown on a tilt. I wasn't prepared to see him.

The morning sun hasn't started to rise yet, so the windows behind him only serve as a dark backdrop, and the light shining down from above him has placed him in a spotlight-like glow. If I was a photographer, I feel that this could be a beautiful photo. As it is, I have just taken a mental picture and will now forever see him sitting in that chair.

If I didn't know any better, from where I am standing, I would say that he is bigger, taller. His legs are slightly stretched out in front of him and they seem so long. His arms and chest are broader and thicker, and his hair is a little on the long side as it curls out from underneath his baseball hat.

Every single part of me inside is screaming. It is screaming at me to go over and hug him, it is screaming at me to demand answers, and it is screaming at me to show him indifference and act as if he doesn't even matter.

The problem, though, with that last thought is . . . he does.

Ali had mentioned a while back ago that he was considering Columbia with Drew, but then she never mentioned it again.

In my mind I have imagined over and over that moment where we would see each other again. I imagined the things that I would say and the things that I would ask him. I would be strong and in control. I would let him know that he no longer has any pull over me, and that I am done. Only, in this little scenario, I never imagined the when and where. Now that it's here, that conversation feels all wrong.

Slowly, I make my way over to him. He doesn't look up at me. He's leaning forward and rubbing the back of his neck.

"What are you doing here?" Beau's hand stops moving on his neck and he pauses. Slowly, his head turns up, and his eyes lock onto mine.

"Leila . . . ," he says in a shocked whisper. He gracefully rises and I can see that he did, in fact, get taller. Neither one of us says anything. We just continue to stare at each other as if we are in a standoff. I can't help but notice the dark circles under his eyes. He looks so tired, almost like he hasn't been sleeping.

"Beau, what are you doing here?" I ask him again. I meant for this to come out a little more forcefully, but instead it sounded weak.

My emotions are all over the place. I'm nervous, I'm angry, and there are butterflies in my stomach. I feel calm for the first time in a long time, yet at the same time, I'm heartbroken. It's this last emotion that I focus on because he has done what no one else has ever done, and that is break my heart over and over again.

"I came in to get a cup of coffee. What are you doing here?" I can feel my eyebrows furrow. Maybe Ali didn't tell him and he didn't know that I work here.

"I work here." He runs his hand across his jaw, which is covered in light stubble. He looks so handsome.

"Why?" What does he mean why? And why does he look so stunned that I would work in a coffee shop? It's not that different from Aunt Ella's.

"Why else? I needed a job."

"Oh," he says, looking at me like he's confused. "Didn't you get a scholarship?"

How is this any of his business? "Yes, I did." Hopefully my tone lets him know that this conversation is closed.

My eyes drift down and I look him over again. I hate to admit this but, to me, he looks like home. This last year has been hard and I didn't realize how much I had been missing home until lately. I glance over at the side table and see his phone, keys, and a brown leather notebook. I instantly recognize the notebook, and he sees my reaction the minute that I do. Both of us reach for it. He gets there first and quickly picks it up, shoving it behind his back.

"Is that the notebook I bought you?"

Panic is written across his face. "Yeah, so?"

I can't believe that he kept this notebook. I gave it to him five and half years ago, right before my family moved away from the island. It was meant for him to write down all of his adventures to share with me, only he didn't, and we didn't talk again for almost three years.

"Can I hold it?"

"No," comes out almost immediately. His eyes harden, his lips pinch down into a thin line, and his jaw is locked tight.

"Why not?" It's not like I plan on reading it. I think I just want to feel it because it connects us to a time when we were happy.

"Because it's private."

"Like a journal?"

"Isn't that what you told me it was for?" He takes a step back, putting more distance between me and journal.

"No, actually; if I remember correctly, that is not what I told you it was for." Understanding flares in his eyes. I let out a deep sigh and drop my gaze to his waist, knowing that the journal is right behind his back. His chest is moving up and down rapidly like he's breathing really hard.

"Yeah, well, you didn't really give me a way to share things with you, now did you?" I can hear anger and sadness blended together in his tone.

"I can't believe that you kept it all of these years," I say as I look back up into his beautiful face.

"You gave it to me. Why wouldn't I keep it?" And this is it. Right here. That one sentence sums up my entire relationship with Beau Hale. It's been twelve years now and he's still sending me mixed signals. He's made so many comments like this one to me over the years, but then he's never wanted to be with me or really given me the time of day. I've never been enough for him.

"Whatever. You came in here. Did you want something?" I can't stand here and look at him anymore. Being reminded of years and years of rejection has me needing to get away from him.

"Coffee would be great. Any kind," he says quietly.

"Still like it bold, two sugars?" I hate that I know how he takes his coffee.

"Yep." His eyes travel up and down the length of me. I can tell by the look on his face that he isn't just looking at me; he is remembering me. I'd like to say that I wish I could forget him but that would be a lie. Most of the best memories that I've ever had include him. I've had enough and I walk off to the back. The coffee is behind the counter but I need a minute to collect myself.

My eyes fill with tears. Tears for a love that I've had for him for so long and tears for a love that has never been wanted or returned. I thought I was doing better. I thought I was getting over him. Nope. One glance from those beautiful hazel eyes and I am right back there again, being consumed by him.

Taking a deep breath, I pull myself together. I walk out of

the saloon doors and see that he hasn't sat back down. I'm try-ing my hardest not to look at him but I can feel him watching me. I grab a large coffee cup, pour in two packets of sugar, and fill it to the top. Time's up, I can't stall anymore. One by one, I place each foot in front of the other and walk back to him. He takes the cup from me but doesn't take a sip and doesn't sit down.

"How are you?" he asks me.

"Good. You?" It's not that I intended to keep my answer so short and brief; I just don't know what to say to him.

"I'm good." His eyes look away from me, he tucks the journal under his arm, and he shifts the coffee cup to his other hand as he says this to me. He's not telling me the truth. Reali-zation of this hurts a little because there used to be a time when he would never lie to me. He always told me the truth.

"I didn't realize that you had moved here already. Ali never mentioned anything."

"Oh, yeah, they don't know yet. I had planned on the middle of the month, but I just needed to get here and get set-tled. Matt drove up with me. He's staying for a few weeks and then will go home with my mom after Drew's beach house weekend."

"How is Matt?" I don't know Matt as well as I do Drew. Matt is so much younger than us. He doesn't talk a lot but eve-ry time I see him, he smiles at me. Beau and Drew have al-ways been very protective of him.

"He's exactly like a thirteen-year-old boy should be: hit-ting puberty, staring at girls, thinks he knows everything, and is full of attitude." Beau smiles a little and it makes my heart squeeze. "He's perfect."

The door pushes open and the tinkling of bell echoes through the café. I should turn to greet whoever it is but I can't take my eyes off of Beau. It's like we are locked in a staring contest that isn't really a contest. Our eyes are making up for lost time.

An arm slides around my waist, and the distinct smell of Charlie drifts up to my nose as he presses a kiss to my forehead. I lean into him.

Beau's eyes harden and leave mine. His whole body has stiffened as he watches every move and every touch Charlie makes. I know the moment that Charlie recognizes him because his hands squeeze me.

I am so glad that Charlie is here. I need some strength to be around Beau, and Charlie is just the person to give it to me.

I slide around in Charlie's arms so we are face to face. He looks down at me and my eyes grow really large. He chuckles. He knows.

"Good morning, sweetheart. Why didn't you wake me before you left? I would have come in with you."

Oh, my God, I know exactly how that sounded.

"I know, but we were up late and I wanted to let you sleep," I say quietly. Even though I know Beau can hear me. I feel like saying it any louder would be as if I was throwing it in his face.

"Yet here you are, looking just as beautiful as always." He smiles down at me and I can see genuine affection in his eyes. I offer a small smile, feeling his confidence and energy sink into me, and I think to myself . . . I can do this.

Chapter Three

BEAU

I HEARD SOMEONE walk over and approach me. I probably should look up to acknowledge them, but at the moment, I just don't care. My eyes are tired, my head is pounding, and I need a cup of coffee.

Of all the voices in the entire world, I never expected to hear hers. Having just heard her screams, for a second I think that I am still in bed and still dreaming.

Her voice has always been like a warm breeze to me; it blows over and calms me. Hearing it so soon after that nightmare, after it has been so long, literally makes me want to cry. I close my eyes for a brief second to freeze this moment.

Looking up and seeing her beautiful face, I think my body goes into shock.

For months I know that I have been somewhat sliding. This past year, being on the island without Drew, Ali, and Leila, was a lot harder than I thought it would be. Drew and I, although we were together daily, it was mostly just in passing and for years we kept to ourselves. It wasn't until a few months before he moved that we finally started talking again. And although, technically, Leila and I weren't together, I didn't realize how much not seeing her on a regular basis would cause me such anxiety.

Every time I see her, she reminds me how dull my world is. I continually move through life in the dark. Everything feels like it is in shades of grays, black, and white. Then she walks into my vision and it bursts with color.

This past year has treated her well and she is more beautiful than I ever imagined. Her hair is still the most amazing strawberry blonde and is long and full of curls. She is thin but toned, and not in a cardio kind of way, more like yoga. She isn't wearing any makeup, just a little lip gloss, and every part of me is reacting to her.

How is it possible that in a city this size, and of all the coffee shops out there, I walk into hers? I've never been one to believe in fate, but why is it that it seems like whenever I need someone the most, she suddenly appears?

I can feel her eyes scan over me and my heart flashes back to the last time that we were together. I never should have walked away from her that night, but I couldn't take her rejection one more time.

I see her spot my journal on the side table next to the chair, and suddenly everything drops into slow motion. She reaches for it and all I know is that I have to beat her to it. She cannot see this, much less open it. Honestly, I never even wanted her to know about it. I grab it quickly and shove it behind my back.

"Is that the notebook I bought you?" Curiosity and astonishment comes through in her voice.

"Yeah, so?"

"Can I hold it?" Not a chance in hell. I don't even want her looking at it. I know there is no way that she can read the contents with it closed and hidden, but just the thought of it scares the shit out of me.

"No." I probably said this a little more harshly than needed, but she needs to understand that there is no way I am going to let her touch it.

"Why not?"

"Because it's private." My fingers are squeezing it so tightly the skin is stretching across my knuckles.

"Like a journal?" Why can't she let this go?

"Isn't that what you told me it was for?" Needing more distance, I take a step back. It's not like I see her tackling me to get it. I just need her to stay away from it.

"No, actually; if I remember correctly, that is not what I told you it was for." The memory of us sitting on the bench down at the end of the dock on Bean Point hits me with such clarity that for a split second I feel pulled back in time.

Bean Point is our place. It is on the very tip of the island, and not a lot of people go there because the riptides and currents are too strong to get in the water. A wooden dock leads over the dunes, held together by sea oats, and down to the beach. Coastal Pines line the backdrop and, throughout the summer months, you will find dozens of undisturbed turtle nests. The beach is quiet, and to us, it is our secret getaway.

Leila's family moved away when we were fourteen. On

the last day that I saw her, we were sharing a bag of salt water taffy, laughing at some of the stupid things we had done together over the years, and that's when she pulls the journal out of her bag.

"So, I bought this for you. We've had years and years of adventures together and, well, I would still like to be a part of yours going forward. If you'll write them down and then share them with me, it'll be like I never left." I take the journal and look down at it. It's leather, light brown, and has a long leather strap that wraps around it to tie it shut. The thoughtfulness of her gift moves me so much that, without thinking, I lean over and kiss her.

It is my first kiss.

Our first kiss.

I know that I startled her, but she doesn't back away. Her lips are warm and her breath, as it fans across my face, smells sweet, just like the salt water taffy. Never wanting to forget this moment, I place my forehead against hers and close my eyes.

"Thank you, Leila. I promise to write in it as much as possible." She pulls back, and her crystal blues eyes sparkle at me with happiness.

I blink and the memory disappears. A fresh rush of anger and sadness sweeps over me.

"Yeah, well, you didn't really give me a way to share things with you, now did you?"

She's watching me and it is unnerving me.

24

"I can't believe that you kept it all of these years," she says quietly.

"You gave it to me. Why wouldn't I keep it?" She pauses and then abruptly ends the conversation and walks away.

I hate watching her walk away from me. It's such a familiar sight that I almost call out to her to stop, but I don't. Instead, I take another look around the café to see what has now become a part of Leila's life.

She slips into the back and I let out a sigh. I need a minute to gather myself.

I know that I should be doing something other than just standing here, but my mind is screaming at me.

What do I say to her? Does she want me to say anything at all? She's so close to where I live. Am I supposed to stop in and see her now? Does she even want me to stop in? It's been a year, we aren't even friends. We haven't been for a long time. Do I want to be friends with her? I know in the end, she will hurt me like she always does.

She comes out from the back, makes the coffee, and walks it over to me. She is so beautiful that even after all these years it still hurts to look at her. She takes my breath away. She hands me the cup and somehow I push through my nerves and attempt to talk to her. Her answers are short and then the spell of the moment is broken by the door opening.

I watch as a guy walks in and wraps his arms around Leila. I think a part of me dies. I knew that she most likely had a boyfriend. How could she not? She is so beautiful. But to have it so suddenly shoved in my face like this, I could throw up all over again.

She turns around in his arms to face him and I feel like a third wheel, an intruder.

I can see by the look on this guy's face that he deeply

25

cares for Leila. They proceed to have a conversation that doesn't include me and I hate every minute of it. I didn't need to know that they were up super late and that he spent the night. Someone may as well take a dull fork and repeatedly stab me in the heart because that is what this feels like.

"You know what, Leila, I'm just gonna take this to go," I say. I've had enough and can't stand here and witness them anymore. She spins back around to face me and my heart slams into my chest. Her crystal blue eyes are piercing and seem to be filled with an apology.

"Oh, you two know each other?" the guy says. He smiles real big at me, stepping out from behind her and extending his hand. "Hi, I'm Charlie."

Being polite, I shake his hand, when all I want to do is rip it off because it touches her. "Beau."

Leila doesn't say anything. She's just watching me.

"So, how do you two know each other?" he asks curiously. I look down at her and can see that she is waiting to hear my response. Her face flushes.

"We grew up together," I say without breaking eye contact with her.

"Really, well that's fantastic. Babe, you were just saying how you were missing home. It must be so nice to see a familiar face." Leila shoots him a look and he smirks at her. I don't understand the look but it does tell me that they aren't new friends. She's been with him for a while.

I need to get out of here.

Reaching into my bag, I pull out my wallet. Leila sees this and takes the cup of coffee back to the counter and pours it into a to-go cup.

"So do you live around here?" Charlie asks me. My eyes swing back to his.

"Uh, yeah, I live just around the corner." Without Leila standing in front of him, I'm able to get a good look at the guy. I would say that we are about the same height. He has really dark brown hair and dark brown eyes. He looks like what I would expect a New Yorker to look like; he even has the accent.

"How convenient," he says with a slight edge. "You'll get to drop in and see Leila regularly."

"Maybe." I can feel him trying to read me and I don't like it. Too many emotions are coursing through and I'll be damned if I let some guy I don't know pass judgment on me or feel threatened by me. Taking my wallet, I walk away from him and toward the counter. Leila sees the money and holds up her hand.

"Coffee's on me. It was nice to see you, Beau."

Nice to see you? That's all she has to say? Of course it is; an easy dismissal. She's got to save face in front of the boyfriend.

My hand shakes as I reach out for the coffee. She sees this and her brows furrow a little.

"Thanks, Leila." I turn, walk back to the chair, grab my things, nod at the guy, because he's given me no reason to be rude to him, and push out the front door.

I can't get out fast enough. The summer humidity slams into me and I take a deep breath. The door closes and I turn to the right to walk away. Squeezing the cup a little too tightly, it bends, and the hot coffee sloshes out. My heart was just ripped out of chest, and my stomach is in knots. There is no way I can drink this coffee. Not wanting it anymore, I drop it into the nearest garbage can and push forward. I'm not sure where I am headed; I just know I need to walk.

The sun has started to lighten the sky and more people

have crowded onto the sidewalks. Who knows where they are all going? I just need to be lost in them.

Seeing her again causes all these familiar emotions that I haven't felt in so long. This is the third time that she has unexpectedly appeared in my life. The first time was when we were eight, the second time when we were sixteen.

All around me things are happening: taxi cabs race down the street, horns blare, dogs are being walked, people laugh, buses whiz by. But as I focus on the pounding of my heart, all of it fades away.

After Leila and her family moved away from the island, I honestly never expected to see her again.

Grant and I were on the beach outside of the café, skimboarding, when Chase walks out and calls over to us. Grant skips off to him as I run after the board.

"Hey, Grant, you remember my cousin Leila, right?" Chase says behind me. My heart stops and I trip over the board. Please tell me that I didn't hear him say what I think he just said.

"Oh yeah! It's good to see you. Are you visiting or did you move back?"

"Moved back." My eyes slide shut. I feel wrecked and I haven't even done anything.

"That's awesome! Beau, you have to come over here and see who it is." I feel all three of them turn to look at me. Of course, Grant thinks that this is good news. I even understand why he would be excited by this . . . I never told him what she did before she moved.

Over and over during those two and a half years, I dreamt about what it would be like to see her again. What type of reunion we would have, or if I would even want one. It's interesting because once the devastation of her leaving wore off, the anger set in. But after so much time, the anger dulled and I seemed to remember so many of the good times. Knowing that she is finally near, the heartache she caused fuels an unexpected rage.

I take a deep breath, looking up and over at them. Grant is smiling and saying something to me but I can't hear him. My ears are thrumming from the blood that is rushing through them. Everything about this moment seems so surreal.

Time stops.

When we were kids, I always thought that she was pretty but, as I look at her now, pretty isn't the right word. She is beautiful. She matured in a way that makes her look classic and gorgeous. She is taller, leaner, and she has curves. Her face is thinner and she's lost what most people would call baby fat.

Pain slices through me. Her standing so close to me after all this time reminds me how much she hurt me.

"Hey, Beau." Her voice touches me. It feels like her fingers are brushing over my heart.

Looking at her, I feel like I am looking at me. For so many years we were inseparable, and all of my best memories include her. How she could have treated me the way that she did after all that time, I will never understand. What I do know though? I will never allow her or anyone else to hurt me like she did ever again.

It's that thought that causes me to narrow my eyes at her, turn, and walk away from them.

"Beau! Where are you going?" I hear Grant call after me. I don't really know where I am going, except that it has to be somewhere far away from her.

My eyes burn. I won't cry. I will never cry over her ever again.

Out of nowhere, Matt skips up next to me. His binoculars are hanging around his neck, so he must have seen me coming.

"What're you doing?" He never talks, so hearing the concern in his voice and seeing the way he's looking at me . . . he knows something is wrong. Then again, maybe it's the look on my face that gives it away.

"Walking."

"Why?" His little legs are trying to keep up.

"Leila's back." He stops walking, but I don't. I need to keep moving and I need to keep moving further away from her.

The sound of screeching tires from a city bus jerks me back into the present. Moving . . . that's what I did that day on the beach, and that's what I'm doing now. Block by block and street by street. With my hands shoved down into the pockets of my shorts, I stretch the distance between the café and me.

LEILA

I COULDN'T WAIT for my shift to end. My heart hasn't stopped racing for the last four hours and pouring coffee is very hard when your hands won't stop shaking.

He didn't know that I worked here. It was obvious once I calmed down from the shock of seeing him. He was just as surprised as I was. I will never understand why our paths continually cross. It's as if the stars have aligned in a way where they want to see how many times they can mess up my life.

Of course, Charlie recognized him, too. Not too long after we became friends, he was over at my apartment one night for dinner and, after two six-packs of wine coolers, he questioned my love life. I broke down, ugly tears and all, and told him why there has never been anyone; anyone else besides Beau, that is. I even pulled out the few pictures that I had of us and couldn't seem to part with.

Charlie told me I was wasting the best years of my life, and maybe I am, but as I watched him stare at the only framed photo of Beau that I have ever put out, I knew that my life couldn't be led differently.

I love that picture. It was taken at my high school graduation. Drew, Ali, and I were all posing together in cap and gown and, right before Drew's mom snapped the photo, Beau jumped in between Drew and me. His arms were wrapped around all three of us in a giant hug and we were laughing. It's such a carefree picture. He is beautiful.

Thinking about Beau, I find myself frowning. For so many years, I did such a great job ignoring him and blocking out all memories and emotions that were tied to him. If only I could remember how to do that now.

One by one, customers form a line at the café counter and I fill their orders. I'm moving on autopilot, staying continually lost in thought. It's seeing a flash of the color teal that takes me back to our little house on Magnolia Street. I'm sixteen years old and it's a warm sunny June afternoon.

My father grew up on Anna Maria Island and, after college, he and Aunt Ella's brother decided to join the military. Once his tour was up, he found himself back at MacDill Air Force Base in Tampa and, while stationed there, he met my mom.

Together they saved every penny they could and when I was eight years old, their dreams came true when they purchased our home on the island, on North Shore Drive. Six years later, our house burned down. My guess is that most will have forgotten why we left but as we pulled back onto the island after two and a half years away, my nerves set in.

Anna Maria Island and Long Boat Key, combined, have a population of around ten thousand residents. That makes us large enough to warrant having our own grocery stores and banks, but leaves us small enough that everyone knows everyone's business. Gossip has always been huge and, on a daily basis, some new tidbit would roll in with the morning tide, only to roll back out by the end of the day.

The plan was always to return. That's where our home, memories, family, and life were meant to be.

My parents talked endlessly about the day we would return and, last week, when they told me that today would be the day, a little part of me squealed with joy. I know that things between Beau and me aren't going to be the same, but just the thought of seeing him again fills me with happiness.

I don't have a lot of clothes, most of them I made, but I try on every dress that I have and settle on a teal one. My mother says it makes my eyes stand out. I'm not sure when the first time we will see each other again might be, but just in case, I need to look good. I also wouldn't be lying if I said that hopefully there will be just some small part of him that will see me and regret the way he ended things.

Seeing him on the beach with Grant, nerves and butterflies fill me up. He is so much taller than I remember, his hair is longer, and his body thinner. He's wearing a pair of board shorts, a sun shirt, and just for a moment, a smile. He laughs at something but I can't tear my eyes away from him to see what.

Chase calls out to them, but Grant is the only one to come over. When Beau finally turns around, faces me, and our eyes lock . . . I could have cried tears of joy. I missed him so desperately. In this moment I would have forgiven him for everything.

"Hey, Beau," I say to him. Seconds pass. He doesn't come any closer and he doesn't say anything in return.

I watch as the expression on his face shifts to one of anger. His look becomes menacing, right before he jerks around and walks away. Grant calls out after him but he never looks back.

Tears fill my eyes. So this is what it looks like to watch him walk away from me. In many ways, this is how he should have done it two and a half years ago. At least this way I can see it, versus being left with a few words and nothing else. After all, seeing is believing, right? Watching him, closure begins to wash over me. I will never understand what I did to him to make him treat me this way, but what I do know is that I deserve more. I deserve to be treated better.

After saying goodbye to Grant and Chase, I calmly walk back to the street until I am out of sight. It's then that I take off running, with tears streaming down my face. My feet in thin sandals pound on the hot pavement, taking me to the one and only place where I feel safe. I run down the dock, onto the sand, and circle back to sit under it, between the dunes in the shade. I don't want anyone to see me. I just need to hide.

I never had any expectations for what a reunion with him might be like, but I didn't think it would be like this. The way he looked at me was almost frightening. Not once in all the years that we were friends had he ever given me any type of look that screamed anger or disgust, like this one did.

Shaking, I pull my knees up into my chest, wrap my arms around them, and bury my face.

Moving away from the island had been the worst experience of my life.

Dad lost his job, so the plan had been to move into a smaller home on the mainland and rent ours out for a while. With the income from the tourists, we would have made triple the monthly mortgage amount, which would've allowed us to pay back the payments missed and leave us a little to live off of. But instead, our home somehow accidentally caught on fire and burned down. With the missed mortgage payments, the insurance company wasn't being paid either, and they denied the fire coverage and personal content coverage. Our home was defaulted to the bank.

We were officially homeless and broke. My family and I still ended up leaving the island, but due to the circumstances, we ended up leaving Florida, too.

And then, to top it all off . . . I lost Beau.

At some point I lift my head and peek through the boards of the dock. I am shocked to see Beau sitting by himself on the beach. His knees are drawn up, too, and he's staring at the water.

Should I go over to him? Should I try to talk to him? I have questions that I need answered. I want to know why. Adrenaline courses through me as I shift to move out from under the dock. Footsteps suddenly come from somewhere behind me and I freeze.

The dock creaks as someone walks toward me, over me, and then down to the beach. Peeking through the cracks again, I see that it is Drew.

"Hey, man, what are you doing?" Drew asks him, sitting down next to him.

"Nothing," Beau says, picking up the sand by his feet and letting it fall through his fingers. The tone of his voice has changed.

"Matt told me about Leila," he says.

"Matt has a big mouth." Anger seeps out in Beau's tone. My mouth and my heart frown.

"Seriously, though, tell me what you are thinking." Drew bumps Beau's shoulder.

"I'm thinking that I hate her!" he says with force and utter disdain.

The air in my lungs stops moving and I feel temporarily suffocated. *He hates me?* Why does he hate me? I could never hate him. Hearing him say this crushes me. My eyes squeeze shut and my hands fold into my chest. I bend over from the excruciating pain that's ripping through me.

After running down here to the Point, and hearing his

words, my whole body overheats and flushes. Tears are running down my face and sweat is trickling down my back. Any thoughts I had of confronting him just deflated. Sitting under here in the dirty sand, I know my dress is ruined and I look disgusting.

"You don't mean that," Drew says gently.

"Oh, yes I do!" Looking back through the crack, I see Beau throw down the rest of the sand and stand up. He starts pacing back and forth in front of Drew.

Drew watches him.

"I don't understand. Why? Why won't you tell me what happened?" Drew's voice is pleading and slightly animated.

Beau stops and stands in front of Drew. "Because! There's no point. I'd like to just forget it all and forget her," Beau yells, throwing his hands out to the side.

Hearing him talk about me this way, I gasp and throw my hands over my face, but not before the sound escapes.

Both Beau and Drew hear the noise and they look my way.

Not moving a muscle, I'm hoping that I am hidden enough that they can't spot me.

"Alright, whatever; we need to get back before Dad starts looking for us." Drew stands and returns his focus to Beau. The two brothers eye each other for a moment. A silent conversation is passing between them and I wish I knew what it was.

Beau lets out a sigh, "Okay. He's the last thing that I need to deal with today."

"I hear you." Drew pats Beau on the back.

Slowly, they come closer to me. I shrink into the furthest, shadiest part that I can and watch their feet as they pass over me. As soon as I can no longer hear the footsteps, tears once again pour out of my eyes. Although my sobs are silent, they are rocking through me. I am devastated. Over and over I repeat his words in my mind.

He said he hates me.

He said he wants to forget me.

I believed in us and I believed in him. How could he have been friends with me for so many years and then say things like that? But, then again, I remember this is what I asked for. My heart shatters and my soul feels lost.

What type of person treats someone that they supposedly care about this way? Maybe that's what I should have been asking myself all along, *did he ever really care about me?*

Conversations flood my mind as time passes and the sun lowers in the sky. I replay my last day here, from two and half years ago. I should have listened to what I was told and not been so hopeful. The truth has been staring me in the face the entire time and I have been hanging on to nothing and for no reason. I feel stupid and naïve.

Anger settles into the bottom of my stomach and slowly the tears stop.

I am not this girl.

I am not the girl who cries over a boy.

Somewhere, somehow, a cool peace slides over me, almost like ice. A wall around my heart builds and hardens.

I know that seeing him on a daily basis is probably going to have its setbacks, but it's in this moment that I decide that it's finally time to move on from Beau Hale.

BEAU

SWEAT DRIPS FROM my hair, over my forehead, and down the side of my face. I'm in the zone and nothing is going to pull me out of it.

I toss the ball high to serve and watch in slow motion as it flies over the net, and Nate responds. His feet are quick but mine are quicker. The muscles in my arms are tense. They're coiled so tight, just waiting to strike. Over and over the ball comes at me. Its speed has to be close to one hundred and fifty miles an hour and all I can think is the faster the better!

Tennis has always been my escape. My brother Drew swims and, over the last few years, I've noticed that Matt has picked up running but, for me . . . I need the impact to release the frustration, anger, and heartache that I am consumed with.

Dad was smart to put me in tennis. Although, I would not and will not ever hit a person, hitting a little yellow ball brings me great relief.

Nate hits the ball, returning the serve, and in slow motion it heads my way. Swinging the racket with as much power as I can, I connect with the ball. It's as if the harder I can hit it, the more tension it releases. I can't even count how many times I have imagined that the ball is my dad's face.

Boxing would probably also do the trick, but then I would be hitting with my fist, and just the thought of that makes my stomach roll.

"Come on, superstar! Is that all you've got?" Nate yells at me from across the net. He loves to try to taunt me, get me all riled up, but little does he know, this morning—my emotions are maxed out.

My eyes connect with him. I've completely lost focus of what he said, and the only word that sticks is *star*. My mind switches to Leila and I grit my teeth. I should have known that it doesn't matter how big the city is; I can't escape her.

Leila is everywhere. She's in my past, my dreams, my daily thoughts, and all over the world around me. When I see candy, bikes, strawberry blonde hair, park benches, a beach towel, glittery things, holiday decorations, just about anything, it somehow has a memory attached to her; and the very worst one . . . the stars.

We spent hours studying the stars, the constellations, different seasonal patterns, and the Greek mythology tied to each one. Night time was our secret time, and for six years, I spent almost every night lying outside with her, telling stories and sharing dreams.

The nights without her have been the hardest. At least now, by living in the city, the glow from the buildings' lights drown out and blur the darkened sky, removing any possibility of seeing them, and for that I am thankful. Regardless, I still find myself looking up, and with the stars gone, it is a reminder that she is, too.

Nate and I continue to play through the sets. I should be focusing on the game but I'm just going through the motions and running through memories of her. This is what happens when I see her, smell her, touch her . . . the memories come flooding in and I'm trapped, remembering a different life. A life that I wanted and now don't have.

When we were kids, after school she would come and watch me practice. Once I started competing, she would sit in the top row behind whatever bench I was placed at and cheer me on. When she moved, I found myself still looking for her in the stands, even though I knew she wouldn't be there. And once she returned, every match I played, I always looked for her just hoping one day she might show.

"Hale, get over here!" Coach's voice echoes across the courts and snaps me out of my reverie. Playing on autopilot, I have no idea how much time has passed.

Walking to the benches, I pick up my towel to wipe my face. Coach is standing near the entrance to the locker rooms and his hands are on his hips. His lips are tightened into a thin line and panic rips through me.

It doesn't matter that we are the same size and I am technically an adult. Will I ever be able to shake the fear that a middle-aged man causes me?

I'm nervous. He sees it and frowns. "Yeah, Coach?"

"What the hell has gotten into you today?" He waves his hand toward the courts.

"Sir, what do you mean?"

"Kid, you are on fire. Keep this up and you could go all the way."

Even though Dad has been in jail and gone for over a year, I still expect the worst. After ten years of emotional abuse, being told how awful and worthless I am, his compliment catches me off guard. "Thank you, sir."

"Same time tomorrow, kid. I'll be expecting a repeat performance." Coach pats me on the shoulder and wanders down the tunnel to head to the offices.

Nate skips up next to me and eyes me with uncertainty. My brows furrow. Why is he looking at me like that?

Nate and I met my first day here on the courts. I had called the coach to let him know that I had arrived early, and he had me paired with him in the sports complex at seven the next morning.

The match was grueling and just what I needed. Instantly we became friends.

Nate was born and raised in the Bronx. He knows all there is about the city, and has spent the last couple of weeks playing tour guide to Matt and me.

"So, what's her name?" he smirks at me.

"What do you mean?" I break eye contact to walk back and grab my things.

"I've been slapping the ball around with you for three weeks and not once have you played like you did today. So, I ask again, what's her name?"

Running my hand through my hair, I contemplate how much I should tell him. He doesn't know her, and sometimes I think that it might be nice to talk about her with someone who is completely uninvolved with our circle of friends.

"Leila," I let out with a sigh.

"Ah, what did she do this time?" He smiles at me knowingly, only he *really* has no idea.

"What you should be asking is what hasn't she done," my tone lets him know that I am completely displeased.

He chuckles. "I didn't think that you had a girlfriend."

41

"I don't." Walking away from him, I'm hoping that he'll end the questioning.

He continues to look at me though; I can feel his eyes boring into the back of me. "Huh."

"It's nothing. Just some girl from my past." If only that was true; more like past, present, and every second in between.

"Doesn't seem like the past after the way you played today."

"Well, she's in the past and I met her new boyfriend today."

The thought of Leila with a boyfriend makes my stomach ache. My father's voice comes crashing through my mind.

No one will ever want you. Even that little girlfriend of yours left you, she didn't want you either. When are you going to learn and how many times do I have to tell you, you are nothing special and no one will ever love you.

For the most part, I've convinced myself that he was wrong, but seeing them together this morning instantly made me remember how I felt when I was fourteen and she moved away. I believed him then. After all, if my father couldn't even love me, why would she?

Nate grabs my arm, pulling me from that depressing thought, to get me to stop walking. "Hold up, she lives here in the city?"

"Yep, goes to Parson's."

"Huh."

"You've said that twice now."

"All you've ever talked about is your brother and his girl. Not once have you mentioned a *Leila*. I'm just wondering how we get this girl to come around more often, especially after today."

"We're not friends." I was wrong. It would not be nice to

talk about her to someone. The way he said her name, in a curious, yet mocking tone, it makes my stomach continue to ache. He doesn't understand the history between us and never will. Having her around would make me nervous.

"Really?"

"Really." My tone lets him know that I am done with this conversation.

His eyes narrow one more time and then he shrugs.

"Well alright then. Let's get cleaned up, pick up Matt, and go grab lunch."

"Lunch sounds good. Matt will be excited to see you."

He grins at me.

"What's the plan for tonight?"

"Don't laugh, but Matt's kind of got this thing for running. He found a 5k dash that runs through Central Park at night. I told him I'd run with him. Kid's pretty fast. You should join us if you think you can keep up."

Nate laughs. "Just because you can kick my ass on the courts doesn't mean you'll beat me in a foot race. Challenge on!"

"It's not me you need to worry about." I slap him on the back.

"Oh, this is going to be good. You're little bro is awesome. I'm going to be sad to see him go."

"Yeah, he is awesome, and me too."

"Oh hey! Did you know that female kangaroos have three vaginas?"

The comment is so unexpected that I throw my head back and bust out laughing. "What are you talking about?"

"Well, I hear you spouting off all these random things all the time, so I thought I would share one that I know." Nate smiles at me.

"That's interesting and gross at the same time. Why am I not surprised that the fact you memorized revolves around female anatomy?"

"What can I say? On the subject matter, I'm pretty much an expert."

"The only part of that statement I'm going to agree with is *whatever you say*. Did you know that cold showers are healthier for you than hot ones?"

He grins back at me.

Walking in to the locker room, Nate punches me on the arm and we part ways to get cleaned up. Standing under the shower, all I can think about is how I told him that Leila and I aren't friends. This actually physically hurts me and it also reminds me of the look on her face the first time I told her she wasn't my friend. I'll never forget that look.

Following the encounter Leila and I had on the beach, I avoid her every time I see her, regardless of whether it's on the beach, at the café, at a party, or once school started. I act like she doesn't even exist, but she does.

Every morning I look for her. I tell myself that I'm not going to, but then I do. It's as if my brain goes on autopilot and, no matter how many pep talks I give myself, the minute I pull into the school parking lot, I look for her.

On this particular day in October, the warning bell rings for Homeroom as Drew, our friends, and I head for the front door. I immediately spot Leila walking from the other direction. Her head is down and she doesn't look as collected as she usually does. Something is wrong with her.

Throughout the day I see her, and each time she looks worse than the time before. I know that I shouldn't, but seeing her this way, looking so distressed, makes me feel very uneasy.

Coming out of the guys' locker room, I see her ahead of me in the hallway. Her posture hasn't changed all day. Walking faster, I catch up to her and wrap my arm around her shoulders, pulling her close to me. She cringes, but just a little, and my side unexpectedly heats up from the contact. Quickly and silently I steer her into the school's darkroom, close the door, and lock it.

"What's wrong with you today?" I ask her as I fold my arms over my chest and lean against the counter. She's watching me very closely. Her eyes are swollen, with dark rings underneath them.

"I've been back now for five months and you haven't spoken to me one time. Why should I tell you anything?" She's angry and she's right. I wasn't thinking. I just reacted when I saw her in the hallway. Not once in this little move did I remember that I haven't talked to her for almost three years. Anger and embarrassment hit me at the same time. I should walk out but, seeing her eyes fill with tears, I just can't.

I don't say anything back to her. There's nothing to say. Her eyes leave mine and the tears roll down her face.

Emotions of the heart are a funny thing. It doesn't matter how badly she has hurt me; seeing her like this crushes me and causes me to temporarily forget everything.

I gently pull her to me and she steps between my legs. Both of my hands wrap around her head as I tilt her face so she'll look at me. Her crystal blue eyes are so clear, watery, *and beautiful*. Using my thumbs, I wipe away some of her tears.

My heart is pounding in my chest. Being this close to her, touching her, makes me feel weak in the knees. I hate this physical reaction to her and want to grit my teeth.

For a split second my eyes leave hers and drop down to her mouth. Her lips are parted and look so inviting. No, clearing that thought, my eyes travel over her face and back to her eyes.

Watching me warily, slowly she leans forward and lays her head on my chest. I wrap my arms around her and memorize how it feels to hold this Leila, the sixteen-year-old Leila, who has curves, is gorgeous, and no longer mine.

"You are so much taller," she says quietly.

Silence lingers in the air between us. I'm afraid to move, breathe, or talk, because even though we are here for her, no matter how much I hate to admit it . . . I need this too.

"My grandmother died," her voice catches on the last word, and my chest instantly aches.

I tighten my hold. I'm not ready for her to pull back.

"I didn't know that you were close to her." I don't ever remember her talking about any other relatives besides Aunt Ella and her cousin Chase.

"I wasn't until we moved to Atlanta."

Atlanta.

"That's where you were, in Atlanta?"

She hears the tone shift in my voice and stiffens.

"Yes, we moved in with her."

"Why?"

"Because we had nowhere else to go."

For some reason, it never occurred to me that they didn't have another home to go to. The plan prior to the fire was to move over to the mainland. I had just assumed that's where she was. All this time, I thought she was somewhat close when she wasn't.

"Oh. Well it's nice that you got to spend some time with her."

"I did. She was a wonderful woman. She taught me how to sew and we spent hours and hours together looking at fabrics and patterns."

"That's cool, I guess. What did you make? Like blankets and pillows or stuff?"

She sighs, "No, clothes." Her hands slide down my chest and she lightly grabs my waist. Having her hands on me almost makes me incoherent.

"For who?"

"Me. I outgrew all of mine and we couldn't afford any more. My grandmother always loved sewing, but her hands became too shaky over the years and eventually she had to give it up. I was lucky because she had kept everything and had an entire room filled with beautiful leftover fabrics."

She couldn't afford any more? I don't know what to say so I don't say anything. It's strange because, in so many ways, I know this girl, everything about her, but then she says stuff like this and I wonder, how well do I know her now?

"Beau, why are you not talking to me? You have to know how much this hurts my feelings."

Her words shake me from the 'what ifs' running through my head, reality slams into me, and I recoil from her. I instantly let her go, push her away from me, and look down at her face.

She flinches at the change in my body language and the expression on my face.

"Hurt *your* feelings? Leila, you were the one who cut me off and told me that you were going to forget me. I will never

47

forget that and you will never know what you did to *me*."

"I'm sorry, I thought it was for the best."

"For the best?! Best for who? No, you aren't sorry or you wouldn't have done it. Did you honestly think that, after everything that happened, you could move back here and I would welcome you with open arms? No way. You and I are no more and you made sure of that."

She was already pale before, but the little color she did have drains away. She looks a little confused, but then a piece of her hair falls over her face and her eyes once again fill with tears.

Just seeing her like this is breaking my heart and I need to get out of this room and away from her.

"Listen, I'm so sorry to hear about your grandmother and for your loss. We may not be friends anymore but that doesn't mean that I don't still care about you."

"So, that's it? We aren't friends anymore?"

"No." I wanted it to sound more firm, but it came out almost like a whisper instead.

She flinches and takes another step back from me as more tears roll down her face. By the way she just pulled away and folds into herself, I know that I made her day worse and now I feel like the biggest jerk in the world. I shouldn't, though; she's the one who sealed our fate, not me.

"Okay, Beau." Defeated is the only word to describe the way she sounds.

LEILA

THE DOORMAN CHECKS his list, sees that I'm on it for Ali, and lets me pass. I pound on the elevator button to her floor, willing it to move faster.

It finally dings open. I sprint down the hallway to her apartment, and bang on the door.

Ali opens it. Shock and alarm are on her face.

"I can't believe you didn't tell me!" I yell at her.

"Tell you what?" She sees how upset I am.

"That Beau is already here." I push past her and walk into the living room, throwing myself onto the couch.

"No he isn't," she says as she follows behind me.

"Oh, wow, so you really didn't know? Well, he is! He came into the café this morning and I felt ambushed. I wasn't ready to see him and I certainly wasn't ready to talk to him after all of this time."

"I didn't know he was here. How does he know where you work?" Ali doesn't sit. She just stares down at me.

"He didn't. It was completely random and right after I opened the door."

"At five in the morning?"

"Yep, and he looked terrible too." Worry lines slowly crease Ali's face.

"Explain that to me," she says as she starts pacing back and forth in front of the couch.

"I don't know; he just didn't look like himself. His usual spark was gone. He looked tired and stressed."

"Maybe he is. I wonder why he didn't tell us he was

49

here." Ali walks over to the window and looks out, although I doubt she is actually looking at anything.

"Matt came with him and he said that he just wanted to get settled in." The hurt on her face is evident and now I feel bad. Here I had been thinking that she was keeping this from me, when really he was keeping this from all of us; not that he would ever tell me but I would have liked to know that he was in town.

"I wonder if Drew knows," she says, more to herself than me.

"Wouldn't he have told you? I got the impression from Beau that he hasn't told anyone. Charlie came in and met him."

She turns back to me and her face is lit up with interest. "How did that go?"

"Of course, Charlie acted like he didn't know who he was, but he did. It was awkward."

"Poor Beau." The worry lines are back.

"What do you mean, poor Beau? Did you forget . . . he is the one who left me?" I can't sit still anymore so I get up and start pacing around the room too.

"I still don't understand why you never asked him why he left."

"Because it doesn't matter." Ali's watching me closely. It does matter. I know this and so does she.

"Come on, I'm going to make you a margarita."

Sitting outside on her little balcony, my heart races. Ali left to take a phone call from her father and now here I sit staring out at the skyline of New York City. This city always seemed so big to me, but now that I know he's here, it feels so small.

Taking a sip of the margarita, I think back to the one and

only time I have ever been drunk.

Grant, a friend of Beau's, is throwing one of his infamous parties and this one is to celebrate the end of the school year. It is the beginning of the summer before my senior year, almost to the day of my return, one year prior.

I don't really want to go to the party, but Chase, my cousin, convinced me that it would be fun. And it is, until about half way through the evening. Every school has that one group of guys and one group of girls, that no matter what, they sit at the top. Of course Beau, Drew, and their friends are those guys; but the girls are Cassidy, Lisa, and their friends.

They are all sitting together and laughing and, as the minutes tick by, Lisa gets closer and closer to Beau. There are always rumors about Beau and Drew with some girl or another, but this is the first time that I am seeing it up close and personal. The margaritas, which are the drink of the evening, are going down a little too easily.

At some point in the evening, I wander inside to go to the bathroom. The door isn't closed all the way so I push it open, only to find Lisa sitting on the counter with her legs and arms wrapped around Beau.

They didn't hear the door open and the way they are kissing breaks every piece of my heart. A noise escapes me, both of them jerk their heads my way, and Beau's eyes lock with mine. I'm certain that I look like a deer in headlights but I am frozen and can't move.

Beau doesn't say anything; he just stares at me.

Beside him, Lisa starts snapping her fingers. "Earth to Leila," she drawls in a sarcastic tone.

My eyes skip to her.

"We're kind of busy here. Can you leave?" Distaste drips from her words.

My eyes jump back to Beau's. My chin trembles. Tears fill my eyes and his brows furrow.

Why?

Why did I have to see this? Maybe this is what I needed, the final nail in the coffin to make me move past him, this— this feeling of hope I carry around for him. All this time, all these years, there really has been no point.

"Sorry." That's all I can get out. One tear falls and Beau's breathing picks up. I can't tell if he looks angry or concerned. It doesn't matter, not any more. I slowly back out of the bathroom. His eyes never leave mine. As I'm closing the door, I hear Lisa call me a freak.

My sudden need to go to the bathroom has left me and I wander back out to the party. I need Chase to take me home but I can't find him. Wandering over to the bar, I pick up two more drinks and take them down to the end of the dock.

There are people everywhere but I just don't care. Before I moved, Beau was my only real friend. I spent all of my time with him and, since I've been back, it's been hard to make new ones.

I wanted to move back here so badly to see him, be near him, just anything that had to do with him but, seeing him to-night, I wish I never had. Throughout this entire year, no matter how hard I tried, I couldn't shake him. He's ignored me, laughed at me and, once again, he's hurt me. And what upsets me the most is that he just doesn't care.

Finishing the first drink, I set the cup down and press the

heels of my hands to my eyes. Everything has started to feel numb and I'm glad. I just want to go home.

"Leila."

I freeze at the sound of his voice. He's behind me. I can feel my heart rate pick up. Saying nothing, I bring the second drink to my lips and then throw my head back to swallow every last drop.

"Leila, why don't you let me take you home?" he says quietly.

Is he joking? Why on earth is he offering this? And, I'm pretty certain that what I saw a few minutes ago meant he is too busy to have to deal with me. Or maybe they've finished; the thought sickens me and breaks me further.

"What makes you think I would go anywhere with you?" I don't look at him. I just continue to stare out across the water, wishing my cup was still full.

"Chase left," he says.

What? My head whips around and my eyes dart up to his. "What do you mean he left?!" Beau's eyes travel over my face and I feel heat spread through my cheeks. His gaze switches to one of pity. He doesn't get to feel that way about me.

"He couldn't find you and told Grant so you would know to get a ride home."

Fury burns in my veins. I'm going to kill Chase. I didn't even want to come to this stupid party in the first place. Mixtures of emotions flip through me; anger, humiliation, sadness, and loneliness.

All of the fight that I have left in me vanishes. I don't know who to ask, and I really don't want to walk home. "Fine, but I want to go now."

"Okay."

Very ungracefully I stand up. Now that I'm moving, I realize these drinks have affected me more than I initially thought. Walking towards Beau, I stumble, and he reaches out to catch me. For a split second, his hands on me calm me, but then I smell Lisa's perfume.

"Don't touch me," I say in a low tone.

He pulls his hands back like I have stung him and has the audacity to look upset.

Together we walk back up the dock and through the party. The music is too loud and the lights are now too bright. My head hurts. My stomach aches. My heart is broken. I can't get home fast enough.

We are silent for most of the ride. I look over at him discreetly and try to memorize every detail of him; his profile, his hand on the steering wheel, the way his jeans fit his thighs. I've never been in a car with him before, where he is driving. How I wish this spot in the passenger seat was mine, but I know it's not and never will be. The thought of Lisa sitting here causes my stomach to clench. I roll down the window so the fresh air can hit my face.

Beau pulls up in front of my little house and puts the car in park. I don't even know how he knows where I live; I've certainly never told him.

He turns and focuses on me. My entire body blushes, and the space in the Tahoe suddenly feels like it's shrinking. I continue to look out the window at my tiny home.

"I'm sorry if what you saw tonight hurt you," he says into the quiet space between us.

Hurt me? He has no idea how much he has hurt me. Using every bit of self-control and strength that I have, I turn to face him.

"You didn't hurt me. You can't hurt me. I stopped allowing that three and half years ago on the day I moved. You lost your right to hurt me." I had been hoping this would have come out more firm and assertive, but it didn't and, knowing him, he probably saw right through my words.

His nostrils flare and his eyes narrow as he lets out a deep sigh, "Whatever you say, Leila."

"Whatever I say?" I repeat. He hears the tone in my voice but doesn't acknowledge it.

A moment of silence passes and neither one of us breaks eye contact. The tension is so thick that the air around us is heating up.

My hands shake as I go to open the door before his warm hand grabs me by the arm, stopping me from climbing out of the Tahoe.

"Leila, I really am sorry you saw that." The look of pity has returned and the air instantly chills.

"Stop saying that to me! You aren't sorry at all! You stopped giving a shit about me a long time ago." His eyes widen and the tears that had been swimming in my eyes spill over. "You never used to lie to me, Beau, so don't start now." I jerk my arm away from his hand but continue to sit there, looking out the windshield.

Part of me knows this is it. We are at an impasse. It's now or never. I should get out, walk away, and keep my mouth shut, but those margaritas either made me super brave, or really stupid.

"Oh, God, Beau, why do I still feel like this? When will all of this go away?" I look up at him and forcefully pat my chest directly over my heart. "Why did you ever become my friend? Why did you call me your best friend, when I really wasn't? Why did you kiss me that day on the bench? I could have given that moment to someone who would have cherished it and me. Why?" My tears still drop.

Beau's face is blank. He's watching me but giving nothing away.

My hands clench into fists and drop to my lap. "I just . . . don't you get it? I know exactly what it feels like to have nothing, and no one. Why? Why did you do it? I lost everything, even the things I had from you. I kept them in this box and I took it to the house to show you before I left but it burned in the fire. And back then, I thought that was going to be the worst of it. But *noooo*, over this last year, you've made me feel so much worse!" I'm bordering on hysterical, but I need him to talk to me, give me answers, something.

"Leila, you need to stop," Beau says; his hands have moved to the steering wheel and his knuckles are white as he grips it.

"No, I know I'm rambling, but you have talked to me once in three and a half years to tell me that you aren't my friend anymore. Well, now it's my turn. Last summer, after I returned and saw you on the beach, you know what you did . . . you walked away from me. That's what you should have done years ago instead of giving me the silent treatment. I missed you so much for so long, and what was the point? You could have ended this the right way, instead of treating me like I am just a nobody. You are a coward!"

His eyes dart back to mine and a flush works its way into his cheeks. The temperature in the car is back on the rise. He's mad and it's radiating off of him.

Good, let him be mad; I know I am!

"You're drunk and you should go inside," he says through gritted teeth.

"Maybe, but what, can't take the truth?" I snap at him.

"You don't know what you're saying. You're slurring your words and, quite frankly, embarrassing yourself."

"Embarrassing myself? I'm sorry if the delivery here isn't perfect enough for you but, then again, I never have been or will be and you remind me of this daily. Why I ever thought you were someone important, someone special, I'll never know. You know what? I'm done. I can't do it anymore. I finally give up; after all this time . . . you, my wasted hope, and everything else about the past year, including your uppity bitch girlfriend, can all just burn in hell for all I care."

Beau gasps and his look changes to one of pain.

I've hurt him. I wanted a reaction from him, and now that I have it, I regret it. My hands are shaking and the visceral change in his body language from my words is almost alarming.

His whiskey eyes glisten back at me and then narrow. "Are you finished?"

Continuing to glare at him, I say nothing.

"Get out of my car," his voice is low but it drips with pure hatred.

And, just like he always does, he gets the last word. I step out onto the road and slam the door, never looking back.

BEAU

I DECIDE TO not drop back into the café. I've thought about it plenty of times, even found myself walking that way, but what would be the point? She has a boyfriend, and knowing this just reminds me that she never cared enough for me to be one.

Mostly, my days consist of the same routine; tennis with Nate in the morning, lunch at the loft with Matt, and then we set out exploring.

New York City in the summer is a great place to be. There are tons of street markets, festivals, and live outdoor concerts. So far, our favorite activities have been to head down to Brooklyn Bridge Park on Sundays to Smorgasburg and over to Washington Square Park for the free music.

Smorgasburg is a weekly food festival that has over 100 different vendors. On each trip down to the park, Matt and I have tried something different and unique. It's no secret to anyone who knows me that I love food but, here, it has been exceptional. My favorite to date is the falafel burger with tatziki sauce. I'm determined to learn how to make it.

Over the last couple of days, I've been watching Matt pretty closely. He's quieted down. It's strange. He goes through these phases where we think he is coming out of his shell, talking and socializing more, but then he'll revert right back. I can't figure out what the trigger is that causes this.

"Little dude, what's wrong with you?" I say, stretching my legs out in the grass of the park. The sun is out today. There's a slight breeze and, lucky for us, we found a spot in the shade.

He looks down and takes a sip of his Vermont maple lemonade.

"I want to stay here with you." He has mentioned this several times, but I know that Mom will never go for it. I wouldn't mind. He's a good kid and I could always threaten with the one slip up and he's shipped back.

"I know you do, pal, and if I thought for one minute that Mom would agree to it, there would be no further discussion. I want you here, you need to know this." We've all spent so much of our lives feeling unwanted. More than anything, I want life to be so much better and different for Matt.

I understand where he's coming from. Just the thought of his being in that house alone with Mom makes me uncomfortable.

Our father was a very abusive man, both emotionally and physically. Well, physically to me, that is. For years we lived in fear of him, and tried to stay as far away from him as much as possible. Month after month, and day by day, though, he seemed to get worse.

He loved being in the public eye and he lived his life like

he was entitled. He worked his sick, twisted charm on unsuspecting people and, over time, had most of the community singing his praises. *Most,* that is.

Drew is a swimmer. Dad never took his frustrations out on him. Only me. So much time has passed that the only two things I will remember of my childhood are Leila and him beating me.

In the end, I wish that I had stood up to him, but instead I cowered down. It was Drew who finally finished our decade of torture. Drew walked into the kitchen that April afternoon, took one look at what he had done to our mother and me, and something in him finally flipped. Drew pulverized our father and saved us. Once all statements were taken, in combination with him running his mouth, the charges filed against him were enough to send him prison for life.

Matt wasn't there and I thank God every day for that. The blood, the destruction, the fear in the air, the police, the ambulance carrying off Mom, no twelve-year-old should have to witness this.

Maybe Drew and I can talk her into selling and buying a new home; one that isn't haunted and tainted with so many horrible memories.

He looks over, his dark hair flops over his eyes, and he smiles at me. God, I love this kid.

The weekend finally arrives for Drew and Ali's birthday beach-house getaway. Matt and I pack up after breakfast and arrive right after lunch. I expected the traffic up into Long Island to be worse than it was, so we actually made pretty good time.

Drew told us that the house he rented is waterfront and out on Dune Road in the West Hamptons. Although I've never been to any of the beaches in New York, it's been almost a month since I have stepped out into the sand and my body is humming with excitement.

As we pull into the circular driveway of the house, I slow the car and double-check my directions. Matt and I are speechless. The house is huge and in the back of my mind, I can't help but wonder how much this is costing Drew.

The home is solid white, elevated up on stilts, and three stories high. It has a gray shingled roof and wrap-around porches on both the first and second levels.

"Whoa! This place is awesome!" Matt jumps out of the car and skips up the steps to the front door. Ali comes out to greet us and Matt jumps into her arms. I know exactly how he feels. Her smiling face and warm eyes have a way of calming a little bit of the storm that has been brewing in me.

Ali came into our lives almost two years ago. She moved to Anna Maria Island after her mother passed away and her father relocated them. Drew used to say he didn't believe in things like love at first sight, but that changed the second his eyes locked onto Ali. All of this was during the darkest time in our family life but, as the months passed, she became a big part in helping all of us heal, and slowly the light filtered back into our days. She is the other half to my brother, and she is perfect for all of us. I couldn't love her anymore if I tried.

"Hey, Tiny; nice place you've got here," I say while grabbing our bags.

"So, I hear you have been in town a lot longer than we realized." She puts her hands on her hips. The look on her face is a mixture of anger and disappointment.

I walk up the steps and stand in front of her. I always forget how small she is, and though she's trying to act pissed, it's not really working.

"What? No hi, hey, hello, how are you?" She raises her eyebrows at me, which causes me to chuckle. "Straight to the point, huh? Yeah, I'm sorry I didn't call. I just needed to get here and get settled. I needed to do this on my own." I lock eyes with her, hoping that she will understand.

"But you aren't on your own; you have us." She isn't moving so I set the bags down. I need to make her understand.

"I know . . . but I needed to do this." She looks me over from head to toe, gives me a small smile, and then jumps. Her arms and legs wrap around me and she squeezes. I should be used to her doing this by now but, every time, she catches me off guard. I return her hug.

"You okay?" she asks as she leans back to look me in the face.

"Of course I am!" I give her one of my signature smirks and her eyes narrow as she studies my face.

"Leila said you didn't look so good when she saw you." And, on that note, I put her down.

"Seems to me that Leila needs to mind her own business." Picking up the bags, we walk into the house together.

"Are you ever going to tell me what happened between the two of you?" I know she is still watching me, but my eyes are taking in the colossal size of this place. Placing my bags at the bottom of the stairs, I walk toward the back of the living room. The entire wall is made up of windows and I take in the view.

"Why do you want to know?" Staring out at the ocean, I contemplate just telling her everything. I've never told anyone everything. The thought terrifies me, and I can't do it. I don't want to be brought back to that time, and I don't want to tell her what her friend did to me. This is between Leila and me, and no one else.

"Because, I happen to love you both and I don't understand. When the two of you are together, there's this crazy vibe running back and forth. It's confusing. I see the way she looks at you and the way you look at her, and I think that the two of you would be perfect together."

Turning to face her, I glance over and see Matt sitting on a stool in the kitchen. He's listening to this conversation, too. "Let it go, Ali. It's never going to happen."

"But why?" I know she doesn't understand, but I just can't go there.

"She's not the person I thought she was, okay?"

She studies me again.

"She's coming this weekend," she says nervously.

I don't want Ali to feel like she can't have her friend around. She doesn't have a lot of them. She's busy with dance, school, and Drew; as for Leila, I know first-hand that when she's someone's friend, she is a really good one.

"Of course she is," I say, adding a little sarcasm to my tone.

She frowns and then I smile.

"Whatever; I'm used to her being around. I'm glad you invited her. It's your birthday and she's your friend. It's not like we don't get along and will cause problems."

"I know, I just wanted to tell you before she gets here."

"No worries, okay?" I wrap my arm around her shoulders and give her a squeeze. "Where's Drew?"

"He went to pick up your mom. Come on, let me show you and Matt to your rooms."

"Tiny! Did you know that cows have four stomachs?"

She giggles. "No, I didn't. Did you know that, on average, Americans consume 18 acres of pizza per day?"

"You know, I think it's evil for you to utter the word pizza in front of me and then not deliver."

"Is that so?" She's mocking me.

"You know it is."

"Well, it just so happens that every Saturday here, there's a farmers' market right down the road. It is supposed to be the best in the Hamptons and I was thinking that you might wanna go with me to pick up some vegetables."

Frowning at her, I let out a pouty sigh. "Vegetables? So not the direction I was hoping you were going."

She giggles again. "I thought you wanted pizza. I'm gonna need some things, like tomatoes."

"Homemade pizza!" I tighten my grip on her shoulder and squeeze again. She has just made my day, no matter if Leila is going to be here or not.

Ali nods her head, smiling.

"And this farmers' market is officially my favorite farmers' market."

Matt decided to stay behind to go for a run on the beach, while we headed to the market. This market is pretty cool. It reminds me of the street fairs we see in the city, with the white tents, but instead of prepared food, it has produce, cheeses, oils, soaps, and breads.

"So how do you like the city so far?" Ali asks, while sorting through the tomatoes.

"I actually like it a lot. It's different than what I expected." She hands me the basket so both of her hands are free.

"That's what Drew said too. The lights and the noise."

"Yeah, those things, but it's the lack of openness. You

can't really see the sky."

Ali looks over at me but I keep looking down at the different vegetables.

"You miss the stars." It isn't a question; it's a statement.

"No."

She punches me in the arm. "Liar."

"Maybe," I smirk at her. The truth is that I'm trying to forget the stars. After Leila left, I would stare out the window at night and watch them twinkle and move across the sky as the hours passed. Every night, I wondered if she was looking at them too. Did they remind her of me? Did she ever think about me?

I pay for the food and we head to the cheese tent.

"She said that you met Charlie. What did you think?"

"What's there to think? He seems nice enough. How long has she known him?"

"They met at a party right after we moved here."

My stomach drops. I was right; they aren't new friends. They've known each other for a while.

"Oh," is all I can think to say.

"Speaking of meeting someone, there's someone I want you to meet." She bats her eyelashes at me and grins.

"Please tell me you're kidding."

"Nope. I'll set it up soon."

"I really don't want to meet anyone; I just want to get settled and play tennis." I'm irritated, not so much at her, just at the idea of some chick being shoved down my throat. I've never had a problem meeting girls, so why she feels the need for this bothers me.

"I thought you were settled; that's why you moved here and didn't tell anyone." She mirrors the irritation in my voice with hers.

I look down at her and see that she is still upset I didn't call her or Drew when we got in.

"Why me?"

"Because, she just moved here and doesn't have a lot of friends."

"Then introduce her to Leila; she can be her friend."

"Alright, Beau, never mind." Her irritation has turned to disappointment.

I hate the thought of disappointing her. She never asks anything of me and, for whatever reason, this must be important to her, so whatever . . .

"Fine, just tell me when and where."

Her face lights up and this makes me smile. I would do anything for her and she knows it.

"Yay! Thank you. Let's go pick out some cheese, and tonight, I will make you your own pizza. You won't even have to share it!"

"Geez, thanks. Nice to know that you were going to punish me if I said no."

"When it comes to you and pizza, I know how to play dirty."

"I'll remember that."

"You better."

LEILA

"ALI! OH MY gosh, girl, I am so excited to be here! This house is gorgeous!" I say as I walk through the front door and hug her.

"I know, right? Drew found it for us and it's perfect. Just wait until you see the back deck. I've been spending most of my time out there. I'm so glad you're here." She is beaming at me.

"I wouldn't have missed this for anything. Gee, let's see . . . it's your birthday and it's a weekend at the beach. Eeeek!"

Ali laughs as we walk through the house.

The home has an open floor plan, and is decorated beautifully in light yellow, gray, and navy blue.

Walking out onto the back deck, I see what she means; this is where I am going to be spending the weekend as well. The view is spectacular and it's decorated just as nicely as inside.

Turning to take in the full view, the air rushes out of my lungs because, on the last lounge chair, is Beau. His eyes lock with mine and my stomach falls. I knew that he would be here this weekend, but seeing him again in person makes my chest and stomach ache. He's so handsome. Neither one of us says anything.

"Do you see what I mean? Isn't this the most relaxing space ever?" Ali says, interrupting the unspoken moment between the two of us.

Breaking eye contact, I turn my attention back to Ali. "Who owns this place?"

"The boyfriend of the girl we rent the apartment from in the city."

"Wow. I can't even imagine what he does for a living."

"I know, right? Where's Charlie? I thought he was coming."

"He was, but his parents called last minute and asked that he come home for a visit, so he did. He would have loved this." I look around at the décor again and laugh to myself. I'll have to take pictures and text them to him. He's going to be so envious.

As much as I don't want to, I can't help looking over at Beau. He's watching the two of us and his eyebrows are furrowed. He looks angry, although I can't imagine why.

Ali pulls on my arm, "Come on; let's get you settled and then you can help me with the pizzas."

Letting out a deep sigh, I give her a small smile, and I know she knows . . . seeing him is hard for me.

"Okay, lead the way."

Not too long after we start the pizzas, Drew arrives with their mom, Diane. She gives me a big hug, and is every bit as polite to me as she usually is; but this time, I feel like there is an underlying edge to her. I used to think that she liked me, but over the years, she's made me feel more and more like she doesn't want me around. I don't understand what I ever did to her.

Ali's pizza dinner is delicious, as always, and I find it adorable that Drew has now added his own twist to the pizza, making them even more delicious—he grills them.

"So, I have some news." Everyone stops talking and turns my way. Why am I so nervous? This news is exciting.

"Oh, we like good news and this is definitely a weekend for celebrating. Can you believe that we are twenty-one? When did that happen?" Ali glances over to Drew and he winks at her.

Taking a deep breath, I look around the table and stop at

Beau. He's looking at me and I momentarily forget what I am saying.

"Spill it, Starling," Drew says.

"Okay, okay. Last spring, I entered a contest hoping to be selected as the "Rising Designer" for this fall's Fashion Week, and well, I won."

Ali squeals and jumps up from the table to hug me. "That's so amazing! I remember you talking about this months ago. Tell us more."

"Well, I had to submit five designs, and they loved them all so much, I get to do a full collection at the start of the show."

"Who's show?"

"BLK's." Ali gasps, and the table grows quiet. All five of them stare at me and I feel a blush spread over my cheeks.

"That's who's presenting you? Wow, this is huge for you! The exposure and possibilities could be endless," Ali says to me.

"I know; Vogue called this morning. I'm going to get a two-page spread in their Fashion Week highlight section."

"Vogue! Oh, my, I'm going to buy out the newsstand and tell everyone I know." Ali is bouncing in her chair.

I giggle at her excitement over this. Charlie already knows that I won, but I couldn't wait to tell Ali.

My smile drops as Beau leans across the table and lays his warm hand on top of mine. He hasn't touched me in over a year, and this contact is almost enough to make me cry.

"I always knew you could do it. I'm so proud of you," he says quietly.

I can see that he is. The emotion in his eyes is a mixture of kindness and awe. He'll never know how much those words mean to me. My eyes fill with tears.

"Thank you," I say softly to him.

He gives me a small smile but doesn't say anything more. I know the moment is over, but he leaves his hand on top of mine for a few seconds longer. I'm glowing on the inside.

The entire table has stopped talking and is watching the two of us, but I just don't care.

After the kitchen clean-up, Diane retires to her room, Matt figured out how to get the Xbox on in the game room, and Ali and Drew go for a walk on the beach. Sucking up my nerve, I wander out to the back deck and sit down on the lounge chair next to Beau. He never looks my way; knowing him like I do, if I don't say something, it's possible that we could sit here all night in silence.

"So, what are you doing out here?" I ask him.

"Truth?" he says without really acknowledging me.

"Of course."

"Looking at the stars."

He still looks at the stars. My heart squeezes. After we moved to Atlanta, every night I would lie out under the stars. It was comforting for me to know that he was out there under them, too.

"You still look at them?" He knows what I am asking, and he pauses to think about his answer.

"No. Living in the city, you can't see them at all."

No. His answer stings and my chest tightens. I always wondered if he continued to gaze at them and now I have my answer. Why are these memories that I have with him so important and prominent to me, when clearly they aren't to him?

Sitting next to him out here, I just can't do it. I thought that, after his kind words at the table, he might treat me a little differently, but nope. I glance over at him and stand up to leave. His presence has always been so much, so overwhelming. Being near him, he makes me feel small and insignificant. Why is it that, after all this time, I still have him built up in my head to be this great person? He isn't a great person; he's just some guy I knew as a kid, and he's turned out to be someone completely different.

"Good night, Leila," I just barely hear him say under his breath as I walk away.

BEAU

I HEARD THE car door slam when she arrived, and I knew the minute she walked out on to the deck. I think my heart stopped beating. Not only could I hear her beautiful voice, but it was as if every nerve ending went on alert. I could physically feel that she was near.

My eyes involuntarily seek her out. I feel like a moth that is constantly being drawn to the flame. Her hair is down and lightly blowing in the breeze that's coming off the water, and she is wearing a pale blue sundress that is the same exact color as her eyes. Why is it that every time I see this girl she gets more and more breathtaking?

She spots me and our eyes connect. I'm so busy looking at her that I haven't paid any attention to their conversation; that is until I hear Ali ask why Charlie didn't come. Instantly, I see red.

Leila was going to bring that guy to our family weekend?

How could she? Part of me had been hoping to get to talk to her a little, see how she's been, but after hearing this . . . there's just no way. The fact that she cares that little for my feelings that she would bring him here, in front of me, just confirms all over again that she's not the girl I thought she was.

Whatever.

They walk back inside and I rub the spot on my chest over my heart.

After Leila went to bed last night, I stayed out on the deck to stare at the night sky. I lied to her about looking at the stars. I look for them and at them any chance I get. I don't know why I still do. I've stopped doing most of the other things that I did as a kid, but not this one.

Most people are nostalgic over something from their childhood; this must be mine. It's what I think about the most and, honestly, when I was the happiest.

I've missed gazing at the stars.

My eyes are instantly drawn to Sirius, the brightest star in the night sky. Sirius, otherwise known as the dog-star, is found in the Canis Major constellation. The Greeks called the time when the star is the most visible, the dog days of summer. To them, these were the hottest days of year, and the most hated. But, Leila and I always thought differently about the star.

Where we lived on the island, it's the law to have the lights out at night due to the loggerhead sea turtles coming on-to shore and nesting. Once the eggs hatch, the babies find their way out of the nest, to the top of the sand. It's the light of the moon and the stars that guide them to the water. The light shines bright for them.

Leila and I watched one nest for months, just waiting for the babies to hatch. Of course, the one night we didn't head out to check on it was the night they dug their way out and swam off. When we saw the scrapings in the sand from their little flippers, Leila threw her hands up in the air and declared that, from now on, we would stick to stargazing. She was such a little spitfire then, even now I guess, when she needs to be.

I love stargazing, especially with her. I should have asked her to stay.

I ended up falling asleep in the chair and Matt woke me up in the morning to ask if I wanted to go for a run with him. Even though every part of me is stiff and tired, I can't say no to him. Tomorrow he leaves and my heart frowns at the impending reality.

For most of the day, everyone does their own thing. I mostly spent my time with Matt but every now and then I catch myself looking at Leila on the back deck, sunbathing. She kept to herself mostly and read a book. Occasionally Ali joined her, but not too often.

Right before dusk, Ali and Drew walk out of the house, hand in hand. Drew thought it would be nice to get a few family photos, and since Leila was here, she could take the pictures. Together, with my mother and Leila, they start to make their way down to the beach. Matt runs out behind them and I watch as my family laughs and moves together. Only, Leila is not my family. She's just this girl we have all known for a long time.

Sometimes when I look at her, I can still see the eight-year-old girl from my memories, and then I blink my eyes and the grown-up version takes her place. I love that I have known her most of her life. No matter what has happened, or what will happen between us, I will always be thankful for this and no one can take it away from me. Just about every good memory and moment in life that I've ever had has involved her, and I wouldn't want it any other way.

Following them down, I look around and see that the beach is empty this evening. The water is calm and the golden lighting is perfect for these pictures. My mother will be happy.

"So, thanks, everyone, for coming down here," Drew says, looking at each of us and stopping on Ali. "I do want to get a few pictures of the family, but what I really wanted you here for, is this ..."

Drew drops to one knee and I think my jaw drops with him. It doesn't surprise me in any way that he is proposing to Ali. I knew it would be coming one day; I just didn't see it being today.

My mother gasps and a moment of silence spreads over the six of us as Drew reaches for Ali.

"Ali . . ." he says calmly and quietly, rubbing his thumbs across the back of her hands. He takes a deep breath and looks up at her with tears in his eyes.

I'm frozen watching him. Seeing this side of him is so foreign to me. It's like snow falling in the middle of a hot summer day. Drew doesn't cry. He shows indifference over emotion.

"I spent years thinking that I would never be good enough and that no one would ever love me...yet here you are. I am in awe of you and so very grateful, every day. I knew the moment I saw you that something about you was going to be life-changing, and it was. You have forever changed me."

"Drew . . ." Ali says on a sigh. She lifts one of her hands

and runs it through his hair and over the side of his face, wiping a tear that has fallen.

He lets out a shaky sigh. "I love you. I love everything about you. I know that usually when guys propose, they talk about how they can't wait to start the rest of their life with that person, but my life with you started a long time ago. I want to make it permanent. I want it forever. Ali, will you marry me?"

Even though I know she's going to say yes, I'm holding my breath, just waiting for her answer.

"Yes! Of course I'll marry you. I love you, too," she says so quietly that I almost don't hear her. Smiling from ear to ear, with tears dripping like crazy, she leans down and wraps her arms around him.

Even my eyes fill with tears as I listen and watch him pour his heart out to her. Drew has always been the type of guy to keep everything bottled inside, and has never been one to share his emotions. The change in him has been so dramatic over the last two years, I can't help but feel a little envious; yet, at the same time, I am so proud of him.

It's with this thought in mind that I glance over to Leila. Her hands are clasped together and pulled up tight next to her chin. Happy tears are streaming down her face. Leila never cries, so this catches me off guard. Seeing her like this makes my heart ache. This is a side she doesn't show many, and certainly not to me anymore.

In the background, my ears perk up at the sound of Ali laughing. Looking back, she is jumping up and down and practically tackles Drew to the ground. They are sitting in the sand when he slips the ring on her finger and brings her hand up to his mouth. Drew's eyes shine again with tears as he kisses her ring finger.

This should be a private moment for the two of them but,

seeing them both this happy, I can't force my gaze away. It makes me wonder if Leila ever thought about me, about us. She had to; after all, how many times did we act this out as kids?

Glancing back to her, I lose myself in thought. She's no longer twenty, but ten and she's running around the beach in a white sundress, looking for wildflowers to make a bouquet.

"Beau, let's play wedding," Leila says to me, while I'm building a sandcastle up on Bean Point.

"Why would I ever want to play that? That's what girls do," I say, frowning.

"Well, I'm not marrying a girl one day, silly. I'm gonna marry you. So let's pretend."

"Fine, but Drew or Grant better never find out about this or they'll make fun of me forever."

"Okay," she giggles, with her eyes sparkling.

I love making her happy and I would do anything for her. I'm starting to think she knows this.

Getting up, I wander through the dunes and find a piece of a dried palm leaf to twist into a ring. If I'm going to be marrying the girl, she needs a ring.

My eyes catch Ali's ring. Did Leila ever save the ones that I made for her? Maybe she did or maybe she didn't. Either way, they most likely would have been in that box that burned in the fire.

Looking out over the water, I can't help but wonder if she dreamed of a happily-ever-after with me. I know that I sure did, even after she moved; as much as I hate to admit it, I still do.

Even though we haven't been together for years, I never saw myself with anyone else. The thought or the possibility that it might be someone who was not her is nonexistent, and the thought that she might marry someone who's not me . . . I'm internally shocked. I shouldn't be, but I am.

"So does this mean you're going to be my sister?" Everyone looks at Matt. His expression is one of hope and happiness.

"Yes, it does," Ali says to him.

Matt grins, his hair flops over his eyes and he jumps at them, landing on Drew's lap between the middle of them. He's hugging them both so tight, my heart clenches. Matt is completely unaffectionate, other than a passing hug here and there. I've never seen him like this before. I hear Mom sniff next to me.

The three of them stand up, and I make my way over to hug them both. I can't possibly be any happier for them than I am at this moment, but that happiness is diluted with the sadness that is consuming me.

Have I been living in such a haze all this time that I've completely lost touch with reality?

Glancing at Leila, I have to walk away from this, from them, from her. My chest has constricted; I can't breathe, and my eyes burn with unshed tears. I don't care if Drew or Ali sees me cry, but there is no way I will ever let Leila see me like this. This is a crushing, debilitating pain that is suffocating me.

She didn't choose me; she's never really chosen me, and she isn't going to. Ever.

I don't even know what I have been hanging on to. We are completely different people and we have been for a long time. The thought of her ultimately building a life with someone who isn't me smothers me with pain. I've never wanted anyone but her. Only her. Now I feel even more alone and vulnerable.

Why didn't I realize this sooner? Boy, do I feel like I have just been smacked with the biggest wake-up call. All these years and all this time, what have I been waiting for? Everyone is moving on with their lives but me. Drew is getting married, Leila has a boyfriend, Mom seems happy, and Matt is finally starting to talk and socialize a little more. I guess it's my turn.

Maybe I shouldn't have come to New York. Oh, well, too late now. Fall classes are paid for. Come January, I think it'll finally be time for me to join the professional tour. Most pro tennis players don't even go to college. They start competing right after high school. In February, I can enter the National Indoor Tournament and, in March, the Sony Open. It will get me on the road and on with my life.

LEILA

BEAU KEPT TO himself this weekend. He hung out with Matt or spent time down on the beach.

This Beau is different from the one that I knew back in Florida. I'm not really sure how to pinpoint exactly what the changes are, but they are there.

I tried to watch him without him knowing, but every time he turned and caught me. Maybe he feels it like I do. I always knew when he was watching me, which was a lot, although I didn't let on.

I knew that Drew was going to propose to Ali. He had asked my opinion on the shape of the diamond a few weeks ago so, when he dropped to one knee, I wasn't surprised.

What did surprise me, though, was that I cried. Seeing them after all that they have been through was a very beautiful and moving moment. However, I think I cried because I've finally come to the realization that this will never be Beau and me.

Beau will never drop to one knee, and he will never tell me how much he loves me.

Why I still dream about him being the one for me, I don't know. I hate that, after twelve years, I still can't let go of him. Yes, the first six were great, but these last six haven't been. Over and over again, he has proved that I am not the one for him.

Charlie asked me once to describe my dream wedding but I just couldn't tell him, so I lied. Every little girl dreams of her wedding and, for most, I imagine it is like a fairytale; mine wasn't. It was real, and deep down I just knew that one day it was going to happen.

Standing here watching the two of them promise forever to each other, my heart breaks all over again. At one point I feel Beau looking at me, but returning the look would have been detrimental. So much so that I'm certain I would have broken down and caused a scene. Instead, I played the surprised, emotionally-moved part because I am Ali's friend.

No one needs to know the truth. After all, who stays in love with the same boy for twelve years? I feel stupid and brokenhearted. I kept thinking that, if I opened up to him, gave myself to him, he would eventually see how much he means to me. Boy was I wrong about that.

What did I do that was so wrong? I don't understand. For six years, we were inseparable. I thought I meant as much to him as he does to me. It hurts to know that I don't. It hurts to love someone and know that they are never going to love you back. It hurts.

After Ali says yes, she lands in Drew's arms and both of them start laughing. Matt is over the moon and the first to get to them. Beau walks over, hugs them both, kisses Ali on the cheek, and then steps back so Diane can congratulate them. Our eyes briefly connect as he glances at me one more time, tucks his hands into his pockets, and turns away to walk down the beach.

Can't he see how I feel? Can't he see that I am devastated on the inside and longing for him? Doesn't he have any compassion for me? After all, he's the one who has broken me repeatedly. Oh, how I wish that he had taken me by the hand and asked me to go with him. All I have ever wanted was to be with him.

More tears drop as I watch him walk away.

Eventually everyone goes inside; everyone but Beau, that is. He's always been so open and in the moment about how he feels about things. I don't understand why he has changed so much, or what could have caused this change.

Slowly, the sky darkens as the sun begins to set. Instead of following the others in, I sit on the boardwalk to the house, and watch the direction that he walked off into. Tomorrow we all leave to head back into the city, and I really would like to talk to him. Who knows when I will see him again?

A lone figure finally emerges, and I know it is him. The sky hasn't completely darkened yet, giving me an opportunity to watch him without him knowing.

Beau is beautiful. He always has been, but seeing him here causes this ache inside of me that I can't get rid of. He's wearing white linen pants, a fitted navy blue T-shirt, and is barefoot. He doesn't even realize how well his clothes fit him or what the sight of him does to me.

His head is down, his hands are in his pockets, and he's completely lost in thought. I wish I knew what he was thinking or, better yet, I wish he wanted to tell me.

"Hey," I say as he approaches the steps. I startle him and his head snaps up at the sound of my voice.

"Hey; what are you doing out here?" His brows furrow. For a second I think he looks concerned, but I know he's not.

"Waiting for you," I say to him.

A breeze blows and his hair falls across his forehead, almost covering his eyes. He presses his lips into a thin line and stares at me.

"Why?"

"I don't know; I just thought that it would be nice to talk to you."

A dark shadow passes over his face, his body language changes, and he looks on edge.

"You know how to reach me," he says sharply.

How do I answer that? I do know how to reach him, but he would probably hurt me. Again.

"I suppose I do," I say, letting out a sigh. A moment of silence passes between us. He runs his hand through his hair and sits down on the step next to me. His leg brushes against mine and I close my eyes. The interactions that I have with him are so far and few between, to now have physical contact makes me want to cry.

We watch the waves lap onto the shore, in silence. I can feel the heat coming off of him and I so badly want to lean into him.

"I'm sorry about the other morning. I was just really surprised to see you," I say to him.

He tenses up and I immediately know that this moment here with him is over.

"What part are you sorry for; the part where you looked like you'd rather be anywhere but there standing next to me or the part where your boyfriend was shoved down my throat?" He's angry.

"What? That's not what happened." I knew that Charlie's little show was going to cause a ripple between us, but I never expected him to be mad over it. I thought I would get attitude and indifference. At least, that's what the old Beau would have given me.

"Oh really?" He shifts to look at me.

"It's not like that." And I don't want him to think that. My eyes lock with his. When we were kids and he would look at me, I could see and feel the affection that he had for me. Now, there's nothing but mistrust and wariness. I still don't understand what really happened for him to think this way about me. He was my best friend until the very end and, unfortunately for me, I thought I was his.

"You know what, it doesn't even matter." He sounds resigned as he stands up abruptly and shoves his hands into his pockets. He looks out toward the water again, takes a deep breath, and lets out a sigh. "I'm happy for you. You look good and it seems that things are going well... I'm going to head in and take a shower." He moves up a few steps and stops. "Oh, here, you always liked these." He pulls something out of his pocket, leans over, and drops it into my lap. I'm so engrossed in watching him that I forget to say thanks. He gives me a small smile and heads up the rest of the steps.

Watching him walk away feels so final that my heart breaks just a bit more. Being here this weekend, I had really hoped things would turn out differently, but they haven't.

The backs of my eyes burn as I look out toward the ocean. Since we are facing east, the sun has set behind us, leaving the sky in front of me a deep lavender.

Looking down, there lying in my lap is a piece of salt water taffy. The tears that had filled my eyes slowly drip out. Some people chew gum, others eat mints, but Beau has always loved taffy.

Slowly, I take the wax paper off of the candy. Biting into it, I eat half and decide to wrap back up the other half and save it for later.

When we were kids, on Sundays we would wander down to Kelly's Kandy Shop to watch her make taffy. Each week she would let us pick a flavor and a color. Then, once the taffy was cool enough to handle, we would Crisco up our hands and pull the taffy like tug-of-war until it became glossy and the color became light. Pulling the taffy fills it with tiny air bubbles, which makes the candy lighter in texture. The pulling process only takes about ten minutes. But each week for ten minutes we would laugh and pull. That is one of my favorite childhood memories.

Ms. Kelly would roll out the taffy into a long skinny rope and then cut it into pieces. She always gave us a bag full of the pieces for helping and, with two bottles of soda, we would hop on our bikes and ride to Bean Point to enjoy the candy. Blueberry was always his favorite and salted caramel was mine.

Back in my room, I pack up my things. If I didn't think that it would be rude, I would leave right now. Ali loves me, I know she does but, being in this house with all of Beau's family, I feel extremely out of place and unwanted. As soon as the morning gets here and I can say goodbye, I'm leaving.

While I'm lying on the bed, staring out at the beach, willing the minutes to tick by, there's a knock on my door.

"Come in." For a split second, my heart actually leaps, thinking it might be Beau, but it isn't. The door opens and Matt steps in. He looks kind of uncomfortable.

"Hey, Matt, come in." I sit up and smile at him.

He steps into my room and stares at me. He must be here for a reason and my curiosity is piqued.

"Have you had a good time in New York?" He comes a little closer and stands at the foot of the bed.

"I have." He smiles a little.

"Are you excited to go home and see your friends?"

The smile drops and now he looks uncomfortable again.

"Not really; I'd rather stay here." His head hangs and he looks at his feet.

"Oh, really? Why?" Matt is so hard to read. He's always been very closed off and quiet.

"Because, I love being with Beau." He looks back up at me and stands a little taller. "Leila, why are you always so mean to him?"

What?

"Why do you think that I'm mean to him?"

"Because . . . every time he's around you, he comes home sad."

This causes me to frown. "I don't understand. Why do you think he's sad?"

85

He pushes the hair out of his face and his cheeks turn a little pink. "Well, let's see; he cried when you moved, he cried when you came back. His entire junior year, especially going into the summer, he was sad. He was sad after he saw you at the coffee shop, and he's been sad this whole weekend. Stop being mean to him."

He cried when I moved? That's not the way things were told to me. And he cried when I moved back? Then why did he ignore me and say we weren't friends? None of this makes any sense to me. Matt is young. He must have it wrong.

"Matt, I don't really know anything about him being sad, but I can tell you that I'm not being mean to him . . . we just aren't friends anymore."

"Well, why not? You two have known each other for a long time and are around each other a lot!" He's confused and getting flustered.

"Have you ever had a girlfriend?" I'm trying to come up with an example where I think he can best understand Beau and me.

"No."

"Well, one day you will and, should the two of you not work out, you'll see how hard it is to be friends."

"You were his girlfriend?"

"Sort of . . . at one time."

"What happened? You two used to be best friends."

"I don't know. I guess you could say he didn't want me to be his best friend anymore." My heart aches and tears fill my eyes. He sees this and freezes.

"What did you do?" he whispers out.

"I don't know." And that's the truth. I have no idea what I ever did to him to make him not want to be friends with me anymore.

"You should ask him."

"Maybe." If only it were that simple.

LEILA

TIME SLIPPED BY and, before I knew it, July was over and August had arrived. The leaves on the trees in the parks were noticeably darker, and the neighborhood slowly began to get more crowded with students returning. Charlie and I fell back into our comfortable routine as the seasons started to change. The excitement that came along with the approach of fall filled the air. With Fashion Week just around the corner, every free second that I had was spent working on my designs to complete the collection, and desperately trying to not think of Beau.

The morning after my conversation with Matt, I quietly said my goodbyes to Ali and Drew, and snuck out of the house without having to see Beau, Matt, or their mom. I didn't get much sleep and most of the night I laid there thinking about the things that Matt said. If he thinks that I'm mean to Beau, do others think that too? I just don't understand anything.

Having nowhere to be, I ended up driving to Charlie's parents' house, and he welcomed me with open arms as I stepped out of the car.

At that moment, being with him, someone who cared for me, I couldn't help the tears as they started to fall.

"Hey, what's this?"

He placed his hands on my face and looked in my eyes. The emotion in his voice was so sincere, I cried even harder.

"Sweetheart, I think maybe I've seen you cry once in the last year. I'm kind of concerned right now, and I think it's time you spill it and tell me truth."

"The truth about what?" I sniffed, secretly willing him to not ask what I know he wants to know.

He pulled back and gave me a knowing look. "Beau."

My shoulders fell.

"You know you'll feel better once you do," he said quietly, still looking at me curiously.

I'd never talked about Beau to anyone, not even Ali. She suspected a few things and I may have mentioned some things in passing, but we'd never had a heart to heart conversation over him. Besides, he's her family now. That made everything different.

"Okay," I said in defeat.

Charlie deserved to know the truth. We'd been together— side by side—for almost a year and a half, and it seemed unfair to keep secrets. If he'd kept them from me, I'd probably feel a little hurt too. He took me by the hand, we walked around the back of his parents' house, curled up in a large wooden swing, and I told him everything. I watched his face as he listened to every detail.

"Leila, I hate to say this to you, but none of it adds up. Don't shoot the messenger here, but as a third party outsider, you called him a coward, but yet you were one just as much as he was. After all that time, and all those years together, you should have demanded answers from him, and only him; no one else."

"Probably, but it's too late now."

"I don't think so. I saw the way he looked at you the other morning in the café."

"How was he looking at me?"

"Like you are the sun, the moon . . . and the stars."

At Charlie's use of the word 'stars', my tears returned. He wrapped his arm around my shoulder and pushed off the ground with his foot. The swing rocked us and I closed my eyes.

Charlie was right; I did feel better after telling him about Beau. The weight of all of the details of our 'relationship' over the years had taken its toll, and it was crushing me. Along with the constant heartache, I felt like I was breaking.

Interestingly, though, since that afternoon Charlie and I have grown closer. It wasn't that we weren't close before, but now he knows all of my secrets and there's nothing left to hide. With him, I don't have to pretend anymore that Beau is just some guy from my past, when he so clearly is a part of my present too. Charlie understands that seeing him and having to interact with him can send me into an emotional tailspin, and as much as I wish I could say that I didn't love him anymore, I still do.

BLK frequently has me drop by their headquarters which, fortunately for me, is fine with my boss. She loves Fashion Week and has been very accommodating and supportive. She just switched my schedule and now has me opening on Saturdays to make up for lost time.

The Saturday crowd is different than that of the weekday

crowd. Patrons wander in and tend to not leave. The tables and chairs are usually filled and it's nice to see the same regulars week after week.

Charlie loves to come and sit in the window while I work, people-watching, and playing 'I spy'.

One night after too many glasses of wine, we were sitting at an outside bistro table, and we turned the classic "I spy" children's game into something more. We would spy on random people as they passed by and then, together, we would make up an elaborate story about who they were, where they were going, or what they did in life. Since then, the game has kind of stuck and we've had hours of laughs together.

"Leila, aren't you off the clock yet?" he asks as I walk his way with two fresh lattes.

"Yep, just finished."

"Perfect, sit for a minute. The scenery this morning has been amazing."

I can't help but giggle. His eyes are playful and happy. I sit in the empty seat next to him.

"I spy something with my big brown eyes, and it's that lady across the street walking her dog. Now what makes this lady so interesting is that the only reason she could possibly be wearing a matching outfit to her dog is because she is headed down to the theater district to audition for a children's show titled, *Here's Why My Owner is Crazy*! And the best part is that they are both wearing animal print. She wrapped her animal in an animal. That is just wrong on so many levels."

I throw my head back and laugh. I hadn't realized they were both in animal print until he pointed it out.

"Theater audition, huh?"

"Most definitely."

I glance back out the window but my eyes catch on someone else. All of the air stops in my lungs and I gasp.

Beau has stopped in front of the café doors and he looks like he is having a conversation with himself about coming in. I haven't seen or spoken to him in weeks and my emotions are split right down the middle. I've become used to missing him, but since that last conversation on the beach, it seems to have become worse. Seeing him makes me so happy. I feel like if my skin wasn't holding me together, I would burst all over the place, but at the same time, instead of my heart slowing down to the peace that I know he can bring me, it speeds up because he also brings heartache. A heartache that is so dull and low-lying, it never leaves and constantly reminds me of what I'll never have.

For a fleeting second, as I watch him, the thought that he might be purposely coming here just to see me enters my mind. I inwardly scold myself because that's doubtful and un-realistic. Knowing Beau, I just gave myself false hope in his sudden appearance.

He shoves one hand into his pocket, reaches for the door, and walks in.

Just like he always has, he takes my breath away. He's wearing khaki pants, a black V-neck T-shirt that makes his arms look lean and strong, and a pair of flip flops. He's recent-ly had a haircut and his face has a light stubble on it. He could easily step off the page of a Calvin Klein ad.

Standing in the doorway, he scans the café and scowls when his eyes land on me. My heart sinks because he looks angry, and I don't know what I've done.

Climbing out of the chair, I slowly approach him, smiling.

"Hey, I saw you stop outside and was wondering if you were going to come in."

"Yeah, I was trying to decide on whether or not I really

want a cup of coffee." He looks past me and at Charlie.

"So what did you decide?" I ask him.

His eyes come back to mine and it's as if they've somehow darkened and become harder.

"I'm here, aren't I?" His tone is sharp and it stings. He lets out a deep sigh, "I'm sorry, Leila, that sounded bad." He looks back toward the door and runs his hand through his hair.

"It's alright. Have a seat and I'll go get it for you." I walk away as quickly as I can. I'm angry at myself for always thinking of him, craving him, and so desperately wanting to see him. Every time, things end badly. Not once in what feels like forever have we had a good moment that hasn't turned sour. If anything, by now, all of these bad moments probably outnumber the good ones.

I pour the coffee and peek up at Beau and Charlie. He has taken my seat, and I can't help but watch the two of them interact. Charlie starts laughing and Beau has stopped scowling. In a perfect world, they would learn to become friends but, then again, in a perfect world he would see me as more than just a girl he once knew and felt a responsibility for.

"Leila, guess what?" Charlie says as I return with the coffee.

"What?" I say, never taking my eyes off of Beau.

"Beau was just saying how he didn't have any plans this afternoon, and I know that you don't either, so the two of you should hang out. You could catch up and reminisce about the good old days."

I'm not sure what type of expression is plastered on my face, but Charlie smirks at me and tilts his head toward Beau. My eyes follow, and Beau is looking at Charlie with complete horror.

Well, there's my answer to if he ever wondered what it

would be like to spend some time together. My heart sinks.

Giving him the easy out, I say, "It's alright, I'm sure you have something that you need to do . . ." Besides, I need to be in my studio all afternoon hand-stitching beads onto the evening wear portion of my collection. Charlie knows this.

Beau blinks and the shutters in his beautiful hazel eyes slam into place. The three of us remain still, while Beau regards me with what looks like caution and annoyance.

"Sure, I was just headed home, if that sounds alright to you."

He wants me to go home with him? He wants to spend time with me? I'm lost in my head, staring at him, until he raises his eyebrows in question.

"Um, sure, I just need to grab my bag from the back." Turning quickly, I fly through the café and the saloon doors to the kitchen, snatch up my things, and head back out front.

Beau is already standing by the door and, when he sees me, he reaches over and shakes Charlie's hand.

"You all set?" he asks me.

"Yep."

I glance at Charlie one last time as I follow Beau out the door. He shoots me a thumbs' up and I roll my eyes.

Standing on the sidewalk, Beau gives me a small smile and starts walking. He doesn't say one word to me as we round the block and stop in front of an old brownstone.

"This is it." He tilts his head toward the building and half-interestedly waves his hand at it.

"You were serious when you said around the corner," I giggle, and for the first time in what feels like forever, he smiles at me. My heart flips over in my chest and squeezes.

He takes his keys out of his pocket and I follow behind him up the steps. Taking a deep breath, I mentally take a picture of this moment.

When I think about us being kids and playing together, the memories are so vivid that they feel like they were just yesterday, not years ago. And now here we are as adults and I'm following him through the front door of his home.

He glances back at me and smiles again. That's two smiles. My heart squeezes again.

"So, the building is rather old and I'm five flights up. Hope you don't mind the stairs."

"Not at all."

He holds the door open, and I slip by. Our eyes lock on to each other, butterflies take flight in my stomach, and I feel that physical pull that I have only ever had with him. I probably move a little slower than necessary, but to be this close to him, I can't help but soak it up. Beau has always been a little on the hot-natured side and the warmth coming off of his skin, oh how I wish I could just lean into him. And he smells like fresh laundry, the outside air, and well—just him.

Together again in silence, we trudge up the stairs, and reach the top level. He unlocks the door and throws it open for me. My jaw drops as I walk in. This loft is one-hundred-percent Beau. Most of it is one wide open space, the back wall is brick, there are windows everywhere to keep it bright, and the ceilings are at least twenty feet high, complete with wood beams. The furniture is chunky and worn. It looks inviting. His table is a large wooden farm table and the couch is a light-brown leather, oversized, complete three-piece sectional. There are a few throw pillows on it and a dark blue rug on the floor. He has one large Jackson Pollock-like painting over the fireplace, and then on the wall going into the kitchen there are black and white photos of the beach from back home too.

"I can't believe this is where you live and how big this

space is. My apartment is a shoebox next to this one." And it really is.

He walks into the kitchen, sets down the coffee, places his phone on the charger, and grabs two bottles of water out of the refrigerator.

"Where do you live?" he asks as he walks into the living room and sits down on the couch.

Standing in the middle of the room, I do one more 360 to take in the space, and then give my attention back to him. "A couple of blocks west, toward the West Village. How did you find this place?" I follow him and sit on the other end of the couch.

"I came up earlier in the spring. My plan was to try and decide which neighborhood I wanted to live in and, as it turned out, the guy next to me on the plane had just been offered a job in Tampa so he was going to need to rent it out. He described the place, we hopped in a cab together, and were brought straight here from the airport. I took one look at the loft, walked through the neighborhood, and I knew. We stopped at Irish 31 for a beer, and an hour later, I wrote him the deposit check. I just knew this was the place for me."

"That's really a great story. So easy for you. I think I searched for two months in this area. Most places are old, small, and expensive."

"I know; I got lucky. This brownstone has been in his family for a long time. That's why this space is so large. It was originally two units, but he tore down the walls, creating this. Next time you come over, I'll show you the best part."

Next time. Just short of him professing his undying love for me, he couldn't have said anything more perfect to me.

"Why can't you show me now?" My curiosity is piqued.

"Because, it's the wrong time of day." He smirks at me.

"Okay, and you're just assuming that I'll want to come back another day." I'm joking with him, but his face falls.

Something flashes across his eyes, but then it's gone. "Maybe; I guess we'll find out," he says flatly.

"If you want me to come back, then just say the word; I'll even bring some food."

His face relaxes. He gives me another smile and leans back into the couch.

"Are you going to Ali's this weekend?" I ask, trying to switch the conversation back to a lighter one.

"Of course; wouldn't miss it. Besides, can you imagine the earful I'd get from her if I didn't show?"

I laugh. I do know her and, for someone so small, she can get super-feisty.

Beau looks at me hesitantly. "So I really don't have anything planned this afternoon. Do you want to stay and watch a movie with me?"

He wants me here.

"Yes, I'd like that." I curl my legs up underneath me and smile back at him.

I should take this as an opportunity to ask him why, but I'm craving time with him and needing a good moment. I don't want to ruin this with questions. He so rarely lets me in . . . maybe next time I'll ask.

BEAU

CLASSES STARTED THE last week in August, and I am grateful for the distraction. Matt went home with Mom after the beach-house weekend and the loft has been pretty quiet. So quiet, I find myself thinking that maybe I could have handled a lot of things with Leila differently over the years, but what good does this do me? I can't change what's done or rewrite history.

Drew and Nate have both stopped over a few times, but really everyone is trying to get settled into the new semester. I know that they are both worried about me, but I'll snap out of this soon. Putting distance between Leila and me will be good for me.

It's been three weeks since I have seen Leila, and knowing that she's so close has been driving me crazy. I shouldn't think about going to the café as much as I do, but it was only a matter of time until I found myself standing outside the front door. Maybe she's working, or maybe not, but I shouldn't be surprised that this is where my feet brought me. I heard her tell Ali at the beach house that she's no longer working weekends, so she most likely won't even be here. I need to just go in and get this over with. My heart races with indecision.

Looking around at the people passing by on the sidewalk, I start laughing at the ridiculousness of this. *Get it together, Hale. She is Ali's best friend and she's always going to be around . . . so get used to it! Stick to the plan, and remember the goal. It's time to move on.* Taking a deep breath, I focus on the last part of my little pep talk: it's time to move on. I shove one hand into my pocket and walk in.

The door closes behind me. I quickly take inventory of who's in the place and my eyes come to a stop on Leila and Charlie. Leila approaches me, smiling.

"Hey, I saw you stop outside and was wondering if you were going to come in."

"Yeah, I was trying to decide whether or not I really want a cup of coffee." My eyes shift past her and I see Charlie sitting in the chair next to the window. It didn't even occur to me that he might be here. I was singularly focused on her and now I'm mad at myself. Seeing him is another reminder of why I never should have come in here.

"So, what did you decide?" her voice snaps me out of my mental scolding.

"I'm here, aren't I?"

She flinches, drops her eyes to the ground, and frowns.

"I'm sorry, Leila, that sounded bad," I say, letting out a sigh. I don't want to be an asshole to her. I just really want to get over her, him, this, how it makes me feel, all of it.

"It's alright. Have a seat and I'll go get it for you."

She walks off and my eyes follow her.

"So, it's Beau, right?" I hear Charlie say from behind me.

"Yep." Looking back at him, he smiles at me and I grit my teeth together.

"Awesome; have a seat."

I walk over and sit down next him. He seems friendly enough; I just don't need or want to be friends with him. A moment of silence passes between us, neither of us really knowing what to say. He's watching me and I'm watching him.

"Did you know that rats can't sweat?" I ask him.

Confusion and humor appear on his face. "What? Why

are you telling me that?"

"No reason. This city is filled with rats . . . and I thought you might find it interesting." I'm certain he hears the double meaning in my reply as he shifts his weight, watches me, and then starts laughing.

"Did you know that bees have five eyes?"

I don't know what type of response I was expecting from him, but it wasn't this. No wonder Drew and Ali like him. He holds his own, I guess.

The corner of my mouth twitches and he smirks back at me. I really don't want to like this guy, but he makes it hard not to. Both times he's been around, he's been nice and, given the right circumstance, I probably would, too.

"Yeah, turns out I'm allergic to the little bastards, so I'm kind of obsessed with them and freaked out at the same time."

"That sucks. What happens if you get stung?"

"Swell up all over."

The thought of buying some bees quickly enters and leaves my mind.

"So, any big plans this weekend?" he asks me.

"No, nothing much." I know that it would be polite to ask him back, but I don't want to hear what they have planned together. Leila walks back over and hands me the coffee in a to-go cup.

"Leila, guess what?" Charlie says to her.

"What?" She's looking at me with her crystal blue eyes and I can feel it all the way down into the bottom of my stomach.

"Beau was just saying how he doesn't have any plans this afternoon, and I know that you don't either, so the two of you should hang out. You could catch up and reminisce about the good old days."

What?

My head swings back to Charlie and I can't believe that he just said this. He has to know that she and I have history. Why would he be pushing us together?

"It's alright; I'm sure you have something that you need to do . . ."

Her voice brings me out of my moment of shock, and I rein in my emotions. Looking at Leila, I know that I have a couple of seconds to decide. Do I decide to let her in, with the possibility of her hurting me further, or do I decide to walk away? Maybe what I need is to spend some time with her. Maybe then I will get some perspective. Maybe then I will decide that all I've done over the years is build her up in my head to be someone else. Either way, she'll be with me and not with him, and I'm okay with that. So much for putting distance between us.

"Sure, I was just headed home, if that sounds alright to you."

Her eyes widen. I've surprised her. She thought I would say no; then again, after the way I dismissed her at the beach, I would probably think that, too.

"Um, sure, I just need to grab my bag from the back."

What did I just do? Part of me is in shock. I invited the girl of my dreams, and from my dreams, to my home. I never thought this would be happening. I just didn't think we were in that place, but maybe we are.

Walking into the loft with her, it immediately feels different, warmer, more like a home. I shouldn't like her being here as much as I do, but I can't help it.

After she looks around the apartment, I know my time is almost up with her. I don't want her to go; I want her to stay, but I don't know what to talk about with her. After all these years, and all the things that have already been said, just coming out and asking her why doesn't seem like a possibility anymore. Does it ever become just too late to ask certain questions? So, just like I did a year and a half ago, I invite her to stay for a movie.

Leila tucks her legs up underneath her and curls up on the couch.

"Here," I reach into the drawer of the end table and pull out a bag of salt water taffy. Her face lights up when she sees what I have.

"You really do love this stuff, don't you?"

"Yep, I don't know what it is but I could eat this stuff nonstop."

She takes the package from me and our fingers brush. My heart rate instantly speeds up. Her eyes catch mine for a second and her cheeks turn a beautiful shade of pink.

"Seems to me, you do eat it nonstop; you always have some on you."

"Yeah, I guess I do. Do you have a preference on the movie?"

"Nope, just something funny or something scary." She used to say this when we were kids. I always opted for funny. I lived everyday with scary and didn't need any more in my life.

The last scary night that I had, I was eighteen. Dad finally went too far. He's getting what he deserves behind bars now. Leila showed up the morning after. I needed her more than ever and somehow she knew this.

Last night, my dad was arrested. I spent most of it sitting next to my mom in the hospital, holding her hand. She cried a lot, and I don't think that she was crying over losing her husband or because she was in pain. I got the feeling from the few things she said, that she was crying out of regret. It really was the first time that I've ever heard her say she wished things had been different for us. Over the years, she always kept her mouth shut and never tried to give us a better life.

The nurse on duty took pity on me. She helped clean and stitch me up. She also mysteriously gave me some pain medicine that, supposedly, my mom refused but she didn't want to go to waste. I'm not gonna lie; my face, my head, my back, where he hit me with the frying pan, everything was screaming at me.

I've replayed over and over in my mind what happened to us earlier at home. Drew has always felt guilty for the things that have happened to Matt and me, but what he doesn't understand is, he's always been my hero. What he did for us, I could never repay him. In many ways, he saved my life. Who knows what would have happened, and I don't think that I could have lived in that house with Drew gone. He has nothing to feel guilty about and I am so happy to see that Drew has Ali. He deserves to be loved and she is the perfect girl for him.

After leaving my mom at the hospital, I drove straight to Ali's. Drew said that he would be there and, like him, I had zero interest in returning to our house. Even the thought of being in that house alone leaves an unsettled feeling in my stomach.

Ali mothers me like she always does, and it's shortly after she serves us breakfast that there is a knock on the door. Ali opens it and my heart stops as I hear her voice. It feels like a cool mist has washed over me, only to be dried by the warm sun. Never in my life has something sounded so good. I hop up off the couch and walk into the foyer. She is talking to Ali, but stops mid-sentence when she sees me.

"Beau," she says, just barely louder than a whisper. Her eyes fill with tears and, for the first time in a long time, I feel like my best friend is back. All I can hope for is that these are not tears of pity for what has become my life, but that they are tears of heartache for what I went through. I don't want her to feel sorry for me but, at the same time, I need her to feel compassion. I need someone to care about me. And, if I'm telling the truth, I don't want just anyone; I want her.

"What do you want, Leila?" I ask her. She needs to know that today is not the day to mess with me.

"I just . . . twenty-four hours." She's fidgeting with her fingers. She always does this when she's nervous.

"Twenty-four hours of what?" I run my hand over the back of my neck. It's stiff from sitting in the hospital chair and from sleeping on the couch.

"A truce, a cease fire, whatever you want to call it. I just . . . please, Beau. Twenty-four hours." I can hear in her voice how desperately she is hoping that I will say yes.

Everyone around me has someone: Drew has Ali, Matt has Aunt Ella, Mom has all of us. Who do I have? I know that I'm not alone, but I feel that way. Standing here looking at her, as much as I don't want to admit that I need her, I do. She was always my person, just mine, and right now I really need her. I need someone for me.

"Okay."

"Okay?" she asks, hopeful yet hesitant at the same time. I nod my head at her and, the next thing I know, she lands in my arms and I feel like I am home.

Just the feel of her up next to me, the way she smells, the

softness of her hair, everything . . . makes this horrible situation feel just a little bit better. I never want to let her go.

"Thank you, Lei," I say into her hair.

She squeezes me tighter and I tuck my face into her neck.

Drew and Ali leave the room and Leila pulls back from me. Slowly, she looks at all of the damage to my face, and I close my eyes. I don't want to see what I am feeling reflected back at me through her eyes. It's bad enough that she can probably see how much her being here is affecting me. I don't want this to be added to my list of memories.

Her hand gently touches the side of my face, "Are you staying here?"

"I am for now. Mom comes home from the hospital a little later today. Now that you're here, Drew and Ali will go get her. Are you really going to be here with me for twenty-four hours?"

"Yes, if you'll let me." Her fingers drift down my face and over my neck to my collarbone. The last time she even came remotely close to touching me, we were standing in the photo lab closet at school. She'll never know how good it feels to be touched by her.

"I need to run home, grab some clothes, and take a shower. I stayed with Mom last night at the hospital and, honestly, I'm just dirty and tired."

"Okay; can I go with you?" she asks.

"Sure."

I decide that it would be best if we go through the front door. I'm not ready to face the kitchen. She follows me up the stairs and into my room. I've never given much thought to Leila being in my room; after all, it's been almost three years. Looking around, I try to imagine how it looks to her. On my nightstand, I spot the journal that she gave me. I quickly walk over to it and shove it into the drawer. I don't want her to see it.

Grabbing some clothes, I turn to face her. "I'll be right out. Will you wait for me?" I don't know why I ask her this. Maybe I feel like if I do, she won't leave and, honestly, that is what I am expecting. I am expecting her to leave.

"Yes, I'll be here. I promise." Giving her a small smile, I head into the bathroom and close the door.

Standing under the water, I'm trying to wrap my head around the fact that Leila is in my bedroom. Even before she moved away, she very rarely came in our house. I never wanted Dad to see her. It was better if he thought I was just outside, being a boy. The more I kept her away from here, the longer I thought I would get to keep her.

Throwing on a long-sleeved T-shirt and a pair of athletic shorts, I apprehensively open the door, and find her sitting on the end of my bed, looking at a magazine she picked up off my desk. She smiles at me and, for the first time in a long time, I feel like things are going to be okay.

As we walk back across the street, she slips her hand into mine. It's such a simple gesture, but it makes me feel like I don't have to cope with this all on my own. I tighten my grip. In this moment, there's no letting go.

"You're in the guest room, right?" she asks me as we walk through the front door of Ali's house.

Ali's home has become my second home, and having Leila here and talking to me all feels surreal. I spend so much time thinking about her that having her here in the flesh is messing with my mind and my heart. I know that we agreed to twenty-four hours, but what am I supposed to do when the twenty-four hours are up?

"Yeah."

"Why don't you head on in there and I'll grab us a couple of waters and a few snacks?"

"Sounds good. Thank you." Before she can pull her hand away, I gently tug her closer to me and lay my forehead on hers. This girl will never understand what her being here means to me.

Lying on my back with my hands under my head, I close my eyes when I hear her coming down the hall. She opens the door and slips in. The bed dips as Leila climbs on and sits right next to me. My senses are immediately invaded by her presence. She smells so good. Her fingertips brush across my cheek bone. The comfort that this gives me causes a lump to form in my throat.

"Does it hurt?"

"Yes. But it will heal. It always does."

"You mean this isn't the first time that he's hit you?" I turn my head so I can look at her beautiful face. I don't say anything. I don't need to. "Why didn't you ever tell me? I could have been there for you or done something. I don't know . . . I just . . . you should have told me."

"When was I going to tell you, Leila? When we were little kids and I was so terrified of him finding out that I told someone that I lived in fear? Or, sometime during the two years that you were gone and I had no way to reach you? Oh, I know . . . when you moved back and our friendship resumed with open arms. Don't you get it? You were never to find out."

She frowns and her eyes dull a little with sadness. "I wish that things had turned out differently for us."

Does she? Does she really wish that? If she did, then why did she say what she did when she moved? Why did she send me that letter? The way she left things and the way she made me feel, I'm not ever going to forget it. Irritation mixed with heartache slips into my already-fragile emotional state.

"Yeah, well, they didn't, which is why, in twenty-three hours, this will be over." As hard as I try, the lump grows bigger, my chest gets tighter and, one by one, tears leak out and roll down the side of my face. I really don't want to cry in front of her but I couldn't stop it if I tried.

Her thumb gently brushes away the tears. I close my eyes and her lips replace her thumb. Running her hand through my hair, she kisses every sore, bruised, and injured spot on my face, including my bottom lip that has stitches. Maybe if this was another time and we were in another place, I might have tried to explore that kiss a little further, but that's not what this moment is all about.

I feel her pull back a little so I open my eyes. She is still hovering directly over me. "I've missed you." This causes my eyes to fill again and become watery; hers do the same.

"Stay with me," my voice catches as I ask her this.

"I'm not going anywhere and, Beau, I will always be here for you." She scoots down next to me, laying her head on my chest. I turn a little and wrap my arms around her.

"Wanna watch a movie?"

"A movie sounds great. You pick, but make it something funny or something scary."

I pull her closer and reach for the remote. I'm sure there are plenty of things that we could talk about, but I'm too tired, and really I just want to lie here curled up with her. Her being here is enough.

When morning comes, I don't even have to open my eyes to know that she is gone. The bed feels empty, and where she was lying next to me is no longer warm. Letting out a deep sigh, I let the pain of this moment absorb me. I'm alone again. Realistically, I knew that she was going to go, but way down deep there is a part of me that really hoped she would stay. I think that maybe, if given the chance, I could have forgiven her for what she did four years ago. But, in the end, I guess I'll never know.

Chapter Eight

BEAU

WALKING INTO DREW'S apartment, every hair of mine seems to stand on end. I knew that Leila would be here and, honestly, this reaction to her is starting to get old.

There is this little bit of me that's excited to see her today. Lately, I have been dreading it more often than not, but having her at the loft was really nice. It was good to get to talk to her again. Maybe I will a little tonight, too.

"Dude, check out all the hot girls here! What did you say your sister-in-law did?" Nate asks.

I love that he calls her that, even though she isn't yet. Just the thought makes me smile. I invited Nate to come along because I know that Tiny is up to something. After our little conversation at the beach house, she's invited me over several times to meet her friend. I politely decline every time, but I know that tonight I probably won't be so lucky.

"She's a dancer at Julliard."

"That's right." He nods his head in agreement now that he remembers, and he grins. "Dancers are flexible . . . mmm, I can just imagine."

"Asshole, gross. That's my brother's girl you're talking about."

"Relax, I'm not talking about her; however, that little blondie over there . . ." He nods and I follow his gaze to a girl across the room. She's standing by herself, with her arms folded over her chest, and she's looking out the window. I have to agree with him; she is something to look at.

"Beau!" A loud squeal comes from behind me. Ali comes skipping over and she throws her arms around me. "I didn't think you were coming." Her face shines up at me.

"Tiny, you know I wouldn't miss one of your parties. Besides, you said the magic word."

"Pizza!" we both say at the same time and she laughs.

"I've missed you," she says, lightly running her hand up and down my arm. This makes me feel bad because I know that she wants the three of us to hang out more.

"You just saw me a few weeks ago."

"I know, but now that you're here in the city, and I know that I can see you more often—we want to, both of us."

"School and tennis have been crazy, but I promise I'll try to make it by more often."

"You better." She punches me in the arm that she was just rubbing.

"Oww!" I always forget how strong she is.

She grins at me.

Nate clears his throat. He's grinning at our interaction.

"Tiny, this is Nate Jackson; he plays on the team with me. Nate, this is Ali."

"Nice to meet you; I take it you're the sister-in-law?"

"Yep, that's me." Her eyes sparkle. "My friend is here and, when you're ready, I want you to meet her."

I can't stop the groan that comes out of me. "Why is this so important to you?"

"Because, she needs friends and you make a pretty good one."

"Alright, bring her over later. First, let me get a beer and find my brother, in that order."

"Okay." She turns to Nate, "It was nice to meet you."

"You too, Ali." He smiles down at her.

I don't like the way he says her name, so I elbow him in the arm.

"What!" he says.

"You know what," I say under my breath.

Ali laughs at the two of us and skips off.

"Come on, let's go grab a beer."

Together we walk through the crowd and out onto the balcony. There, standing next to the cooler full of beer, is Leila . . . and Charlie. His arm is wrapped around her shoulders and he's laughing at something Drew said. My gut calls Drew a traitor, even though I know he's not. So much for talking to her tonight.

Leila looks at Nate, and then at me. She watches me approach but doesn't say anything.

"Beau! About time you got here." Drew slaps me on the back and we bump forearms, pretending our arms are fighting swords. It's something we've done since we were kids.

"What do you mean? The party just started," I say to him.

"For you, maybe, pizzas hit the grill over three hours ago."

I narrow my eyes at him, "Whatever, keep rubbing it in, but hand me a beer while you're at it."

He laughs and grabs two bottles out of the cooler.

"Hi, I'm Charlie, and this is Leila," Charlie says to Nate, while removing his arm from around Leila and extending his hand. Why is this guy always so nice?

Nate's eyebrows shoot up. He must remember her name from over a month ago. Of course, her name has to be unique, not something like Sarah or Michelle. He glances my way and whatever he sees on my face causes him to grin.

"Nate," he shakes Charlie's hand and then turns his attention to Leila. "Beau and I are on the tennis team together. It's nice to meet you." His eyes flick to Charlie and then back to her. "And it's really nice to meet you, Leila," he says, smiling at her.

She frowns at him, but takes his hand. I imagine that I am frowning, too.

"Yeah, I'm Drew, this one's older brother." He slaps me on the back again and smirks at me, too.

"So, how is the season going?" Charlie asks us.

"Awesome for Beau, here. He hasn't lost yet," Nate says, still giving me a sly smile. I know he's thinking about that practice and our conversation. I never should have told him her name.

"Really? That doesn't surprise me. He's always had the talent and the ability to get exactly what he wants." Drew's eyes flare with mischief; the smirk is still in place. Charlie is watching the three of us.

I know there's a double meaning to this, but I don't want to hear any more. I look at Leila and give her a small smile.

"Hey," I say to her.

Her eyes widen, and she lights up just a little bit. "Hey."

And then that awkward moment happens where the five of us are standing on the balcony and not one person says anything. The three of them are watching us; if they are waiting for Leila and me to engage in some kind of conversation, it's never going to happen. Not with Charlie standing here. Visions of his arm around her come back to me and, just like that, I'm done with this little scene.

"Well, I'll be inside looking for pizza." My eyes lock with Leila's one more time, and my stomach bottoms out at how blue and familiar they are to me. I know those eyes just as much as I know my own, and I hate how she no longer sees me; then again, I'm not really sure she ever did. I turn around and leave.

It takes Nate about three seconds to ask the question that I know he is dying to. "So, that's Leila?" he asks, following me into the condo.

"Yep."

"Wow, I can see why she has you all torn up."

I stop walking and shoot him a look to let him know that he's crossing the line. I don't want him or anyone else to look at her.

"Seriously? Ease up, dude. Poaching my friends' girls, whether they are current or in the past, is not my thing."

I let out a sigh and he sees me relax.

"You do realize the girl that I just met is by no means over you. Did you see the way she was looking at you?"

"Whatever; it doesn't really matter anyway." Didn't he see the way Charlie had his arm wrapped around her?

"Are you sure about that?" he asks.

"Yeah, I'm sure."

Any little sliver of hope that I had from last weekend just vanished.

Walking toward the kitchen, my eye catches Drew's and he smirks again at me. He's up to something.

"Hey, Beau, come over here for a minute. I want to introduce you Ali's friend, Camille," he says to me.

And there it is. Here we go . . .

Leaving Drew and Ali's party, I sigh in relief. It's funny how I used to love to go to parties. Now I just want to avoid them as much as possible. Three quarters of the night I spent thinking about Leila, and the other quarter I spent thinking about when I could make my escape to head home.

"Hey, Beau! Wait up!"

I turn around and see Camille jogging toward me. I stop to wait for her, shoving my hands into my pockets. She really is a pretty girl, but I'm just not the one for her, and I need to make that clear pretty quickly.

"I saw you leave and I thought maybe we could walk together for a while," she says.

"Alright, I was just walking home. Where do you live?"

"East side actually, straight across the park."

"Lead the way." I gesture with my hand.

She smiles at me.

"So, you play tennis at Columbia?"

I'm not surprised that she knows this, "Yep, what else did Ali tell you?"

She chuckles. "Not a lot, just that you didn't know very many people in the city; neither do I, and she thought that we might get along."

"Yeah, well, what Ali seems to be overlooking is that I choose not to know a lot of people. I like things just the way they are." That probably came out a little harsher than it needed to. It wasn't really directed at her but more at the way I want to live my life.

When I look over at Camille, her eyebrows are raised at me. "Look, your message just came through loud and clear, but no worries, I have a boyfriend."

"You do?" I suddenly feel like an idiot. "Does Ali know this, because she's been all 'I'm all about pushing Camille Beau's way' for the last couple of weeks."

She giggles. "No, I haven't told her. Here, in the city, I get to be somebody completely different than I have to be at home and, well, here . . . I'm free."

"That doesn't make sense to me." Why would she choose to hide her boyfriend?

"Let's just say that where I come from, he is the family-approved boyfriend and expected to be husband one day."

"You make it sound like it's arranged."

"May as well be." She frowns and wraps her arms around her middle.

"So, where is this guy?"

"Harvard."

I look down at her and that's when I see it. She isn't just a pretty girl; she's of a high society pedigree. Everything about her is perfect, from her southern accent, to her posture, her gleaming white smile, and her clothes. I instantly feel bad for her. Why is it that we allow parents to have so much influence over us?

"I see. How about we hop in a cab since it's dark out? Better to be safe than sorry crossing the park."

"Sure. Thanks for taking me home."

"Anytime, Camille, and maybe being friends won't be so bad." I look down at her and give her a small smile.

She smiles back at me and I can see genuine relief in her face. She must really need friends and not know how to make them. There must be more to her story than she's telling me.

The cab ride is quick. We talk a little but not too much. Most of it is just the basic where are you from type questions. She seems a little sad. I should definitely have her hang out with Nate some. He'll get her laughing.

Dropping her off in front of her building, she waves goodbye before walking into her building. She seems like a really nice girl. I wonder if this guy even realizes what he has, or if he is just as caught up in the charade as their parents are.

Glancing up to the sky, there's a single star dotting the night and shining down. My mind instantly drifts and Leila's thirteen-year-old voice takes over.

"Do you see it?" she asks, handing me a piece of taffy. We've snuck out again and are down on the beach at Bean Point.

"What, the Summer Triangle? Of course I see it. We look for it every time we come out here."

"I wish that we could see it year-round," she says as she lies back on the towel to stare up at the sky.

"I don't know, I kind of like only seeing it during the summer. It's like it belongs to us."

She tilts her head to look at me and the moonlight has made her eyes a silver color. They are beautiful. She is beautiful.

"Beau, why do you like the stars so much?"

"Because they remind me of you," I say, looking out over the water and not at her. I don't want her to see exactly how I am feeling about her.

She reaches over, grabs my hand, and hugs it to her chest. This causes me to blush. I'm so glad that it's dark out.

"They remind me of you, too," she whispers.

"Did you know that Vega, from the Lyra constellation, is the fifth-brightest star in the night sky?"

She's still looking at me. "Which star is the second-brightest?"

"Why didn't you ask me about the brightest star?"

Looking down at her she giggles.

"Because you talked about it last week, remember? The dog days of summer."

"Oh, yeah, well Canopus is the second-brightest star in the sky. We can see it so well because it is located in the southern sky. People who live north of Virginia can't see it at all. Its name means keel of a ship; it used to belong to a larger constellation called Argo Navis. Story has it, the ship, which belonged to Jason and the Argonauts, was used to hunt for a golden fleece that was supposed to help make him king. Only, you know how these stories go, the glory days didn't last too long."

"Why do you know all of these things? You are always telling me interesting facts and stories."

"Because, I like to read. When I'm at home, I always stay in my room, and since I don't have a TV, it's the next best thing. Mom gave me an old set of encyclopedias; they probably aren't too up-to-date, but I think they're alright. Some of the things that I've read in them are so funny. Like, did you know that, on average, a chocolate bar has eight insect legs in it?"

"Ewww, that's gross." She giggles, still holding my hand.

"Anyway, I like learning all of these things and you always seem to like hearing them, so as far as I see it, it's a win-win."

"I guess so. You are, by far, the smartest person I know."

"I don't know about that, but if you think so, okay."

Watching her, under the stars, while she holds my hand . . . I couldn't be happier.

LEILA

IT'S THE FIRST weekend in September, and Drew and Ali decide to throw a party. Ali had called earlier in the week to remind us, and I assured her that Charlie and I would be there, even though I needed to spend the time finalizing the last minute details on the Fashion Week collection. And honestly, after spending the afternoon with Beau a few days before, I needed the entire week to prepare myself to see him again. Beau's different; he's changed, and this new Beau has my head spinning.

It was easy to ignore him before. He's always been a little on the loud side and lacked the ability to use a filter. He liked to be the center of attention. He was funny and smiled a lot. Everyone wanted to be friends with him and he was friends with everyone.

But this Beau is quiet and reserved. He sits off to the side more and seems to shy away from the spotlight. He's still funny if you get him going but he never smiles or laughs anymore. Even Drew and Ali commented on how he never talks about any friends, mostly it's just Matt; here at Ali's party is the first time any of us have seen or heard of a Nate.

"I thought that you said the two of you got along last weekend," Charlie says to me as we watch Drew leave the patio and follow Beau into the condo.

"We did; at least that's what I thought."

"Huh." Charlie leans back against the railing.

Every time that Beau and I are together, it's like we are in a bubble where it's just him and me. But the minute you put us out into the real world, the bubble pops.

"Do you think that he thinks we're together?" Charlie asks me.

I consider this. The first time he saw us, Charlie made it seem like we were together, and even today we were standing pretty close. "Maybe; except for the beach, he's seen me three times and all three times I've been with you."

"You should tell him that we're not together then."

"I really don't know if it would make much of a difference. Anyway, I've got two weeks left until the show and I need to focus on the collection. You know that for years I've wanted to be a designer. This is my future and I can't let anything get in the way of it . . . even him."

"I still think you should tell him, especially before it's too late." He nods his head and I look over to see Drew introducing him to a very beautiful girl. He shakes her hand, smiles at her, and I feel like a part of me dies. Since I first saw him again, almost two months ago, he hasn't smiled at me much at all, but with her it just came out so easily.

When we were kids, his face used to light up every time he saw me. He would smile and wave and it was the best feeling in the world to know that he was happy because of me.

I should have known that Ali would have invited some of her dancing friends. I spent so much time thinking about seeing Beau and how I would react to him, that I never considered that I might have to see him with someone else.

Ali walks out on to the porch and, without thinking, I ask, "Who's that?"

She follows my gaze and pauses.

"Oh, she's a friend of mine from school. Her name is Camille, and she's in the dance program with me." I can feel Ali looking at me, so I stop staring at the girl and give Ali my attention. Ali's expression is one of remorse. I hate that she knows me so well.

"Is she nice or fake?"

"She's nice," Ali says quietly.

Camille is such a pretty name, and I'm reminded me of the time Beau asked me about mine.

"How did you get your name? I've never met anyone named Leila before," Beau asks.

"My mom and dad went on their honeymoon to Hawaii. When they got to the hotel they each were given a necklace made of orchids, called a lei. My mom said that since they had such a memorable time there, and because I was born just a couple of months shy of their first anniversary, that it was the perfect name. She said she loves my name because it reminds her of one of the best times in her life."

"I've seen those flower necklaces before."

"Aren't they just beautiful? Orchids are my favorite flower. It's why I love purple so much."

"Oh, I didn't know that," Beau says, looking at me thoughtfully.

The next day, Beau shows up to Bean Point with a potted orchid plant. He had ridden his bike down to the local nursery and bought it for me. His smiled from ear to ear when he handed it to me. He has always been so thoughtful, and I loved that plant. When we were rummaging through the remains from the fire, I looked for the pot, but never found it.

Blinking out of the memory, I look back and continue to observe them. Beau's friend Nate walks up and introduces himself. They all laugh and my heart breaks; I've always loved Beau's laugh.

I really do only want the best for him.

This sucks.

Chapter Nine

BEAU

I HAD ANOTHER nightmare last night. It's been almost two months since I've had one this bad and I hate how real it feels. The unavoidable terror, Matt's cries, and Leila's screams all echo in my mind nonstop, leaving me no way to escape it.

I understand the dreams. I've never wondered why I have them—they are my biggest fears. Drew has never appeared in any of them but, then again, I've never worried about him. He always did exactly what he needed to do to fly under the radar and focus on getting out. I knew he would. But it's my mother, Matt, and Leila that I always feared for.

My mother was always weak. She never stood up for herself and demanded to be treated better. My dad walked all over her like a door mat, and he was physical with her more times than I care to remember. That last day, when I walked into the kitchen and saw him strangling her, it is a day I'll never forget. The image is burned into my memory. Her eyes were huge, her mouth was open, and he had her head tipped at an awkward angle. He was going to kill her . . . and then he saw me.

Usually after school, I headed straight for the courts to get a few sets in with Grant; however, on this particular day, he canceled at the last minute to go help his grandmother with her yard. Instead of finding something else to do, like dropping into the Beachside Café, I chose to go home. Leila always worked there for a few hours after school, and mostly I don't mind seeing her, but after watching Drew fall in love and finally find some peace with himself, I just couldn't go there.

Matt was so small and helpless. Both my mother and my father pretended like he didn't exist and he was always by himself. Drew and I tried to talk to him and show him some attention when we could, but we were busy trying to survive. No one ever talked to Matt or showed him love. I remember, before Matt was born, Mom hugging me, loving on me, and protecting me. I can't imagine what childhood would be like without that.

And then there's Leila. She was always the one thing that was mine, only mine. Every day I woke up in fear that he would tell me I couldn't see her anymore. I just knew that he was going to take her away from me somehow. She brought me happiness in a way that was indescribable, and the thought of not having her left me anxious more often than not.

As for the fire, that's an obvious one.

Today, I got up and went about my normal day; practice with Nate, then to class, but now . . . the rest of the day is mine.

Taking the subway over to midtown, I get off at the 42nd street stop and walk up into Times Square.

It's here that I can be no one in the midst of everyone.

Drew once mentioned how he always felt like he had to wear a mask around people to keep up the perfect appearance. Well, I wore mine but for a different reason. Who wants people to know that they mean so little to someone, that they're used as a personal punching bag?

Getting lost in the crowds here is so easy. They say that Times Square is one of the most visited places in the world, and it's because of this that I've found a place where I can hide, and still be in plain sight.

In a park, at the beach, on a regular street, any of these types of places, people are relaxing and looking around to see what others are doing. I mean who hasn't laid on the beach at some point and stared at the people walking by? But, here, in this part of the city, that usually doesn't happen.

There are always so many people here from so many different parts of the world, that people- watching gives me an escape. It's watching them look around in wonder, it's watching them laugh, and it's watching them be happy with friends and family. I don't pretend that I'm someone else or that I was given a different life. These are the cards that I was dealt, but seeing that there are other ways to live . . . that gives me hope.

A billboard for HBO catches my eye, advertising a fight between two boxers. I know that boxing is a huge sport and a lot of people really enjoy it, but after being on the receiving end of a fist for so long, I just couldn't do it.

Or maybe I could. It's this thought that frightens me on a pretty regular basis.

My mother hates snakes. She is so afraid of them, that the closer she is to one, the more she panics.

We had this one that was living under the front porch, but for some reason it would come up and sunbathe. Mom would open the front door, see the snake, and by the way she screamed you would have thought someone was trying to pry off her fingernails.

One afternoon, Matt and I had just come in from a run, and there it was. Something had happened earlier that day, I don't remember what it was, but I was in a bad mood, and seeing it made me snap. I walked into the garage, grabbed a large flat-head shovel, and then proceeded to swing the shovel as hard as I could to kill that snake.

Matt watched in horror.

Dad must have heard the noise, and came outside. From behind me, I heard clapping and his laugh; the same laugh that haunts my dreams.

Every time, his laugh creeps up my spine and makes the hair on my arms stand up. It's not a normal laugh. It has this evil, sinister cadence to it.

"Well, well, well; what do we have here?"

I turn to face him. We've all been taught that, when he speaks, we're to give him our undivided attention. He wore a condescending smirk and his eyes were lit up. If I believed in paranormal beings, I would say his eyes almost look like they are glowing.

"Maybe you are my son after all . . ." he laughs again and then looks over to Matt, "but don't worry; you aren't." Then he wandered back into the house.

Fear settled into the pit of my stomach and I felt like ice water had just been thrown on me. For years, I always thought to myself that I could never treat anyone the way he treats us, but what if I could? He's right. I am his son. As much as I wanted to ignore it, the expression, "the apple doesn't fall far from the tree," comes to mind.

Mom decided after Dad went to jail last year that she was finally going to step in and try to fix the years and years of damage that had been done. She took us to some family counselor and, in a typical professional setting, this person asked questions that immediately went right to the core of me. Of course, we are the stereotypical abused family, and she was educated on how to help us move forward, but to hear her verbalize my fears as if they were normal, it just bothered me because, to me, the things that I felt and experienced aren't normal.

I listened to her talk about how abused kids hardly ever grow up to be abusers themselves. It's all just a myth that is usually created by the abuser, in hopes of creating fear and doubt in the child. She said that most children grow up to be kind, loving, and the best parents because they have this fierce motivation to protect those that they love.

The only person I have ever truly loved is Leila. Walking through the streets, people bump into me, but I just don't care. Block after block, my feet keep moving. They have a one-track mind and that's to get to her. The need to see her is so overwhelming, there's a lump in my chest that is pushing on my heart.

By the time I reach the café, the sun has dropped behind me and my reflection on the windows bounces back at me. I can't see in to see if she is there, and I take this as a sign; a sign that I shouldn't be seeing her, shouldn't be thinking about her, and in general I should be remembering that everyone is moving on.

Letting out a sigh, I turn, walk away from the café, and head around the corner to my loft.

Tossing my keys on the counter, I slip off my shoes, and walk straight to the couch. Without even turning the TV on, I flop down on the spot where she sat and close my eyes.

I'm tired—physically and emotionally.

There's a loud knocking on the door that wakes me up. Wandering over and peeking through the eyehole, I come face to face with a messenger kid. I throw the door open, and the kid looks me over from head to toe. I get it; I'm tall, thick through the arms, chest, shoulders, and can come across as intimidating.

"Are you Beau Hale?" he asks as he swallows.

"Yes."

"Sign here, please." He lifts a small clipboard. I sign next to my name. He hands me an envelope and runs off.

The envelope is black with three silver letters embossed in the middle on the front, BLK.

Inside is an all-black invitation with the same silver script. It is to attend BLK's premier show at the end of Fashion Week. The show is invitation-only, and three quarters of the way down I see why I have received this—highlighting our "Rising Designer" of the year, Leila Starling.

A surge of pride fills me. She has worked so hard for this

and for so long. The number of doors that will probably open for her after this will be unlimited.

Walking over to the refrigerator, I hang the invitation. I am a little surprised that she invited me, but if she wants me there then I will be there. After all, I've never been able to tell her no.

LEILA

AFTER THE ANNOUNCEMENT of the "Rising Designer," a representative from the BLK label called and offered me the use of a vacant studio. Honestly, I had been tossing around the idea of looking for a separate place to work, and this couldn't have come at a more opportune time.

The warehouse is located a few blocks from the school, so ideally this is perfect. Inside the warehouse, the space is broken down into individual design studios. One whole wall is made up of windows, allowing as much natural light as possible into the room.

Charlie was over the moon with the new space, and immediately ran out and found a few signature pieces to complete the space and make it mine. He always thinks one step ahead and knew that, eventually, people would be stopping by to see what I am working on. And, also, inside the studio, the models would need a place to change.

My favorite of the pieces he brought in is a chandelier. It looks vintage Victorian, and he hung it right in the middle of the room. It's huge and covered in crystals and mirrors. At night, the light bounces off of the ceiling and, although they are just tiny reflections, I feel like I am under the stars.

"Have I told you how much I love this space?" he says.

"Yes, you have," I giggle at Charlie as he takes in every detail of the room. "I can't believe that they offered it to me, and at such a good price, too."

"They must see something great in you . . . I've always said one day you'd be famous."

"I don't know about famous, but I've had a lot of fun doing this, and that's what matters, right?"

"Absolutely. So these are your selections for the show?"

Against the inside wall of the studio, I have ten mannequins on one side of the door and ten on the other. This keeps them out of the sunlight and also gives me the ability to wander back and forth between them for any last minute changes. They should probably be zipped up tight in garment bags, but I'm a visual girl and I need them on display.

"I think so. I've been staring at them for the last week, wondering if I should do anything more or less with them." Walking over, I finger the sheer batiste cover-up for the first model. I had spent the last three months trying to decide on the perfect embroidery that would enhance not only the figure of the person wearing it, but also the swimsuit underneath, and I couldn't be more pleased with how it turned out.

"I think that you should leave them. They look perfect to me. The stitching and beading are exquisite, and the patterns and colors make them desirable for any body type. I mean, who wouldn't want to wear these?"

"You always know how to make me smile." And he really does. I can't imagine what my life would have been like without him over the last year and half. Most graduate from high school and go off to college, not knowing anyone and, even though I have Ali and Drew, being here in the city has always been a bit overwhelming and intimidating. I'm just so thankful for Charlie. He makes everything better.

"Show me what you plan on wearing." Charlie walks over to one of the two oversized plush velvet purple chairs that he found and sits down.

I walk to the back, open the closet doors, and pull out a silver, strapless, knee-length dress.

"So, who all have you invited?"

"No one really. Just you, Ali, and Drew."

"I see."

I know that he's curious about Beau, but I can't talk about him. Walking behind the tri-fold screen, I slip on the dress and step out. Charlie's eyes grow soft and he smiles.

He pauses before saying, "You look stunning in that dress."

"Thank you. Do you like the sweetheart neckline?"

"Very much; it accentuates all of your *beautiful* curves perfectly. What jewelry are you going to accent it with?"

My fingers drift to my neck and run across my collarbone. Standing in front of the three-way mirror, the thought of the necklace stalls me, and behind me I no longer see the studio, but I'm standing in my front doorway of my home on Anna Maria Island.

I haven't spoken to Beau since the morning after I spent the night with him. I could tell that there was a big part of him hoping that, even though I called it a twenty-four hour truce, it might become permanent. Nope, the next morning I walked out the door and it was as if nothing between us had even happened. This hurt more than I realized, but if I let Beau in, I know that he will break my heart all over again.

I've tried to not be as rude to him over the last couple of weeks, but really we just continue as if nothing has changed. He's tried to talk to me, but I give him one of my classic 'leave me alone' looks, which he is the master of. He always sighs in defeat and then walks off.

I hear a car door slam in front of our house. The driveway is only meant for one car and it pulls up to a carport, so most people just park on the street. I walk over to the curtains; they are thin enough for me to see out, but thick enough where people can't see in. I watch him skip up the steps to the front porch, pull open the screen door, and knock. The screen door flings back, making a loud bang, and I jump at the noise.

What is he doing here?

Slowly, I walk over to the front door and pull it open. Beau is standing on the other side of the screen door and he takes my breath away. He's wearing a pair of gray dress pants and a light purple button-down with the sleeves rolled up. Purple is my favorite color and he knows this.

I watch as his gaze travels down the length of me and, even though I am at home, I suddenly feel very exposed. My hair is pulled up into a ponytail, I have on a little purple tank top, and a pair of denim shorts that are cut short, frayed on the edges, and the pockets are sticking out underneath. His eyes linger on my legs and this causes me to shift my weight from side to side, nervously.

I don't say anything. He just stares at me and I stare back at him

"Hi," he says quietly.

I can't help but raise my eyebrows at him.

"What do you want?" If he was hoping that I would be happy to see him, or at least be a little pleasant, that's not going to be the case.

"Another twenty-four hour truce," he says, getting straight to the point.

Panic instantly floods through me and my eyes drop and run over the length of him. I'm looking for injuries, and then I remember his dad is in jail, and that he is safe. My eyes return to his and his eyebrows shoot up in question. He can see the worry as it turns to relief and then curiosity on my face.

"Why?" I have to know.

He takes a deep breath, "Because, I wanted to know if you would like to go to prom with me."

Prom.

My heart is pounding in my chest and I can feel my hands shaking. I'm trying to process what he just said to me, and it just doesn't make any sense.

"You want me to go to prom with you?" The tone of my voice gives away my bewilderment. He's looking at me like he doesn't understand why I would be surprised by this.

"Yes . . . please say yes." He sounds so pleading, yet hopeful at the same time.

"I don't understand. You can go with anyone that you want. I'm sure there are a ton of girls just hoping that you'll ask them."

"Maybe," he ponders with a half shrug, but doesn't appear any less determined, "but the only person I want to go with is you." He lets out a deep sigh. He looks defeated, like he believes I am going to say no. "All these years, Leila, I only ever saw myself going with you."

And isn't that the truth. I only ever saw myself with him.

I lean my hip against the edge of the door frame and

slowly push open the screen door. He catches it and pushes it the rest of the way with his foot, to keep it propped open. A warm breeze blows over us and coconut drifts off of his skin and over to me. I will forever associate the smell of coconut and sunblock with him.

"What if I already have a date?" For some reason, this must not have occurred to him because now he looks nervous. He looks away from me and down at the ground. He shoves his hands into his pants pockets and I see him ball them into fists.

"I . . . umm . . . do you?" Why am I making this so hard on him? Oh, well. He's hurt me enough that making him sweat a little isn't such a bad thing.

"I almost did, but I told him no." I can see his body physically relax. The stiffness that had built up eased away.

"Oh." He looks back up at me and our eyes lock. His eyes are a mixture of colors that make them such a unique shade of hazel that he hypnotizes me without even knowing it. A moment of silence passes between us and I watch as he pulls his bottom lip between his teeth.

He's watching me think about my decision, and I can feel him memorizing the details of my face. I can't help it when I slowly start to smile. "Yes, Beau, I'll go to prom with you."

He smiles back at me and sparks of electricity flash in my heart.

"Thank you, Leila. You'll never know how much this means to me." He reaches into his back pocket and pulls out a long skinny box. It is wrapped in white paper and tied up with a purple bow. "This is for you. You don't have to wear it if you have something else planned; that's not why I'm giving it to you . . . it's just, I saw it a while ago and it reminded me of you, so I bought it." I take the box. I can feel him studying my shaking fingers as I begin to unwrap it.

"You bought me a gift?" I glance back up at him and his eyes are warm as he gives me a shy smile.

"Yes."

"No one has ever bought me a gift before." I look up at him. "Well, at least not in a long time." When we were kids, he used to buy me things everywhere we went. I stuff the wrapping paper into my pocket and lift the lid. A small gasp slips out as I remove from the box the most beautiful necklace I have ever seen.

"You're always wearing bright colors. You light up the world and you don't even know it, actually. It's not much, but I thought it was beautiful, just like you." Tears fill my eyes as I look up at him. "I had taken my mom to a winter art festival a few months ago, down in Sarasota, and this one vendor had hand-designed jewelry made with Swarovski crystals. I hope you like it." The necklace is made up of different colored crystals that are wired and set together to make beautiful flowers. The flowers are all linked together and they are a little on the large side. It is so sparkly and beautiful that I am at a loss of words for him. There's a pair of earrings in the box, too.

"Beau, it's so beautiful. I love it more than you will ever know." Overwhelmed with emotion, I lean forward, lay my head on his chest, wrap my arms around his waist, and hug him. I can tell that he wasn't expecting this as his body stiffens, but he doesn't push me off.

I pull back and look up at him. "I'm confused. I don't understand all of this. Why me? We aren't nice to each other. You tease me and I hate you. This isn't us. We don't spend time together, make plans together, and we certainly don't buy each other gifts."

"I know. But it should have been us, and these are the re-

grets and decisions that I have to live with. You don't hate me. You entertain the idea of it because I've hurt you. I have been a complete asshole to you for the past two years, and I'm sorry. I don't expect things to change between us, and I don't expect you to understand the reasons why I have behaved the way I have; like I said before, I have only ever seen you with me for prom. Twenty-four hours. Thank you for saying yes." He hesitantly leans forward and places a kiss on my cheek. His lips are warm, and I freeze. He takes a step back away from me and slowly starts retreating toward the Tahoe. My eyes watch his every move. He gives me a small smile before he climbs in and closes the door. I don't say anything else to him. I don't have to.

Chapter Ten

BEAU

"HEY, MAN; THANKS for inviting me over. I can't think of very many things I would rather be doing on a Sunday than kicking it with my feet up and watching some football."

"Yeah, thanks for coming over."

Nate wanders through the loft and into the kitchen to shove a twelve-pack into the refrigerator.

"I love getting to live at home and not having to worry about the added expense of a place to live but, sometimes, I just need to get out and away."

"You know you're welcome here anytime you want."

"I know, and I appreciate it, but Mom still needs help at night with my sister."

"How's she doing?"

"She's good; a brat, but she's good."

Nate finishes unpacking the beer, closes the fridge, and pauses as he reads the invitation hanging on the middle of the door.

"What's this?"

"What does it look like?"

"So, she's going to be, like, the opening act for BLK?"

"I don't know. I guess something like that."

"Wow. That's so awesome."

"She's pretty excited."

"So, you've talked to her?"

"A little. You know I saw her at the beach and then she stopped by for a little bit two weekends ago."

"So you saw her and spent time with her the weekend before Drew's party?"

"Yep."

"Then, why didn't you talk to her? I thought you two were essentially strangers now."

"I don't know; she was with that Charlie guy, and I guess in a way we are strangers now."

"How long have you known her?"

"Since I was eight."

Nate lets out a whistle and glances back at the invitation. "This looks like fun and I bet she'll be all dressed up and looking smoking hot, too."

My eyebrows furrow down, "Stop thinking about her and the way she looks."

He starts laughing and shakes his head at me. "You should stop thinking about the past and go get her."

"It's not that simple."

"Why not?"

"You can't make someone want to be with you."

"How do you know she doesn't want to be with you?"

"She never has before."

"And you've asked her?"

"Well, no."

"Man, how do you know that she doesn't think the same thing about you?"

I study the remote for a second to think about his question. "Because she could have had me, but she left."

"Left to go where?"

"Atlanta."

"But she moved back, right? I mean, I've seen the picture of you and her over there," he points to my desk. "And where was that taken? Prom?"

"Yeah, so?"

"All I'm saying is, if the girl had left you and didn't want to be with you, why would she ever go to prom with you? She's gorgeous enough; I'm sure she had options."

She did have options and she did pick me. The day I invited her on her front porch, she asked me why her, after she said yes, I should have asked her why me.

"Whatever, dude, enough about her. Grab me a beer, too, and let's watch the game."

When I think back to all of the days and nights that I've had with Leila over the years, by far, prom night is one of my favorites. I couldn't believe that she said yes. For some reason, I had convinced myself she would say no, and I was shocked and elated when those few simple words slipped out of her mouth.

Drew and I picked up Ali first, since she lived across the street and, together, the three of us drove to Leila's house to pick her up. I had already called her when we were on our way but, deep down, there is this little part of me that fears she might change her mind.

As I walk to her front door, sweat is dripping down my back. I am so nervous. I hear the click of the lock and the door flies open. Leila is standing on the other side of the screen door and, I swear, she causes my heart to stop beating.

I should have guessed that she would be wearing purple, but it's lighter than that; almost like lavender. Her dress is strapless, cut low enough in the front to show off a lot of her ivory skin, there's a belt/sash thing around her waist, and the skirt is short but full of layers. Her hair is down and full of those beautiful curls. Her shoes are tall, nude-colored, and strappy, and she's wearing the jewelry that I gave her. She looks stunning, elegant, and beautiful all at once.

She steps outside, and never in my entire life have I seen anything more beautiful than the sight before me.

We spend most of the night laughing and dancing with Drew and Ali. There are a few people who give us strange looks, but then there are others like Grant who just look at us knowingly.

By the time the night ends, I drop Drew and Ali off at her house so I can have a few more minutes with Leila.

"Do you want to go down to Bean Point?" she asks.

I'm shocked. We haven't been there together in years. I'm glad that she wants to extend our night together, but to end up there, a place that's filled with so many memories, causes me to feel anxious.

I park the Tahoe at the entrance and turn off the engine.

"I'm going to leave my shoes in the car, okay?"

"Yeah, I should do the same."

Leila pulls her legs into the seat, and her dress slides up

toward her waist. I know I shouldn't be checking her out, but she has always had a killer body, and those legs make me need to take a moment.

Gripping the steering wheel, I close my eyes and remind myself again why this girl and I can never happen. She broke me once, has already left me twice, and if I let her in I am certain she would only do it again.

In the back of my mind, I hear my dad whisper, "No one will ever want you."

"What's wrong?" she asks me.

"Nothing, just a little tired." I look over at her and she's watching me.

"Oh, I'm sorry; we can go home if you want," she says quietly.

"No, I'm good; just needed a moment."

"Alright."

I throw open the door, slip off my shoes and socks, and walk around to her side of the car.

"Piggy-back ride?" I ask.

She giggles. "Okay"

Her arms slide around my neck. I feel her lean into me and wrap her legs around my waist.

Slowly, in the dark, I take us down the familiar dirt trail, over the wooden walkway, and down to the beach.

Once we reach the water's edge, she slides down the back of me until her feet hit the sand. Her hands are still on my arms and she hugs me from behind. I'm frozen from the alarm bells that are going off in my head. She's pressing her face on my back. I should hug her back, but I don't. She drops her hands and steps away.

"Come on, let's walk." I hold my hand out for hers. The moonlight sparkles off of the necklace, her beautiful long hair is curled and blowing around in the breeze, and her eyes shine up at me with happiness. I want to burn this moment into my memory.

Her fingers slide in between mine, and together we walk the beach, listening to the quiet sounds of the Gulf as it laps onto the shore.

"I had a really great time tonight. Thank you for asking me, Beau."

I look down at her and squeeze her hand.

"Do you ever come out here?" I'm not sure why I asked her this, but I am curious.

"All the time. Do you?"

Her answer surprises me.

"Yes, I do. I like to see the stars." She tilts her head up, our eyes lock, and she smiles at me knowingly. The stars weren't just my thing; they were our thing. Seeing the stars made me feel closer to her, even though we weren't anymore.

"Will you do something for me?"

"Sure, what?"

She stops walking and pulls on my hand so I am facing her.

"Will you kiss me?" she looks at me hesitantly.

"Lei . . ." The nerves in the bottom of my stomach start bouncing.

"I've…I've never really been kissed before," she says before I can say anything further. Her gaze drops to the ground and I feel her twitch her fingers against my hand. She's nervous.

"What do you mean? Why not?"

Leila is, by far, the most beautiful person I have ever seen. I've heard guys at school talk about her and, although I've never seen her with any of them, I just find it so hard to believe that none of them have had the balls enough to try and kiss her.

"Truth?" she whispers, while tilting her head to the side.

"Please."

"Well, you kissed me when I was fourteen and I've never wanted to kiss anyone else. I always wanted it to be you."

She says things like this to me and, although my heart is rejoicing, she confuses me so much. If she's always wanted it to be me, then why didn't she come to me so many years ago, and why did she send me that letter?

Blinking, I clear away the confusion, and my eyes drop to her mouth. She doesn't need to ask me twice. I've dreamt of this moment more times than I care to admit.

I let go of her hand, move mine to the small of her back, and slowly pull her into me. Her body is flush with mine and she arches her back so she can look at me. Wrapping my other hand around the side of her face, I tilt it up. "Are you sure?"

"Yes," she answers, in barely a whisper.

I know that I should be gentle with her but I just can't. I have wanted to kiss her for years and, now that I am about to, I know I'm never going to want to stop.

Lowering my head, my mouth hovers over hers. She licks her lips and, with just that small glimpse of her tongue, I'm lost.

"Leila, this isn't going to be sweet and romantic."

"I don't want that, I just want you . . . to kiss me."

The underlying message in that statement comes through loud and clear, and my fingers tighten in her hair.

Closing the distance, my mouth connects with hers. An electric shock, almost like one that comes from static, shoots straight down to my toes.

My lips attach to her upper one, sucking on it slightly and

then my tongue slides across lower one. She opens her mouth and I take what should have always been mine.

Her skin, her hair, her smell, her lips, her tongue, her taste . . . I am lost in it all.

In a way, I feel bad that she isn't getting the Hollywood leg-popping kiss, but at the same time, she asked for me, and this is me. I'm not just kissing her; I am devouring her.

Once the shock of my assault on her has settled in, her arms wrap around my neck, and she presses her body even closer and completely into mine.

Leila kisses me like she was created just for me. There's no awkwardness or fumbling. The way her lips, tongue, and breath melt into mine, I can't help but feel somewhat proud that I am the first and only one to do this with her. She has given me both of her first kisses and this fuels my love for her even more.

"Beau . . ." she says my name with adoration and my heart cracks.

I slow the kiss down a little and attempt to give her sweet. I don't know how much time has passed, but I could stand here and kiss her all night.

My forehead rests on hers; both of us are panting. "You should let me take you home," I whisper against her lips.

"But, I don't want to go home."

That's the best thing she has said to me all night.

Pulling back, I look at her and tuck a loose piece of hair behind her ear. "Oh, well, where did you want to go?"

She pauses for a minute and her eyes drop back to my mouth. "I want to go with you."

Hell yeah! The thought of making out with her most of the night makes my blood to race.

"I'm headed back to Ali's."

"Is that okay? Would she mind?" she asks hesitantly.

"Yes, that's okay and, no, I don't think she'll mind at all."

Together we turn and, with our fingers laced together, we start walking back toward my Tahoe.

"I don't have anything to change into, though." Her look is sheepish.

I can't help the grin that flashes on my face.

She turns beet red.

"No worries; I'll give you a T-shirt."

LEILA

SHORTLY AFTER ALI and I moved to the city, we were out walking through Central Park and we happened to spot this place across the street, Sarabeth's Central Park West. It turns out that it is pretty well known, but to us, it was a find, and we have loved it ever since.

Sarabeth's is unique and lovely at the same time. It has a full menu but we love to come for afternoon tea. The seats are covered in a zebra fabric and there are old black and white photos hanging on the walls, some of which are of Audrey Hepburn. It's beautifully lit and always covered in gorgeous flower arrangements.

Every second Sunday of the month, I meet Ali for some

girl time. I'm running a few minutes late, so when I walk through the front door and see both her and Camille sitting there, I almost turn around and walk out.

Why did she invite that girl to our lunch? Not that there is anything wrong with her. She seems nice enough, but Ali has to know how it made me feel to watch her leave right after Beau the other night.

It's been eating away at me, just the thought of him with her. She's so tiny and beautiful, and well, I'm just me.

I'm not quick enough to duck out. Ali spots me and waves.

I weave my way around the tables and give her a look that lets her know I'm not happy.

"Yay, I'm so glad you made it. I was starting to wonder if you were going to cancel." She stands up and gives me a hug.

"I know, I'm sorry. Time got away from me and the bus today seemed to take forever." I sit down at the little four-top table. Ali is to my left and Camille is directly across from me. Just great. There's no avoiding her now. I may as well just stare at her.

"Leila, you remember my friend, Camille, right?" She smiles her million-dollar megawatt smile and I want to cringe.

Putting on my best fake face, I smile back, "Yes, I do. How are you?"

"I'm great. Thank you so much for letting me crash your lunch today. I never get out and have any fun, so this is super exciting for me."

"Why don't you ever get out?" Now that she's here in front of me, I'm actually a little curious about her. After Ali's party, all I could think about was her looks, how perfect she and Beau would look together, and how, essentially, she was spending time with Beau and I wasn't. But there must be more to her if Ali is friends with her.

"No time, I guess. My parents were extremely strict with my schedule when I was growing up and it's all I really know how to do: dance, school, and dance." She drops her gaze and picks up the teacup. When you first look at her, you are blinded by her beauty, but once you see past that, she looks really sad. I'm starting to think that maybe Ali was right; she does need friends.

"Well, you should give me your number and we should try to get together for coffee sometime." Her eyes light up and she smiles so big that I smile back.

"I would really like that, but enough about me; we're here to talk about you." She takes the tea pot and pours me a cup.

"I can't even begin to tell you both how crazy this last week has been, and how crazy next week will be. In six days, all of this will be over. Ali, did you get your tickets?" I drop in a few sugar cubes and stir.

"I did."

Suddenly, I feel bad for mentioning this in front of Camille. She'd probably love to go to the show, only I don't have tickets. They asked for names and addresses from me and that's it. There's nothing to hand out.

"I'm sorry I don't have any extra tickets, Camille, or I would give you one," I say, looking at her apologetically.

"That's okay. I'll hold you to that coffee and you can tell me all about it afterward." She takes a sip of her tea.

"Did you invite Beau?" Ali asks.

"No." Ali frowns and, out of the corner of my eye, I see Camille watching us. Ali just stares at me.

"Speaking of Beau, what's his story?" Camille asks with a little too much interest.

Both Ali and I look at each other, neither one of us saying

anything, and Camille looks back and forth between the two of us.

"Oh, I see. For the record, I'm not interested in dating him. I was just curious."

She looks at me and gives me another one of her genuinely beautiful smiles.

"Besides, he made it pretty clear that he wasn't interested either."

Wait, did she hit on him? Whatever; if he wasn't interested in her, that's all I need to hear. Relief washes over me and I smile back at her. She sees my smile and that's her cue to continue.

"Not to sound conceited or anything, but I know I'm not bad to look at. I get hit on at least ten times a day, which makes it easy to spot the good ones. It's the guys who go out of their way to make it known that they are not looking for a quick hookup that makes my heart happy for the girl on the other end. And there is always one on the other end, whether they know it or not." She tilts her head to look at me more closely.

"You followed him out the other night. Why?" I had to ask. I had to know.

"Because I hate being outside in the dark by myself. He hailed us a cab and had the driver drop me off in front of my building."

"Well, you picked the perfect guy to take you home. Beau loves the dark and being outside at night," I say to her.

She shakes her head at me like I'm crazy, and shivers. Like Beau, I've always loved the night-time too. I can't imagine not being able to sit outside and look at the stars. I guess that everyone has that one thing that scares them. I used to think I was fearless; that is, until we lost our home and everything. Now I fear having nothing. No money, no home, no way to pay for school, just all of it. I've lived and seen how quickly things can turn south and go bad, and I never want to live through that again.

"Leila, are you sure you didn't invite Beau to go to the show?" Ali asks again.

"Yeah, I'm sure. The only address I gave to BLK was yours."

"Huh." She looks confused and I'm about to ask her why, but Camille jumps in.

"So, tell us about the models. I always wanted to be a model, but I am way to short."

"I actually got to sit in on the interview process at BLK this week for the models and I learned a lot. There were three different directors there who would be working the show, one person from marketing, me, and, of course, Brandeth—who is BLK. She is so nice. I kind of expected her to be a little haughty, but she wasn't like that at all."

"BLK are her initials?"

"Yep, pretty brilliant if you think about it. From a marketing standpoint, she gets the uniqueness of black, which is what most people think it stands for, and then her name."

"Her logo is pretty awesome. Now to me, except for skin color, all of those runway models look pretty much the same. How does selection work? What did you do to interview them?"

"Mostly, the people from BLK were looking at their knees, ankles, and neck. You would think that they are all pretty similar, but once they started pointing out the differences, I saw it immediately with all of them. Another thing that the directors were looking for was personality. Anyone can walk an outfit down the runway, but BLK is looking for spark and genuine interest in being there. Brandeth said that it's these models who can own the outfits; they give them extra life. We must have interviewed 300 models, and the ones who came in with blank expressions, nothing behind the eyes, just there to do the walk, didn't even get considered."

"This whole process to me is crazy." Camille's watching me and shaking her head in disbelief.

"I know, right? Usually, there are twelve to fifteen models per show, but BLK decided that we should have twenty. For my collection, they will only dress once; there won't be a change of outfits, but I do believe that there will be for BLK."

"What are you most excited about?" Ali asks.

"I think what I'm most excited for is how the energy of the audience and the excitement of introducing something so new, fresh, and never seen before makes me feel alive. It can be very rewarding, as I suppose it is with any artist who is showing their work to an audience for the first time. I'm not sure if you've ever been to a fashion show." I look at Camille and she shakes her head. "When the music starts and the models line up, it's like you know something great and magical is about to happen. Backstage can be chaotic, hectic, and just downright nerve-wracking, but as soon as the first model hits the runway it's an intoxicating moment."

"Wow."

"A couple of days ago, Vogue came to my studio for the interview and to shoot a few pictures of the ensembles, but that part is kind of boring. Yes, it's exciting to know that I'm going to be in Vogue, but it's editorial and it's delayed. The person they sent over raved about the pieces, which was wonderful to hear, but that's just one person. The excitement doesn't come until the magazine is released to the world, and even then, it's me standing on the street corner by myself. During the show, you can feel the buildup of the anticipation from the crowd, and it's an instant gratification that floods through you at a live event."

A waitress walks over, sets down the three-tiered tray and refreshes our pot of tea. My grandmother introduced me to different delicious types of teas when we lived with her and I've loved them ever since.

"So, something really awesome that BLK is doing this year; they will be streaming the show live and giving the fashion bloggers an extra hour after the show for any questions that they have. It's so crazy how much the industry is expanding due to the bloggers, and all of the ones I have met are just so nice."

"Where is the show going to be?" Camille asks.

"This year, BLK has decided to break out of Lincoln Center and put up a tent back in Bryant Park. The show used to be there. They moved it in 2010."

"I remember my mom saying something about them moving it. My mother is a southern socialite and uses my father's political connections to help her stay in the know with fashion. Heaven forbid she wears something that's currently not in season. But that's neither here nor there; I think it's amazing that they are moving locations to the park." There was a slight edge to her tone when she mentioned her mother that makes me sad for her. I love my mother.

"A lot of designers have been branching out to different locations, but this one has definitely created a buzz."

"Did you tell your mom? Is she going to watch the show?" Ali asks as she takes a sip of her tea.

"Oh, Aunt Ella bought a projector, and they're closing the café to have a private 'fashion party' of their own. I think they're dressing up and serving champagne."

"Ahh, that's fun. I love your aunt. Drew and the guys love her, too."

"She *is* pretty amazing. I hope everyone likes the show."

"How could they not? You're crazy; I don't know why you're worried. Your designs are brilliant," Ali says to me.

"So the twenty models will walk one at a time, then the entire collection will come out all at once at the end of the show, and then me. Some designers just wave, others walk the runway. I haven't decided what I'm going to do yet. Most people would probably be excited about this, but I'd be lying if I said I wasn't afraid of falling on my face."

"Leila, for as long as I have known you, you've always worn tall, fancy shoes. You have nothing to worry about."

"I hope not."

"Well, I think we should toast," says Camille. She raises her glass and we follow suit. "Here's to you, Leila; may your show be flawless and may all your dreams come true."

"Thank you, Camille, and here's to new friends."

Her smile stretches from ear to ear.

Giggling, the three of us clink our glasses together.

Chapter Eleven

BEAU

CLIMBING OUT OF the cab at Bryant Park, I am awed by the grandiose production that is taking place before me. I knew that Fashion Week was a big deal here, but all of this is just wow.

Drew and Ali are already waiting for me as I approach the grill. He hands me a beer and Ali's eyes light up.

"Oh, my God! I forget how nicely you clean up." She smiles at me.

"You don't look so bad yourself, Tiny."

Drew forcefully shoves me in the arm while scowling at me.

"Really?" I say to him.

Ali giggles and his expression relaxes. He clinks his bottle with mine and we raise them in a silent toast.

"So, have you talked to her at all?" I ask Ali.

"No, not since last weekend; BLK pretty much swooped

in and took her hostage. I do know that she is equally excited and nervous about today."

"She'll be fine. She always is, and I'm certain what she's put together will be amazing."

Ali tilts her head and I can see that she wants to ask questions, but she won't today.

"I'm still surprised she sent me an invitation. I honestly didn't expect to get one."

Neither she nor Drew says anything. I take a swallow of the beer and look at all the chaos going on across the street. We wait about fifteen more minutes and then decide to make our way over.

As we walk up to the entrance of the tent, there are a lot of people standing around: assorted celebrities, fashion press, fashionistas, bloggers, buyers, and spectators. The paparazzi are swarming and snapping photos of just about anyone and everyone.

"Beau, did you know that the first fashion show was held in 1943, because fashion experts at the time could not travel to France to see the French shows during World War II?"

"Tiny, did you know that bikini designer Louis Reard said a two-piece bathing suit couldn't be called a bikini "unless it could be pulled through a wedding ring."

"Of course a guy would say something like that."

I grin at her.

"I'm impressed you did your fashion homework."

"I couldn't come here empty-handed."

Handing in our invitations, the three of us are ushered down a black carpet that stops in front of a wall with the Mercedes-Benz logo splattered around and a photographer. The three of us pose together and then the guy laughs as I hand over my cell phone. I want a picture of us, too. It's not very often we get so dressed up.

Once inside the tent, we see that it's broken down into three sections. There is the main center room where the catwalk is set up for the show, and then there are two smaller sections; one off to each side. On the left is where the cocktail party is and on the right is The Gallery, which will be open after the show for spectators to wander through and look at the designs presented.

A gong rings throughout the tent, alerting everyone that the show is about to begin. As Ali and I follow Drew and make our way to our seats, waiters appear, handing out champagne. The runway isn't your typical catwalk. It's shaped more like a horseshoe, allowing photographers access to the middle.

There are about 400 white wooden chairs strategically placed around the runway. As we sit down in our front-row seats, several people point and frown at us. I'm certain these seats are prestigious, and now that we are here it would take a team of wild horses to drag me away.

Once everyone is in their seats, the lights dim . . .

"BLK proudly presents 'Rising Designer', Leila Starling." All the lights in the room go out, leaving it pitch black except for the ceiling. Tiny stars are projected onto the roof of the tent, which has been covered in large swathes of black fabric. The illusion she's created of being outside at night is spectacular, and I gasp at the sight. Ali must hear me, because she reaches over and squeezes my leg.

Very faintly, music from Modern Symphony fills the air and, as the music grows louder, Leila's name comes into view on both sides of the runway on the back wall. Her name is done in an elegant script, surrounded by three shooting stars. I know that there's no coincidence in the three stars, but I can't help but think about the summer triangle.

KATHRYN ✪ ANDREWS

Staring at her name on the wall, which has now become her brand, a lump forms in the back of my throat and my eyes begin to burn. I know that I am witnessing what is going to be a very long and successful career for her. I'm so proud of her.

A spotlight hits the corner of the stage that runs across the back wall and, under her name, sitting there with his violin perched and ready, is Josh Vietti. The energy in the room picks up as he strikes his bow across the strings and the runway lights up. Ali squeals a little, and even I, who know nothing about fashion, can't help but feel excited.

The entrance to the runway glows hot pink, and standing there is the first model. She's wearing a bikini with a long sheer cover-up, a large brimmed hat, carrying some type of beach bag. She descends toward us in sky-high heels. It's a very classy look—it's very Leila.

Her entire show lasts no longer than thirty minutes. As each model stepped out and down the runway, her designs became more detailed, intricate, and beautiful. All three of us could hear the surprised and pleased murmurs around us and my heart swelled with pride.

At the end of the show, Leila appears on the runway and the room erupts in applause. The smile that breaks out on her face is infectious and I'm certain everyone in this tent smiles with her. BLK walks out from the other direction and wraps Leila up in a congratulatory hug. She points down the runway and Leila laughs. The clicks from the media cameras in the room are firing off and I soak up this moment for her.

Gracefully and confidently, she makes her celebratory walk. The dress she's wearing is silver and stunning, her heels are navy blue, and that's when I see it. She's wearing the jewelry that I gave her a year and a half ago. My breath catches in my throat and I just stare.

156

As she gets closer to us, her eyes lock on to mine, and not once does she glance at Drew and Ali. She smiles at me and my heart thunders in my chest. What she did tonight was amazing—she is amazing.

LEILA

THE GONG SOUNDS and echoes through the back of the tent. The director calls "first outfits" and immediately there is buzz amongst the models, dressers, hairstylists, and makeup artists. I can't help but to take one last peek from behind the curtains to the crowd. I have waited years for this moment and finally my dreams are becoming a reality.

I scan the audience and look for Ali. She said that she would be here, but what I didn't expect was to find her standing between Drew and Beau.

Beau came.

My heart flutters in my chest and my eyes fill with tears. I am so happy that he is here. I will never tell him how much, but he just made this entire event complete for me.

The nerves that I was feeling when I walked in this morning dissipate and in their place butterflies take over.

"Girl! Who are you staring at?" Charlie had walked up behind me and he peeks over my shoulder. "Oh, my, Mr. Beautiful himself is here. Did you know that he was coming?"

"No." I can't tear my eyes away from him.

"I don't know why you insist on dragging this out. You are possibly the most stubborn girl I have ever met. Do you realize how much time you have wasted not being with him?

Just think of all the memories you could be making together."

"You don't understand. I know that he's interested in me, he always has been. The problem is he leaves me. Every. Single. Time. I just don't know if I can do it again."

"Leila, that boy loves you. When are you going to ask him why? From what I have seen, you should be giving him the benefit of the doubt."

"I don't know."

"What do you have to lose?"

"I already lost it."

"Well, maybe you know exactly where to find it."

I know that he's right. Beau and I have never once talked about the fire or why he didn't wait around to say goodbye to me. The more time that passes, the more I find myself doubting the way I left things with him. I know what I said in my letter to him was mean, but he hurt me. Or did he?

BLK walks up next me, along with the backstage director.

"Are you ready?" she asks.

"More than you can even imagine. I was born ready for this."

Her face lights up and she gives me a thoroughly pleased smile.

"This right here, your attitude that screams 'I'm gonna own this moment,' is exactly why you will become a huge success. Your designs are stunning and I know I speak for everyone at the label when I say we are so proud of you."

"Thank you so much. You will never know what that means to me."

"Congratulations, darling, and good luck." She leans forward and kisses me on the cheek.

The entrance to the runway begins to glow and behind me the models line up. The director squeezes the first one's shoulder, I give her a once-over, and then gently she is pushed forward.

The show has begun.

The next half hour whips by in a blur. I'm so focused on each and every detail that I don't even see Charlie come up from behind me to hand me my heels.

Locking eyes with him, I grab his shoulder for support, and slip out of my flats and into my five-inch heels.

The director comes to stand next to me and, just like with the models, she squeezes my shoulder until it's my turn to take to the catwalk.

Stepping out under the lights, I breathe in the moment, and my heart bursts with happiness. Any plans that I had of remaining calm just flew out the window. I smile from ear to ear.

Brandeth meets me on the runway, gives me a hug, and encourages me to take the walk. I had decided against it, but now I just have to.

Mostly, as I'm walking down the line, the spectators blur together. That is, until I see Beau. He gives me the courage that I need to hold my head a little higher and to walk a little fiercer. Watching him smile at me, and being able to share part of this moment with him, I am beyond elated.

At the end of the runway, I am met with a four-by-four-person square of photographers. I strike what I will forever refer to as my victory pose, and the cameras go wild. The flashing, clicks, and applause are all just so amazing.

The second I make it into the back of the tent, the lights go black and the charge in the air changes for BLK's new spring collection. Charlie reaches for me, wraps me up in his arms, and pulls me to the side. There are tears in his eyes.

"I'm so proud of you," he whispers in my ear.

"Thank you."

He squeezes me tighter, takes a deep breath, and sets me down so we can watch as the models line up to go again.

Thirty minutes later, the show is complete, and everyone relaxes.

As I move to my portion of the tent to make sure that the dressers have appropriately packed up the pieces that are going with me, and prepped the pieces that are to be displayed in the gallery tent off to the side, the bloggers and photographers swoop in.

The show was a huge success. Champagne is passed around to all of us in the back and, as the hour passes for the media meet and greet, three different magazines approach me about doing an interview. I don't think that I can possibly be any happier.

Little by little the tent clears out. Most of my team has already headed over to Bin 52 for an after-party, but I just needed to stay and soak up the atmosphere a little longer.

Hearing a throat clear to my right, I turn and see Beau.

"Hi."

I jump off of the chair to stand in front of him.

"Hi."

He smiles at me and I can feel my cheeks get pink.

Beau is wearing a charcoal gray suit, with a black button-down dress shirt underneath. It's open at the neck and a silver Rolex is peeking out from under the sleeve. His hair is styled and he looks so freaking good I could stare at him all day.

"I won't take up too much of your time, but I wanted to say congratulations and give you these." From behind his back he pulls out a beautiful bouquet of orchids. He remembered, and I'm so touched.

"Thank you for these. They're beautiful. And thank you

for coming. It really means a lot to me."

He shoves his hands into his pockets and takes a step back. "Of course. When the invitation came, I was really happy to be included in this with you. Thank you."

Without thinking, I take the two steps needed and walk into him. His arms wrap around me and he just holds me.

"Congratulations, Leila," someone says from behind me and Beau pulls back.

"I'll see you around, alright?" He smiles at me and starts walking away.

"Beau, wait!" He stops and turns back around. "There's an after-party at Bin 52. Would you like to go with me?"

He turns his body halfway back toward me. "Are you sure? I don't want to get in the way of you celebrating with your friends."

"You're my friend."

He doesn't say anything and a moment of silence passes between us.

"Hey, Leila!" I turn and see Charlie headed straight toward me. "There you are. Let's get going; I need a drink." He picks me up, hugs me, and swings me around in his arms before putting me down. "Hey, Beau. Are you going to Bin 52 with us?"

"I just asked him to go. Don't you think he should go with us?"

"I most definitely do. We all want to celebrate you and your successful night. You really were fabulous tonight."

"So you'll go?" I ask Beau again.

"Of course he's going," Charlie says with mischief in his eyes. "Listen, I'm gonna catch up with Jacob. I'll meet you two there." With that, Charlie kisses me on the forehead and walks out of the tent, leaving Beau and me staring after him.

BEAU

THE PLACE THAT was chosen for the after-party isn't very large, but the ambiance is definitely Leila. The two side walls are brick, the back is painted maroon, and the front is covered with two large bay windows. One is on each side of the front door and they open up to a sidewalk lounge section. The ceiling is covered with different chandeliers. They really are beautiful and they make this place glow.

The group that arrived before us cheers as we walk through the door. I sit back and watch as all of these people who I have no idea who they are, one by one come over to hug and congratulate Leila.

Watching her smile and laugh the way she is tonight makes my heart feel warm. I am so happy for her.

I also can't help but feel a little left out. I know that this is my fault; after all, I'm the one who has chosen to keep this distance between us. Maybe Nate's right. Maybe it is time to put the past behind us and try to get back to somehow being friends, or just maybe something more.

Charlie arrived about fifteen minutes after us. He immediately walked straight into the crowd and scooped her up. He whispers something in her ear and she throws her head back and laughs. I do love the sound of her laughing; however, I wish that it was me making her laugh that way, not him.

Watching the two of them, I really don't understand what kind of relationship she has with this Charlie guy. They both seem to genuinely care about each other and they are very affectionate with each other. I heard them, first-hand, talking about late nights, but yet there is this distance between them that isn't usually there between two people who are a couple.

Weaving my way through the crowd, I wander back to bar. The bartender comes over, I order an IPA, and take a long pull on it.

"Do you want to cash out now or start a tab?" the bartender asks me.

"Actually, open the tab up to five hundred for this group right here. Just make sure that the girl with the strawberry blonde hair in the silver dress gets whatever she wants."

"No problem," he says.

"Well, that was very generous of you." I turn to see Charlie standing next to me.

"I'm proud of her. I want her to have a good time." Looking back, I find her sitting up front in the bay window.

"So, I'm glad that you decided to come today," Charlie says, eyeing me.

"I guess I didn't realize that you would care one way or another."

"You're kidding, right?" He looks away from me and across the room over to Leila. I can tell he is contemplating what to say next. "I'm the one who sent you the ticket."

What? That doesn't make any sense to me.

"The ticket was from you? I thought that Leila had sent it over."

"Nope; you were a very welcome surprise to her today."

My eyebrows furrow. "I don't understand the two of you."

"What do you mean?" He smirks at me. He knows why I am asking this question.

"I thought that the two of you were dating." He throws his head back and laughs.

"Beau, you need to know that Leila, as beautiful as she is, just doesn't do it for me. She's not my type. You, on the other hand, I would not say no to." He looks me over from head to toe and I take a step back.

"You're gay," I say this as a statement, but it could be a question, too.

"Yep; have been for as long as I can remember." He props an elbow against the bar and leans into it.

"I had just assumed . . .," I run my hand through my hair and take a sip of my beer.

"I know you did and that's the biggest problem right there. The two of you don't communicate or talk at all; you just assume." I don't appreciate his tone or the way he is speaking to me. He pauses and looks at me hesitantly, as if he's not sure what or how much he wants to say. "I met Leila at an orientation party before the first day of classes last year. I am also at Parson's, but for interior design. I adore her, and she instantly became one of my best friends. She is also my roommate."

Roommate.

Shaking my head, a small laugh escapes. "Well, I guess

that clears up some of the questions I had been wondering about."

He tilts his head to the side and studies me. "Funny, none of the questions that I have about you have been answered."

"Why would you have questions about me?"

"Are you serious?"

I raise my eyebrows in annoyance.

"Leila is the most amazing girl I have ever met. She's beautiful, both inside and out. She's bright, smart, funny, and so kind. At least once a day, I wish that I was into girls because, if I was, I would make her mine and never let her go."

"You don't need to tell me these things about her; I already know them. I've known her most of my life."

He stands to his full height and looks me right in the eye. "If you know, then what are you doing?"

I can't say anything back to him. He will never know how many times I have asked myself that same question. Reality is, though, what happened between her and me is our business and not his. I understand that he is looking out for his friend, but all of this is so much bigger than his questions and misunderstandings.

"Hey, what's going on over here?" I didn't even notice Leila approach. She's standing next to us and I realize that Charlie and I must look like we are in a face-off.

Charlie breaks the eye contact and looks down at her. "Nothing; I'm just having a nice little chat with our friend Beau, here." He smiles at her and I can't help but let out a sharp chuckle. Both of them glance over at me. "Listen, love, I'm going to go find Jacob." He claps me on the shoulder, kisses her forehead, and walks off.

Leila moves into his spot and looks up at me. My heart flutters and I realize I'm nervous. She's not dating anyone.

She's free. What I really need to decide now is if I'm going to do anything about this or not.

"Why didn't you tell me that Charlie was gay and your roommate?" I ask her.

Confusion and then understanding register on her face. A small smile graces one side of her mouth.

"First off, it's kind of obvious that he's gay, so I didn't think that I needed to, and second it's never come up. Why?"

Suddenly, I feel kind of stupid. Thinking back to the few interactions that we've had, he hasn't given me any reason to think that he wasn't into her. He always has his hands on her and he always kisses her on the forehead, so why should it have been obvious?

"I thought you two were dating." She giggles and then stops when she sees that I don't think this is funny.

"Ah . . . all this time, were you jealous?"

I want to scoff at her and tell her no, but that would be a lie. Instead, I say nothing. An emotion flashes across her face and it shifts from amusement to pain. She looks slightly haunted and I don't understand what she is remembering or seeing.

"You know, Beau, for years I watched you parade other girls in front of me. You always made it very clear what you thought of me, and that you weren't interested, by screwing your way across the island. You don't get to be angry or jealous, especially of someone who is just my friend, and a good one at that."

Part of what she says is true; I did parade other girls around in front of her. However, I've always been interested in her, but what do you do when the girl who owns your heart breaks it, won't talk to you, and you can't trust her? Nothing; that's what. I wanted her to know that even though she didn't want me, others did. Why she thinks that I 'screwed my way across the island', though, I don't understand. I wasn't that guy and there isn't one girl out there who could say I was. I might have been jealous over Charlie, but now, after that statement, I'm just hurt.

Looking her over from head to toe, I remember why we are here tonight, and it's time for me to go. I don't want her to look back on this evening and remember us arguing; I want her to remember her successes. After all, she deserves them. She was spectacular tonight.

My eyes leave her and land on the front door. "You don't know anything. But, then again, I'm not surprised; you've never cared enough to know the truth. Congratulations on your show tonight, Leila. I hope you enjoy the rest of your evening." I just can't take any more. I turn to walk away from her but she grabs my arm.

"Then why don't you tell me what I don't know because you seem to have forgotten, Beau . . . I was there! You were never alone." This place has become more crowded. Someone bumps into the back of her, pushing her forward and into me. Reflexes have me wrapping my arms around her. She doesn't move away from me.

"Lei . . ." How much do I tell her? How much does she deserve to know? I can't look her in the eyes as I say this. I lean down and put my mouth next to her ear. "You may have seen me with other people, but the only person that I have *ever* been with is you. You were my first . . . and, to date, my only." She tenses and we become engulfed in the silence between us.

"I don't understand. How?" she whispers. Her breath is warm as it brushes across my cheek.

"How what?" I lean back a little to see her face.

"How was I your first? And I don't understand why I'm your only."

"Because, Leila. I may have messed around with girls but doesn't mean that I slept with them. You were my first because that moment was always meant to be with you too. You weren't the only one who felt that way. And as for you being my only, I have my reasons."

"What reasons?" Somewhere in the midst of this conversation, she and I have moved closer. I am instantly aware of how near she is to me and how good it feels to have her in my arms after all this time. She is wearing really tall shoes tonight that make her only a few inches shorter than me, and the lavender scent that is coming off of her hair and skin is almost enough to send me over the edge. I love the smell of her.

"I don't want to talk about this anymore tonight." My hand on her lower back pulls her in tighter to me and my other hand wraps around the side of her face and into her hair. My eyes drop to her mouth and she licks her bottom lip.

This moment feels like Deja' vu. My thumb follows her tongue and rubs across her bottom lip.

Slowly, I tilt her head and lean down. Our breath is now shared, and as my eyes slip shut I feel the pressure of her fingertips on my back. I didn't even notice that her hands and arms had slipped underneath my suit jacket coat, and panic washes over me.

I jerk away from her, causing her hands to drop to my hips. She sees the panic on my face and I see the confusion on hers.

"What's wrong?" she asks me. One of her hands moves to my arm and I continue to stare at her. No one touches my back. Ever! What if she felt the scars? They aren't flat and smooth. If she was to run her hand down my back, she would feel them. They are very noticeable. She knows they are there, hell everyone does, but she's never asked me about them and we aren't going to start talking about them now.

"Nothing." I give her a small smile and she knows me well enough to know that I am lying. Leaning back toward her, I kiss her on the cheek and then step away. "Listen, I've got an early practice tomorrow, so I'm going to take off. I'm really proud of you. What you did tonight was amazing. I really do love watching this person that you are becoming."

"Thanks, Beau. That means a lot to me." I can see her eyes glisten from the light of the chandeliers. This girl will never know what she does to me. I take another step back from her and then turn away.

Pushing my way through crowd, I spot Charlie. He sees me and lifts his eyebrows. I shrug my shoulders, shake my head, and walk out the front door.

Standing on the sidewalk, I take a deep breath and run my hand through my hair. The temperature has dropped a little and the cool air calms my nerves. I can't believe that I almost kissed her. Night after night, I lie in bed and think about the few times that I have kissed her and what it would be like to kiss her again, taste her again, and hold her again. I rub my hand over the sharp pain in my chest.

"Hey, Beau?"

I turn around and see Leila standing right behind me. My eyes lock onto hers.

"Yeah?"

She's fidgeting with her fingers, and this reminds me of the first day that I met her, when we were eight. She's nervous and trying so hard not to show it. She lets out a deep sigh like she's holding her breath, and looks at the ground. "Can I see you tomorrow?"

I'm so busy watching her that I almost don't hear her question. "Yes." Her eyes shoot back up to mine and she smiles. "If you are free for dinner tomorrow, you can come over and I'll cook."

Her eyes grow wide. "Really?"

"Yes."

"I'd love to come over for dinner," she says quietly. A slow smile stretches across her beautiful face and, this time, I can't help it. I lean in and kiss the corner of her mouth.

"Then I'll see you tomorrow . . ."

LEILA

I WATCH AS Beau turns and walks away. The city is busy tonight; as people pass and bump into me on the sidewalk, I don't even care. My eyes are locked onto the back of him.

He wants to see me. He said yes. On the inside I'm bursting with happiness and I'm certain that the smile on my face has never been bigger.

I feel someone walk up next to me and I immediately know that it is Charlie.

"Well, someone looks like they've found the pot of gold at the end of the rainbow."

I bust out laughing at his crazy statement and turn to look at him.

"You are glowing and I know for certain that nothing kinky went down here on the sidewalk."

"No, but he did invite me over for dinner tomorrow." I grin at him.

"Well, well, maybe this is a pre-glow." He circles my face with his finger. I slap his arm; he chuckles, and then wraps it around my shoulders. "Just kidding, beautiful; I hope this works out for you two. It seems it has been a long time coming."

"We'll see. For years he has kept this impenetrable wall up when it comes to me . . . I just don't know."

"Well, I do know. It's there, but you have got to talk to him. At some point, the two of you are going to need to clear the air."

"I know." And I do. Charlie's right. Tonight I learned that, all this time, Beau has been going around thinking that Charlie and I were together. As ridiculous as that idea is to me, it makes me wonder, how many other miscommunications and misunderstandings are hanging between us?

BEAU

WHY AM I so nervous to have her over? I've known her forever and she's already been here. This is not a new thing, but even as I think this thought, I know that's not the truth. Whatever this is tonight, it may or may not be the start of us.

She's right; I'm not the same person that I was before. What if she doesn't like this version of me? I mean, how do you explain to someone just how different you are? When I look at her, I see strong, determined, creative, glass half full, and love. She's perfect and whole, whereas I feel broken; most days, I'm struggling just to hold all of the pieces together.

The change occurred over the last year, after my dad went to jail. When I was younger, the things that my dad said and did to me, I thought I deserved; that, for some reason, I hadn't earned his love and affection. In my mind, as a kid, from day to day, it was what it was because I believed him.

Now that I'm older, I've slowly been able to put things

into a little bit better perspective. I know what he did is all on him but it doesn't change the fact that I was his chosen target and I was never loved. Who doesn't want to love their own child?

This is a hard pill to swallow.

But then I think what if she's changed, too, and I don't like this new version of her? I really don't know much about her anymore, and maybe I've built her up into being someone that she isn't.

The doorbell rings and I run my hand through my hair.

Taking a deep breath, I walk over and open the door.

I'm met with huge sparkling blue eyes and wild long strawberry-blonde curls. She smiles at me and once again, my whole world bursts into color. She brightens everything. She always has.

"Hey," I say to her.

Her smile widens and I find myself smiling back.

"Come on in."

"Thanks; it smells amazing in here."

I want to tell her that she smells amazing as she walks past me and I'm hit with her scent of lavender.

"So, I'm still trying to wrap my head around the fact that you cook." She hands me a bottle of wine and looks around the loft.

"You brought wine?" I grin at her.

"Yeah, Ali came over and told me that I couldn't come here empty-handed and that I needed to bring wine. She gave that to me." She's looking at me a little sheepishly and I let out a laugh.

"That's funny, because she came over here earlier and brought me a wine opener, along with four glasses, telling me that I must always be prepared."

Her eyes light up and she grins.

"Do you know anything about wine?" she asks, following me into the kitchen to grab Ali's opener.

"Nope. I guess we can learn about it together." I pour us both a glass and hand her one. We tap them together and say, "Cheers."

She smiles at me while we do this. I will never get tired of watching her smile.

"Did you know the ritual of bumping glasses with a "cheers" started way back in ancient Greece? They did this to make sure no one was trying to poison them. Bumping the glasses together at the right angle makes the drink spill from one into the other. Basically, it was a courtesy of the host to drink the first cup of wine to show his guests that he didn't intend to poison them."

Leila nods her head slowly as if she is seriously pondering my factoid. "I didn't know that. But I did read once that if women drink wine, it increases their sex drive."

I choke a little on the wine and chuckle at this. "I think I like yours better."

"You would," she says, grinning at me and leaning against the kitchen counter.

"So, back to your original question of why I know how to cook: After Drew and Ali left, Mom slipped in and out of these depression spells, so someone had to take care of her and Matt."

She frowns.

"How is Matt?"

"He's okay I guess. He texts me nonstop throughout the day. He's never really had friends that I know of, so I always try to text him back as soon as I can. He wants to come here for Thanksgiving and Christmas. I told him okay."

"So, you're not planning on going home for the holidays?"

"No. I think that Drew and Ali are headed home for Christmas and New Year's. They did the whole Times Square thing last year and once was enough for them."

"She mentioned that. I guess I had just assumed you would go too."

"Nope." There's disappointment on her face. Was she hoping to spend the holidays with me?

She twirls the glass between her fingers. She just got nervous, and I don't want her to be nervous here.

"Dinner's ready if you're hungry."

"I'm starving. How can I help?"

"You can grab the wine, our glasses, and I'll get the rest.

"Okay."

Leila walks to the table and takes a seat. In the middle of the table I set down steaks, asparagus, french fries, and cupcakes. She watches me and smiles. My heart skips a beat. I'm so happy she's here.

To me, dinner was a huge success. Leila and I spent most of it really just trying to play catch- up. We talked about everything from how I was liking New York, how school was going for both of us, the publicity she's received after the fashion show, my tennis schedule, and even who has the best takeout pizza in the neighborhood.

After dinner, I decide it's time to start having a few bigger conversations with her. I'm not going to ask her every question that I have, but there are a lot of holes, and I think we need to open up a little more about the past. Some answers would be nice.

"So, tell me about Atlanta. What happened to you after you moved?"

Her face falls a little and I wonder if I've asked the wrong question. She pushes her plate to the side and reaches over for a cupcake.

"Well, remember how we were going to move over to the mainland and rent a house?"

I nod at her.

"After the fire, because my dad couldn't pay the mortgage, the insurance company wouldn't pay us. We lost everything. My dad didn't have a job, we were living off of his very tiny retirement savings from the military, and all of our belongings were gone, except for what we took to Aunt Ella's. What were we to do? Where were we supposed to go?"

Watching her relive this in her mind breaks my heart for her. As a kid, something like a fire and the house burning down is really sad, but we don't understand the grownup responsibility side about what comes next. If our house had burned down, we had enough money to move into another one. It never occurred to me that Leila's parents didn't.

"My dad sold my mother's car and the three of us headed to Atlanta." She peels the paper off of the cake and takes a bite.

"Wow."

"Yeah, I overheard my dad and mom talking on the drive up. They thought I was sleeping, but I wasn't. If staying at my grandmother's didn't work out, there was a shelter nearby that took families until they could get back on their feet."

"A shelter?"

"For homeless families," she whispers, looking away from me.

The thought of Leila being homeless and having nowhere to live makes my stomach hurt. I've always had this need down deep to want to take care of her. It wasn't like I had to; it was because I've always wanted to.

"So tell me about your grandmother's place," I ask, trying to change the subject.

"She lived in a retirement community. You know, one of those fifty-five and older places. Her home was one half of a duplex and it was a two-bedroom, one bath, with a small kitchen and a tiny sunroom that she turned into her sewing room."

"Who was on the other side?"

"This little old man who I think was sweet on my grand-mother." She smiles at the memory.

"What was his name?"

"Paul Douglas." She dips her finger into the icing of the cupcake, swipes some, and then licks it off her finger. She looks at me and I realize I haven't said anything, as I'm staring at her mouth in a haze-induced stupor.

"That's awesome." I finally get out after clearing my throat.

"Yeah, he has a son who works at Coca Cola, and he found my dad a job right away. We couldn't have been more grateful or thankful."

"So, did you guys ever get into trouble for staying there?"

"No, we only had the one car, we kept to ourselves, and Mr. Paul liked us so it worked out okay."

"You said the place was a two-bedroom; where did you sleep?"

"On the couch. It wasn't so bad after I got used to it. The only problem we ever had was after we got there I wanted to sleep all the time, and they wanted to sit around and rehash everything that had happened over the last couple of weeks leading up to that point."

"You slept on the couch for two years?"

She nods her head taking another bite.

"That must have sucked."

"It did." She lets out a sad sigh.

"So, tell me what it was that you couldn't show me the last time that I was here." She sits up a little straighter and curiosity shines in her eyes.

"Nah, I'm not going to tell you; I'm going to show you. Come on."

She shoves another bite of the cupcake into her mouth and looks at the table. "What about the dishes?" she says around a full mouth of cupcake.

I chuckle. "I'll get them later or tomorrow. Don't worry about them."

"You cooked, I should clean."

"Next time." I stand up from the table and go grab a beer out of the refrigerator. I'm hoping my message came through loud and clear that I want there to be a next time.

She follows and grabs her glass of wine, refilling it. We walk into my closet. I push the clothes to the side and show her the door.

"I never asked the guy who owns this place why the door is in the closet. I like to think it's because there were shady mob activities going on here back in the day."

"Sounds good to me; I like your theory, and this is seriously pretty cool."

I unlock the door, push it open, and together we climb up two flights of steps to get the top. At the top, I flip on a switch, unlock the bolt, and open the door. This door swings to the inside. Must be because of the snow. There is no way to shovel it from the other side and should it pile up, the door wouldn't push open.

Leila and I walk out on to the roof and she gasps at the

sight.

After I moved in, I purchased an outdoor living room set, along with a table and chairs. Matt helped me put it together. We strung up some white Christmas lights and we spent hours up here talking and listening to the sounds of the city.

"Beau, this is amazing." I watch her take it all in.

"Thanks; Matt helped."

"Do you come up here a lot?"

"Yes."

She looks up and tonight there is a cloud cover preventing any star-gazing.

"Can you see the stars from here?"

"Sometimes, not too often."

She shivers and I walk over and grab a blanket out of a trunk. She smiles at me as I hand it to her.

"You know who else would love this? Camille."

"Oh yeah? Why?"

"She's from the south. She always talks about how she misses the wide open space."

"Well, I'm not inviting her over, but you can if you want to. You girls can have all the fun up here you want."

"I just might." Her eyes sparkle as she curls up on the couch.

Leila and I spend most of the night laughing and reminiscing about the crazy things we did as kids. I don't know if it was the wine, being outside, or just her getting comfortable with me, but she giggled and laughed so much that I wanted to bottle this night up and save it.

Sometime around 1 a.m., Leila looks over at me and tells me it's late and she needs to go. As much as I would like to ask her to stay, I know that neither one of us is ready for that.

As we walk to the front door, the energy changes between

us. She feels it and so do I.

She turns around, faces me, and looks up at me with her crystal blue eyes.

"Thank you for having me over tonight and for cooking dinner. I had a really great time."

"I'm glad, and me, too. Maybe you'll come back soon." I give her a one-sided smile.

"I'd like that." She softly smiles, which causes my eyes to drop to her mouth.

Should I or should I not kiss her good night? Is it too soon?

To hell with it.

I close the distance between us and her back hits the wall.

LEILA

HE HASN'T CALLED me. I thought that he would. We got along so well at his place for dinner. Ali tells me that he's been busy with school and tennis, but still, I thought that I would hear from him by now. I know it's only been a couple of days, but if you like someone, shouldn't you call them?

Then again, I haven't called him either . . .

Lying on my bed, in my mind, I replay Beau kissing me goodnight after dinner at his loft, and my heart squeezes.

Standing by his front door, I looked up at him and felt a current pass between us. The silence was electrically charged and the longer we stood there facing each other, the stronger it felt. With hesitation mixed into his hooded eyes, I watched as he rocked up on his toes, and then took that final step into me, pushing me back up against the wall. Cautiously, he leaned forward and placed both of his hands next to my shoulders, trapping me, his beautiful eyes never leaving mine.

I don't know if I have ever been more aware of him than I was in that moment.

Slowly, he lowered and tucked his head into the nape of my neck. My eyes drifted shut at the sensation of his warm breath tickling each and every nerve ending as he breathed in and out. My hands landed on his ribcage and slid down to his waist. Time passed and eventually we both relaxed into each other.

His head turned and his mouth softly latched onto my neck, sucking it in slightly. His tongue brushed against my skin, and I exhaled a moan and shivered at the same time.

He shifted, leaned forward, and his chest brushed up against mine. His heartbeat was thundering through his chest and I was elated to see that this was affecting him as much as it was me.

One hand leaves the wall and wraps around my lower back. He pulls us tighter together and he kisses the spot directly under my ear. His lips are warm and the softness of his hair brushes my cheek. I love being close to him. In his arms, wrapped up around him, he's the only one that I have ever wanted this from.

Pulling back, I search and memorize his beautiful face. The whiskey color of his eyes that are usually shining at me, have deepened to a brown. His cheeks are pink and his lips are already parted and ready for mine.

Slowly, he leans in and kisses me. His lips are full and his kiss is so gentle, so tender, so affectionate that a lump forms in the back of my throat and I feel my eyes prick with tears.

Beau has always had this way about him, where he could give me just one look and I would instantly feel stripped and raw. He can see through every layer that is in me like no one else can. It's moments like this where I know that I made the wrong decision all those years ago. I should have confronted him and demanded to know why he didn't show up. Why he didn't keep his promise.

His kiss doesn't stay gentle for long, but then again, it's Beau and it wouldn't. Beau is a very passionate person, which makes him very tenacious. When he wants something, he takes it unapologetically, and I love that about him. Years ago, he lit the flame between us and as his lips press harder and his tongue pushes deeper, the heat inside of me erupts.

Arching my back into him, both of his hands slid down my backside, lifting to press me into the wall.

And press he does. I can feel all the best parts of him as my legs and arms wrap around him. If I had my way, I'd never let go.

My phone dings, pulling me out of the memory. I look down to see that it's Ali. She's asking if I have plans tonight. Deciding to take things into my own hands, I answer yes without any explanation.

Pulling up the match schedule for Columbia, I find that

Beau has a game tonight. I need to see him and I don't know any other way to. I need to see if he has been thinking of me and is just slightly preoccupied, or if he has moved on.

Charlie thinks that I should just go back over to his loft, but he's wrong. He doesn't know Beau like I do. If Beau wanted me to come over, he would ask. He's always been very private with his space, and I'm afraid showing up unannounced would upset him.

The sports complex is packed. I'm relieved because I don't want him to know that I am here. I just want to be able to watch him.

Over the last couple of months, Beau has become a big name here on campus. He is undefeated, and has earned the backing of most of the student body. All around me are girls, and every one of them is talking about how gorgeous he is.

The announcer calls his name and the crowd explodes. Adrenaline is coursing through me; partly, because I am excited to be here, and partly because there is no way to not get caught up in the energy of this place.

The coin is tossed and it lands in Beau's favor. He smirks at his opponent and chooses to receive. Everyone in this place knows that Beau is exceptional when it comes to serving, but being undefeated, he's trying to unnerve and intimidate his opponent. For a brief second, there was confusion on the poor guy's face, but he quickly masked it. Beau crosses his arms over his chest and his smile grows. He saw it too.

The umpire hands a ball to the opponent. He walks to the center of his baseline and bounces it while tracking Beau. Beau tosses his racket between his hands and shifts his weight from side to side. He is in the zone and he smirks again at the poor guy across the net from him.

The opponent tosses the ball high, the racket comes down,

and the set begins. Within five minutes the umpire calls 'love-30'. This match isn't going to last long.

It's been a good year and a half since I have watched Beau play, and it's easy for me to see how much he has grown into this sport. He makes it look so easy and effortless.

The second set ends and he walks to the sidelines to get a drink of water. He picks up his towel, runs it over his face and neck, and freezes. He looks straight up into the stands and right at me.

How did he know I was here? Heat spreads up my neck and into my cheeks. I feel busted for doing something wrong, even though I'm not.

Our eyes are lock and he takes my breath away. Slowly, I lift my hand, give a small wave, and a smile. He smiles back and my eyes fill with tears, tears of relief.

In high school I used to go to his matches but he never knew. Only once did he see me, but then he didn't smile, he scowled. After that, I sat in a different place and he never saw me again. I saw him look up to that spot where I used to sit at every match though.

"Wait for me," he mouths.

I nod my head, thinking that I would wait for him forever.

He smiles at me one more time and then puts his competitor-face back on.

"Hey, do you know him?" The girl behind me taps on my shoulder and asks.

That's such a loaded question. "Yep." I answer without looking back at her.

"That's awesome, how?" Her voice is louder. She's leaned closer to me.

"We grew up together."

"Wow, so you like really know him."

"Yes, I do."

Beau finishes the third set in record time and the match is called. The crowd cheers and I watch with pride as he smiles and waves. He glances at me once, winks, and then runs off to the locker room. One by one the people file out and leave, except the girls sitting behind me.

Twenty minutes later, Beau jogs out of the tunnel and onto the courts. He sees me and smiles from ear to ear. He's wearing the same jeans from the other night and a plaid button-down with the sleeves rolled up. His hair is wet and he looks so good.

Skipping up the stadium steps, he stops right in front of me, smiling. "Hi."

"Hi. Nice win." A breeze blows and the scent of fresh soap fills the air around me.

"Thanks, you know how it is."

The girls from behind me giggle and he glances up at them.

"Hi," he says, all three of them freeze.

"Can I have my picture taken with you?" I recognize the voice of the girl who was asking me the questions.

He laughs and looks at me. I shrug my shoulders. Turning around I see that the three girls are watching us very closely.

"Okay," he says.

The girl jumps up and wraps her arm around him while her friend takes the photo.

"Thank you," she says, while batting her eyelashes at him.

Her friends giggle again.

"No problem." He looks back to me and holds out his hand. "Ready to go?"

I immediately take it and he links his fingers through

mine. "Yes."

Together we walk down the steps and away from the three girls. I know I shouldn't feel this surge of pride that I do but I can't help it. He didn't even look twice at them. He was singularly focused on me.

"I didn't know you were coming today; you should have called or texted me."

"Maybe."

He looks down at me and I know he understands. We don't have that type of relationship where we pick up the phone to call each other. At least . . . not yet.

"If you come to any more, will you let me know? I liked seeing you today."

"Sure."

He smiles again and his thumb rubs over the back of my hand.

"So, what do you want to do tonight?" I know I'm being presumptuous, but I want him to know that I want to spend time with him.

His hand tightens around mine and the butterflies take off.

"I have an idea, but first I need to know if you are hungry. I'm starving."

"I could eat."

"Perfect."

Together, in silence, we walk out of the stadium and he hails us a cab.

"Please take us to Canal and Mulberry Street. Drop us as close as you can to the feast."

The cab driver nods his head and off we go.

"What's the feast?"

"Oh, if you don't know, I'm not telling you. You'll have to wait and see."

"Well, that's not fair."

He grins at me, wraps his arm around my shoulder, and pulls me closer to him. My hand lands on his thigh and that grin turns into a full smile. He's so gorgeous. We're in the cab for about fifteen minutes as it heads downtown. Neither one of us says anything, but it's a familiar, comfortable silence.

After the cab driver drops us off, we walk two blocks down Canal, and I come to a complete stop. "Where are we?"

"Little Italy," he says.

"I know that, but what is all this?"

Looking around I see that there are hundreds of people crammed onto the street. Lights are arched over the road and street food vendors are lined up one after the other. Outside the restaurants are little tables with red-and-white-checkered table cloths, there's music floating in the air, and overall the atmosphere is calling to me.

"It's the Feast of San Gennaro. This feast is the longest running religious festival in the city. They do all this for eleven days."

"How did you hear about this? I've been here over a year and it's new to me."

"I like food. Nate knows this and he told me about it. He's from the Bronx and knows everything about living in the city."

"Sounds like a good friend to have."

"He is. So, I know this is all a little cheesy and over the top, but I thought it would be fun and we'll get to eat some great food," he says, turning to face me.

"No, it's perfect. Thank you for bringing me here."

"One more thing . . ." He wraps his hands around my face, steps into me, and lowers his lips to mine. Standing in the middle of the street, under the festival lights, with old Italian music playing in the background, he kisses me and it's a kiss that couldn't have been more romantic.

Beau deepens the kiss just enough to not make it offensive in public, but enough to set off a thousand butterflies in my stomach. He takes my breath away.

Leaning his forehead against mine, he pulls back slightly, and I'm met with light colored hazel eyes. He smiles at me and runs his thumbs over my cheek bones.

"Yeah, so since the second I saw you from the courts, I've wanted to kiss you. It's kind of all I've been thinking about."

"Feel free to kiss me anytime you want."

His smile grows and the corners of his eyes crinkle. "Okay." He leans down again and brushes his warm lips against mine.

Beau is kissing me in public. In front of other people. Other than prom, we've never been anywhere or done anything in front of other people. My heart has wings, and at the moment, it is soaring.

"Alright, beautiful, are you ready to eat some meatballs and a cannoli?"

"Absolutely."

His hand finds mine and together we walk under the lit-up San Genarro arched entrance.

"Can I tell you something?"

"Of course." He squeezes my hand.

"I've never been on a date before."

He stops in the street and looks down at me with a frown on his face.

"I'm sorry," he says barely louder than a whisper.

"Why are you sorry?"

"Because at this moment, I'm wishing that I had taken you on a hundred dates."

His words are so genuine. I don't know what to say to him. He pulls me into him, tucks his face into my neck, and hugs me. Being flush up against him and in his arms I wonder, what do I need to do, and how many stars do I need to make wishes on to make this last forever?

"For the record, I never have either."

BEAU

"DO YOU WANT to come up?"

I'm pretty certain that I've just had one of the best nights of my life. It isn't lost on me either that it's with Leila. All of my best nights have been with her. Looking down at her, with her strawberry blonde hair blowing all around and her bright blue eyes, I'm spellbound. I would love to follow her into her apartment. However, knowing all of the things that I want to do to her, it's best if I don't.

"Yes . . . but I'm not going to."

"Oh." She drops her gaze from mine to her hands. She looks embarrassed.

"Hey, listen, don't do that," I say and lightly press my thumb up against her chin so she'll look back at me. "I really do want to come up, but if you and I are going to try to do this, then it's not time . . . not yet at least." I give her a one-sided grin.

As much as I would like to see where tonight could go, we do have some things we need to talk about. We've been completely avoiding the elephant in the room.

"I had a really great time." She reaches out and rubs her hand down my arm.

"I did too."

"Will you call me?" She looks so hopeful my chest aches. She wants me to call her. She wants me.

"Yes."

A smile splits across her face and her eyes light up.

"Okay, well, good night then." She rises up on her tiptoes and leans forward. Her lips lightly brush mine. This kiss is sweet, just like her. Oh, what this girl does to me.

"Goodnight, Leila." I stuff my hands into my pockets, and she slowly backs away from me.

Watching Leila walk away and into her building, I hate the feeling that I get in the pit of my stomach. As much as I'm trying to let go of the past, part of me wonders if I'll ever get over how she left me.

Right before the door closes, she turns back around and gives me one more small wave good night. I wink at her and my chest aches again.

Walking away from her building, and off toward mine, I'm stuck on the possibility that I could be upstairs with her right this second. I know it's not the right time, but her skin, her curves, the way she feels, the sounds she makes . . . all of it takes me back to the last night I spent with her before she moved up here with Drew and Ali.

In typical Grant fashion, he hosts a party to say farewell to Drew, Ali, and Leila. Drew and Ali have already lined up an apartment, and Leila plans on staying with them until the dorms open up at her new school. They decided that they didn't need both cars, so the three of them are driving up in Ali's and Drew is leaving the Jeep behind. Drew hired movers to transfer their things and the apartment should be set up by the time they get there.

Walking into the party, I scan the crowd and take a deep breath. I really didn't want to come tonight but I'm trying to set aside my feelings for them. Everyone is so excited about their move to New York City, and yes, I am too, but the feeling of loss that I have outweighs any joy. Scanning the crowd, I can't help but frown as I think how different things are going to be. There are a lot of seniors here who are all going to be gone over the next couple of weeks.

"Beau! Come over here!" I hear Ali yell over the music. I find her and Drew in our usual place around the stone fire pit. Sitting next to Ali is Leila. My heart speeds up just looking at her.

I bump arms with Drew and take a seat.

Looking at Ali, she smiles at me. She knows what's coming. "Tiny, did you know that when someone is 86'd—escorted out and told to not come back—that phrase actually came from back in the day in Vegas, when the mob ran the town. It meant to take that person eight miles out and six feet down."

"Did you know that stars don't actually twinkle? The light from the star passes through the atmosphere and the light gets deflected before it reaches your eyes, making you think it's twinkling."

"Oh, Tiny, you'll never beat me at the star facts." I smirk

at her. "Did you know there is no such thing as a shooting star? What happens is a meteor, which is nothing but rock and debris left over from an asteroid, hits that same atmosphere and burns up. The effect looks like a shooting star. So all those years when we were kids making wishes really was kind of pointless."

Yeah, after I say this, hearing the tone in my own voice, I realize how much of a pissy mood I'm in. Maybe I shouldn't have come. I look over at Leila and see that my words have hurt her feelings. Whatever; she's hurt mine plenty enough.

The crowd around us has quieted. Ali looks at me with her big brown eyes. They're sad. She shouldn't be sad for me. It is what it is.

"Sea otters hold hands when they sleep so they don't drift apart," she says very innocently, in her sweet little voice. The tension breaks, a few 'ahs' are said, and everyone around us goes back to their previous conversations.

"What took you so long to get here?" Drew asks.

I relax into the chair. "I don't know. Originally, I wasn't planning on coming." I look at him and he knows. Nothing needs to be said between us. He gets me and the fact that this final party is hard.

"Well, I'm glad you came." Ali leans over and squeezes my arm.

I give her a small smile and not once do I look over at Leila.

Most of the party is pretty typical, just like all of the others. Grant's attempt for the drink of the evening is a Manhattan. He bought cheap bourbon and mixed it with sweet vermouth and bitters. I imagine that done properly it's not too bad, but he made a cooler size vat of it and it just tastes awful. Eventually, cherry grenadine is mixed in, and slowly people begin drinking it.

Leila keeps to herself most of the evening. She speaks when spoken to, but in general she is pretty quiet, more so than usual. I'm trying not to notice her or what she's doing, but I can't help it. She has on a little blue sundress that fits her perfectly. That dress and her long legs have me thinking all kinds of thoughts.

After prom, I thought that things might change between us, but once again, they didn't. I don't know why I am so hopeful for this change; I should know better by now. That's twice in the last six weeks she has left me the next morning like nothing ever happened. Even from day to day, she still treats me as if I'm just another random guy to her, and not someone who supposedly used to mean so much to her. I don't get it, I really don't.

Walking down the dock, I board Drew's and my boat. All of the laughter from the party is starting to get to me, and I really just need to step away for a few minutes. Thinking about tomorrow, I don't feel like there's anything left to laugh about.

"Hey, what are you doing all the way down here?" I open my eyes and see Leila standing on the dock. It doesn't matter how many times I look at her; each time she makes my heart skip a beat. The sadness that I am already feeling intensifies.

I look up at the sky and spot the Summer Triangle. I'd rather look at the stars than her. It hurts to look at her. "Nothing much, just decided to step away for a bit."

"Care if I join you?" To date, Ali is the only girl who has ever been on this boat.

I look back over at her and hesitate. "Sure."

"Actually . . . let's get out of here and go down to the beach. Will you go for a walk with me?" I eye her warily. She's hardly spoken to me in weeks, and not at all tonight.

"Why?" I have to ask her. Her cheeks flush pink and she looks away from me.

"For some reason, it just seems important since I'm leaving...I don't know. I feel like one of my last memories of this place should be with you."

I can't argue with this and, honestly, I want her last memories to be of me too.

"Okay." I still can't say no to her.

Silently and together, we walk back up the dock. Ali sees us and watches us walk over to the side entrance. She doesn't make a single facial expression, so I have no idea what she is thinking. Not that it matters anyway.

When we reach the Tahoe, I open the door for her and she climbs in.

Neither one of us has yet to say anything as I drive us toward the tip of the island. She said beach but I know that she means Bean Point. I'm not sure what she is thinking about, but what my mind is stuck on is that I don't know when I will see her again. She's leaving . . . again. And, although I will never tell her, this time hurts too.

I park the car. We both climb out and I grab a blanket from the back. Leila has already walked over to the entrance and she is just standing there, staring down the trail into the darkness. There is a breeze blowing. Her hair ruffles across her back and the skirt of her dress lifts just a little, showing me more of her gorgeous legs.

I take a mental picture as I walk to stand next to her. After a long silence, she finally looks up at me, and there are tears in her eyes.

"Beau..."

"Don't, Leila. What's the point?"

Her face falls and she lets out a sigh. I understand how

she feels, I really do, but like she said, this is going to be her last memory on the island and I don't want it to be a bad one.

I take her hand, lace my fingers through hers and, together, we walk under the canopy of the island trees, across the dunes, and down to the water.

It's June, meaning sea-turtle nesting season, so all of the lights on the island are out. I look up at the night sky and smile at how bright the moon and the stars are. Of course the stars are out.

"Do you remember all the times we used to come down here to stargaze?"

"Mmm hmm." She already knows from the last time we were here that I still come down here, but there is no way that I'm going to tell her that I've still been coming down here, at least once a week, for the last four and half years. I've always hated myself for it, but I just couldn't stay away.

"Did you mean what you said about the shooting stars?"

"I don't know anymore." That's the best and most honest answer I can give her.

Slowly, we walk around the tip of the island and back. We're both quiet as we watch the tide roll the water onto and off of the shore. I'm still holding her hand and occasionally she leans into my arm.

When we get back to the trail, she pulls on my hand, causing me to stop.

"I don't want to go back yet. Can we just sit down over there like we used to?"

"That's why I brought the blanket. I just wasn't sure how long you wanted to be out here."

"I don't care how long . . . I just want to be with you."

We walk into the dunes and I lay down the blanket on a flat area. Leila sits down on the blanket first and I can't help but stare down at her. Part of me is so happy to be here with her right now, but another part of me hurts, knowing that, when the sun rises tomorrow, she'll pretend like this night never existed, and she'll be gone.

"Are you going to join me?" She looks up at me.

"Yeah, sorry." Sitting next to her out here, where there is no one around, and no one can see us in the midst of all of the sea oats, my body begins to hum with awareness.

"Can I ask you a question?" She doesn't face me. She just stares out at the water.

"Sure," I say while lying down, tucking my hands under my head.

"What happened to us?" she asks softly.

"You know what happened to us. You were there . . ."

"I just don't understand. Why didn't yo—"

I can't get in to this with her. Not right now. I move one of my hands and place it on her back.

"Hey," I say to her.

She turns, angling her body toward mine and looks down at me. I can see the tears shimmering in her eyes and I feel exactly the same way.

"Let's not do this tonight, okay? It's a really beautiful night and with you leaving . . . I'd rather remember things this way, with you under the stars, wouldn't you?"

She nods her head and I pull on her. She shifts her weight, curls up next to me on her side, and lays her head down on my chest.

Time passes and I run my hand up and down her arm that's draped over me. Her hand runs across my chest and down over my stomach. There is no way I can stop the reaction that this is causing; my stomach muscles tighten and my whole body freezes.

"Beau . . ."

"Mmm hmm."

She hesitates before speaking and her fingers tangle in my shirt. "I want you to be my first." She says this so quietly, that I'm certain she didn't just say what I think she said. I don't say anything in response, and Leila tenses, pulls away from me, sits up, and wraps her arms around her legs. She looks back out to the water and her face is so sad.

"Wait. What?" I sit up so I'm more on her level. She looks at me. There's embarrassment written all over her face and I'm sure she can see the confusion on mine.

"I want it to be you," she whispers again.

"Want me to be what?" A breeze blows over us and I tuck a few loose strands of her hair behind her ear.

She doesn't say anything. She just looks at me with trepidation.

I'm stunned into silence.

"Lei, you don't know what you're asking of me."

"I do know what I'm asking. I've done nothing but think about this and . . . please, it has to be you."

I understand why she is saying this, I really do. Despite all of the problems that the two of us have had over the years, this pull, this connection between us, we've always had it. I think back to when we were younger. I would've done anything for her then, and it seems I will now too.

For just a moment, she leans forward and rests her forehead against mine. Her eyes are closed and her hand reaches up to touch my face. Her fingertips still and her pulse lightly thumps on my skin. It's beating fast and it matches mine. She lets out a small sigh and I breathe in the sweetness of her breath. She's nervous, but then again, so am I.

I'm not going to make her beg. I'm sure it was hard

enough for her to ask me this, and the truth is I want it with her too. I've always wanted her.

Leaning closer, my thumbs press up under her chin and my lips brush against hers. Her fingers slip around and into my hair, bringing us closer. It's official . . . I'm done.

"Please make love to me," she mumbles against my lips.

Shifting slightly, I pull back and look at her beautiful face. She's always been so easy for me to read that I need to know for certain that she really wants this.

Her eyes are warm and excited. She gives me a small smile and I fall in love with her all over again right here, under our stars.

"Okay," I whisper.

Her smile widens.

My fingers trace down her neck, over her collarbone, to the swell of her breasts. Endless amounts of time I have spent fantasizing over what it would be like to taste her skin, see her, be with her, and now, within two months, she's given it all to me—all of her.

Slowly, with trembling fingers, I pull on one of her dress straps and it slips over her shoulder. Just this one tiny section where the indent between her collarbone, shoulder, and neck meet is so sexy.

I lower my mouth, my tongue swipes across her skin, and she moans. With very clear purpose, I kiss and lick my way up her neck and back to her mouth. She doesn't hesitate kissing me in return. She really does want this.

Leila lies back on the blanket and I lean over her. Between Sirius and the moon, up close, I can see every detail of her perfectly—even her tiny freckles.

"You are so beautiful."

"So are you," she whispers back to me. My heart squeezes because I wonder if she would still think that if she saw all of me.

"You alright?" she asks.

"Yeah, sorry," I say blinking away the image.

"Thought I lost you there for a second."

"No, I'm here. I'm very here."

She pulls me down and her lips and mouth steal my breath. I'm trying to remember to breathe, but being this close to her and knowing what is about to happen, I keep forgetting.

My hand moves over her breast and I pause to take in the changes to her body from over the last couple of years. Her body really is something amazing, and knowing that I get to do this with her excites me even further. Through the fabric of her dress, my thumb runs over her and her grip on me tightens.

Pulling down the other strap, my fingers trail along the freckles on her collarbone, and then dip inside the edge of her dress. Slowly, I pull it down and leave her top half in nothing but a strapless bra. Her breathing picks up as I lean over and run my nose across her skin. It's so warm and she smells so good.

Moving one cup of her bra away, I get my first glimpse of Leila in an intimate way. I'm speechless at the perfection of her. She fills my hand. I squeeze her lightly and I just can't wait any longer to taste her.

My mouth closes over her and she arches her back and moans. It's the sexiest thing I have ever heard. Spending equal amounts of time on both sides, I can't get enough of her.

Eventually, I push the bra back into place and I return to her mouth. A few weeks ago, we perfected kissing each other, so there's no hesitation here. Just complete desire.

My hands tangle in her hair and no part of her mouth is left unexplored. Her lips are so soft and she tastes better than anything I have ever tasted. My need to completely devour every part of her is overwhelming.

I lie down next to her; her hand moves from my hip, across my stomach, and lower. There's no hiding how much I want to be with her. Tentatively, her fingers brush against me and then she cups me through my jeans. I push into her hand. It feels so good to be touched by her.

At the same time, I gently caress her outer thigh, pushing her dress up and out of the way. Slowly, my fingers drift to the inside of her legs. Her reflexes have her attempting to close them for a breath, but she opens up wider for me.

Higher and higher, my fingers slide up her smooth skin, until I reach the lace edge of her underwear. Placing my hand on her, I run it over her backside, and then move to the front. She lets out a sigh as my fingers drift down over the sensitive parts of her.

Pulling away, I look into her beautiful eyes and smile.

She smiles back, unbuckling my belt. The leather easily gives. She undoes the button and lowers the zipper.

I can't believe this is about to happen and then it does. Her hand finds its way into my pants and wraps around me. I'm momentarily frozen as she explores all of me and then begins to move her hand up and down.

She snuggles in a little closer to me and my fingers slide down between her legs. This snaps me out of my trance.

Gently pushing her underwear to the side, my fingers brush over her and take their time memorizing every detail. Slipping in and out, she's so soft and responsive. If I thought she was going to be uncomfortable with me touching her, my uneasiness is put to rest by the serene look I find spread across her face.

I'm not sure how much time passes while we lie here

learning and enjoying the way each other feels and how we react to each other's touch. Her hand moves at the perfect speed with the perfect amount of tension, and her mouth makes me delirious. I'm so close to going over the edge and I can feel the same from her. Mirroring the movement with purpose, her breathing picks up.

Turning her head, she tucks it into my neck, and her hand comes to a stop. Rolling her hips against my hand, her back arches, and she breathes out a small moan. Every muscle in her tenses and so do I.

I stand corrected; this is the sexiest sound I have ever heard.

Her body is on fire. I can feel every one of her pulse points throb against me at a thunderous pace. Her neck where she's lying on my arm, her wrist as it sits against my lower abdomen, and of course my hand. A smile stretches across my face, and a swell of pride surges through my system that I can make her feel this way. Leila owns me, she always has, but in this moment, right here, right now, I feel like she belongs to me too. She's finally mine.

She eventually relaxes, and I sit up. I can't take it anymore. Moving between her legs, I sit back on my heels and look down at her. Her lips are swollen from being thoroughly kissed, her cheeks are flushed, and she's breathing hard. Her eyes are so big and bright, if I didn't know any better, I would swear that there was love shining out of them.

Reaching under the skirt of her dress, I hook on to her underwear, pulling it down and off. I don't know which one of us is trembling more. Grabbing a condom out of my wallet, she watches my every move as I slip it on.

"Are you sure about this?" I ask her as I lean down over her.

"Yes," she whispers.

The tip of me brushes against her and I think there's a good possibility that I might die in this moment.

Easing into her just a little bit; she closes her eyes, and lets out another moan. "Beau, that feels so good."

Wrapping my hands around her head, her beautiful blue eyes open and lock onto mine. She knows what's coming and I hope she can see that I'm sorry I'm about to hurt her.

Slowly, I move in and out, letting her adjust to me, pushing further each time until finally, I slide all the way into her and through that last barrier. She feels incredible and my body is screaming for me to move, but my heart has me paused as I'm realizing that just when I've made her mine, she's leaving. A lump forms in the back of my throat and she stiffens underneath me. I stop breathing to keep us completely still.

"Are you okay?" I ask her, just barely in a whisper. Her eyes are squeezed shut.

"Mmm hmm. Just give me second." Her voice shakes.

A second. I would give her forever.

She shifts slightly as she begins to relax underneath me, and I'm struggling. "Lei, you need to lie completely still, or let me start moving because I don't think that I'm going to last too long."

She opens her eyes again and gives me a small smile. "That's okay. I've already gotten what I asked for . . . you."

Lowering my head, my lips brush against hers.

"Leila . . ." My chest aches.

"I know, Beau," she says with tears in her eyes.

Tucking my head into her neck, I slowly slide back out. She feels so good. Instinctually, I want to grab on and move, but this isn't about just me, and this moment is so much bigger than an instinct. Gently, I begin making love to the only girl I have ever loved, under the stars.

Her moves match mine, like we were born to be together this way. The feel of her, her touch, her taste, the sounds she's making, I know I will wake up in the middle of the night remembering and reliving this moment with her.

Kissing Leila, I don't know where one of us begins and the other ends. We are completely connected. In my mind, it's like we are a circle, a ring, two complete halves that make a whole.

She lifts her legs, wraps them around my waist, and I'm done for. I couldn't stop if I tried. Together we move exactly the way I need us to.

Every part of me is tense to the point it's almost unbearable. The need for this, the need for her, I'm chasing release in so many different ways. Keeping one arm next to her head to hold my weight up, my other hand slips under her to tilt her hips up, and my world explodes.

As always with Leila, my world bursts into different colors and those tiny sparks one by one land on my skin.

Slowing down to ride out this accomplished sensation, Leila squeezes her legs around me to hold me in place.

"Don't pull out yet, please."

"Okay, I won't." I'm still breathing hard and I lay my head on the blanket next to hers. Wetness hits my cheek, and I turn to see Leila's eyes closed and tears are leaking out. I kiss my way up her face, over the tears, and lace my fingers through hers.

"Thank you," she says to me, and all I can think to say back is the same.

"Thank you."

I'm not sure how long I end up lying there with her wrapped up in my arms. This night is permanently etched not only in my mind but in my heart: the sound of the water, the sea oats as they sway in the breeze, and endless number of stars against the midnight sky.

At some point while sleeping, Leila moves off of me, and rolls onto her side facing me. It was this movement that woke me, leaving me feeling completely vulnerable. Never in my wildest dreams did I think tonight would end like this. Surely, it should be our beginning.

The moonlight is bright enough that I can memorize every detail of her beautiful face. There's a slight breeze blowing and her hair keeps fluttering across her skin. Her eyelashes are resting on her cheeks and her lips are slightly parted. She is breathtaking to me. There isn't a person on this planet who could ever compare.

I watch her for what feels like hours and eventually roll over onto my back to stare up at the stars. Immediately, the Summer Triangle comes into view. Focusing in on Vega, the fifth-brightest star, I remember that the constellation Lyra also has a Ring Nebula. A ring. Only, this ring doesn't mean a coming together, it's coming apart. It represents the death of a star, and, as it burns out, it expels a ring of glowing gas.

My heart frowns, because all this does is remind me that no matter what, everything ends.

I have to get up and walk away from her. I can't lie here, go to sleep, and be hopeful that she'll be here in the morning. I know that if I stay, she won't be. And after tonight, it'll destroy me. It's literally the worst feeling in the world to always be reminded that I just don't mean enough to her. It's not that I'm looking to hurt her, because I'm not. And it's not that I don't care for her, because I do. I care too much. But at some point I have to think about me.

Maybe she would want me to stay, or maybe she

wouldn't. After the last couple of mornings that we've had together, she just might be relieved to wake up and find me not here. I can only hope that it's not the opposite. Then again, she's leaving tomorrow. What good would come of her having a change of heart now? . . . nothing.

As the sun's glow slowly begins to light up the sky, I very carefully move away from her. I'm afraid if I lie here much longer, she'll wake, but there was no way I was going to leave her out here by herself in the dark.

Unbuttoning and slipping off the shirt that I have on over my T-shirt, I gently lay it on top of her. It's not really cool out but it isn't warm either. Who knows, maybe she'll hang on to this shirt to remember me.

Stepping back away from her, my chest tightens to the point of aching. I shove my hands into my pockets and my eyes blur with tears. She's leaving today, and with her she takes my heart. I don't know when I will see her again, if ever. Yes, she and Ali are friends but people change and drift apart. I know that there's a good possibility that she'll meet someone new, and she'll store me away with all of her other past memories.

A memory, that's what I'll become.

This was goodbye. I now see that's what she was trying to say. Goodbye is what last night was all about and I have no regrets. Well, maybe I wish that I would have held her a little tighter for just a little longer.

As I'm watching her, she stirs. Any minute now she'll wake and I know it's time for me to go.

One by one, tears begin to roll down my face. In my heart, I tell her that I'll always love her and I'll miss her forever.

Turning away, I will my feet to move, placing one in front

of the other. The coolness of the morning sand sinks between my toes and I involuntarily shiver. Thinking back to the pain that I felt four years ago, the first time she left me, although this is different, hurts just as much.

Chapter Fifteen

LEILA

"SO, WHAT ARE we doing this weekend?" Charlie asks me as he flops down on the couch and flips on the TV.

Living with him kind of reminds me of living with my dad. As much as Charlie loves fashion and design, he's all dude. ESPN Sports Center blares throughout the room. He turns down the volume and tosses the remote down next to him.

"Nothing; I picked up a few shifts at the café," I say as I load our breakfast dishes into the dishwasher.

Charlie and I hunted for this apartment for almost two months. We wanted to be close to school, so that didn't leave us very many blocks to comb through.

This apartment we finally found is off of MacDougal. It's not much but it works for us. All of the units in this building are mostly filled with college students, being that it's across the street from NYU. It kind of reminds me of last year's dorm life, only it's a little quieter.

"Why?"

"Because I need the money; I spent more than I should have on materials for the fashion show and now I'm paying for it, pun intended."

"You know, I bet if you looked into the details of your scholarship you might find that it includes things like supplies. I know that most include textbooks, so why wouldn't fabric and thread be included as well?"

"You might be right. I never did try to figure out all of the fine details. I'll have to drop by the administration building later this afternoon."

"So, how's the man?" Charlie smirks at me.

A blush rises into my cheeks at the mention of Beau.

"He's good," I say, walking into the living room to join him on the couch.

"That's it? That's all you're going to give me?"

"There's not really much to tell yet."

"But you've spent a lot of time with him." He phrases this as a statement, but it could be a question too.

"I know. He says he's making up for lost time in the date department."

"Well, that's romantic." He smiles at me again.

"I think so. He even bought me those flowers over there." I point to the new white orchid plant sitting in the window. As much as I love purple, I'm glad that he bought white. It feels fresh, clean, and new, just like us. The plan is to keep it inside during the winter, and next to the window. We'll see if it lasts or not.

"Every day I like him more and more."

"Me too."

"So, have you asked him yet?"

Without realizing it, my hands fall to my lap and I start wringing my fingers. The thought of bringing up the past with Beau makes me nervous.

"No, we haven't talked about any of it." I pause, looking at the orchid plant. "Things have been going so well between us. He's talking to me, wanting to spend time with me, and I'm learning all about who he is now. I'm afraid that if I bring it up, it'll remind him of why he didn't want to be with me in the first place, and it could ruin everything."

"You should ask him soon. The longer you spend time with him, the more whatever he has to say could hurt you. Besides, whatever he says, it may actually sway you on how you feel about him. Wouldn't you rather know?"

"Some days I think yes, I would like to know why he felt I didn't even deserve a goodbye, but then there are others when everything feels so perfect and right, and I just don't want to pop that bubble."

"Leila, based on the things you've told me, you shouldn't be worrying about it popping; it's going to explode."

I frown at him and he looks back at the TV.

"Oh! Did you see that? He didn't just tackle that guy; he crushed him!"

Charlie has always loved football, but Beau's friend Nate told us in passing, at Ali's party, that his brother Reid plays in the NFL for Jacksonville, and this, of course, made Charlie's night. When we got home later that evening, we watched YouTube clips of him playing, and Charlie became an instant fan.

"You really could just sit here and watch this all day, couldn't you?"

"You know it."

Shaking my head at him, I get up and walk over to our

kitchen table where my things are. "Well, I'm off to class."

"Grab a coat. There's some weather moving in."

"Thanks . . . see you later."

The admissions office is busy today.

After I walked in, I was told to take a number and have a seat. I sat here for an hour before I was called up, only to be told that I would have to wait even longer because the finance department was in a meeting. Normally I wouldn't have minded, but I needed to get into the studio and get started on my end of the semester project. The fashion show took up a lot of my time, and although a few of my professors were sympathetic to this, others were not.

Two hours later, I'm called into another office at the end of the hall, and I'm slightly angry.

"Good afternoon, Ms. Starling. I hear you have a few questions about the details of your scholarship," says a very chipper lady behind the counter.

"Yes. I'm wondering what it covers. I know that my classes and books are paid for, and last year's housing, but does it include supplies too?"

"Well, let me pull your account and we'll take a look."

She jots down my social security number and I watch as she walks into another room and begins typing on her computer. Her eyebrows shoot up. She glances at me as she walks to a filing cabinet and pulls out a red folder.

"Okay, Ms. Starling, I'm not sure why this wasn't reviewed and given to you sooner but I guess now is better than never. You did receive a scholarship, but it is untraditional."

"What does that mean?"

She lays the folder on the counter between the two of us and looks me right in the eye. "It means that all of your expenses are paid, through a benefactor."

A benefactor? I only applied for scholarships through large corporations. I didn't seek out individual help. Maybe some board member from one of the companies liked my essay and took an interest.

"Is this common?" I ask her.

"We have had a few of these over the years. Usually it's a past alumna who wants to sponsor a student. Didn't they tell you when you were accepted that all expenses were paid for?"

"Yes; this is why I haven't received any bills from the school."

"That's correct, but you shouldn't have paid for anything. Your benefactor has provided you with a credit card. I'm not sure why it wasn't sent to you, but here it is." She holds it up for me to see. "All of your school-related expenses, including cost of living, on campus or off, are to be charged to this card."

"What? But that's crazy. How did I get picked for this?" Suddenly, the room feels warmer, my fingers begin to cramp, and I start rubbing them.

"I'm not so sure. Oh, wait a minute; actually it says here that the benefactor asked for you specifically."

"Who is it?" I have to know who did this so I can thank them.

"We aren't supposed to disclose that information. If the benefactor wanted you to know then they would have told you." The woman watches me closely. "Here's your credit card. You know, you are one very lucky girl."

Without even thinking, instead of grabbing the card, I

snatch the folder from her and take a step away from the counter and out of her reach.

"Now, you give that back to me this instant!" Several papers slip out of the folder and fall to the floor. I bend over to pick them up and glance at the top one. It's a bank funds transfer receipt to the school from a Mr. B. Hale.

Mr. B. Hale.

I can't help but gasp in shock. The woman freezes in front of me but I can't take my eyes off of his name. Slowly, she reaches out and takes the folder from me. Heat fills my face as I let it go, and tears fill my eyes. How did he do this? Why did he do this?

"Is there any way to return the money?" I ask quietly. My throat is so tight, it hurts to speak.

"No dear." She looks at me sympathetically. "I take it you know this person."

"Yes. Is there any way to stop payment going forward?"

She flips through the papers again. "No, he's paid in full."

Of course he has. My hands are balled into fists. "Can I please have the credit card?" She picks it up off of the counter and hands it to me. "Thank you for your time."

Without making eye contact, I turn around and walk out of the school, and head straight for the studio. Charlie was right. Clouds have moved in and the temperature has dropped drastically. Wrapping my scarf a little tighter around me, my eyes again fill with tears.

I don't understand why he did this.

After I moved back to the island, Beau made it very clear that he hated me for years. Occasionally, I would catch him looking at me, but he always turned away. Mostly, he just pretended like I never even existed, and that hurt so much.

Wracking my brain, I try to place when and where Beau

213

would have even heard or known about my acceptance to Parson's. I didn't tell anyone, except for Chase, until after the money was secured. Chase wouldn't have told him. They've always been friends but I can't see them sitting down and talking about me. Chase was pissed as it was with the way things went down between Beau and me. He saw firsthand how heartbroken I was after the fire, before we moved. The thing is, too, with all of this, Beau wasn't even talking to me when he would have paid the tuition. We weren't friends. Why would he do this? And where did he get the money?

The shock of him being behind this slowly wears off, and anger seeps in. I am so frustrated, I am shaking. He has been a part of every single major event in my life, one way or another. I was so proud that I did this on my own. I worked hard, got into the school of my dreams, and I made it all happen. *Me.* And now I'm faced with knowing that I didn't. I'm devastated and furious at the same time.

He's got some explaining to do.

Pulling out my cell phone, I fire off a text to him.

BEAU

I'M JUST FINISHING up with Nate when Leila's text comes in. She's invited me to her studio and wants to know if and when I might drop by. Of course I'll stop by. I've been trying to think up an excuse to see her today anyway. Her text surprises me a little bit, but after the last couple of weeks, maybe she wants to see me as much as I want to see her. I smile at the thought.

Taking a quick shower, I head out of the school. There's a light dusting of snow on the ground and I'm surprised by how quickly the temperature has dropped and the weather's changed. It's only October. Isn't that early for snow? Little flurries are swirling all around.

Instead of taking the train, I hop in a cab. It'll take less time to get to her and I really want to see her.

The warehouse building isn't too far from Parson's. I make a mental note to myself that she really doesn't have that far of a walk between work, school, the studio, and her apartment. Entering the building, I skip the elevator and take the stairs two at a time. She's on the third floor.

I knock on the door and from behind it she hollers, "Come in."

Walking into her studio, my heart smiles at how much the interior looks just like her; from the colors, the décor, the organization around her workstation, and even the chandelier. Another wave of pride swells in my chest for her. She's worked so hard and done so well to get here.

She's standing by the back wall, which is all windows, and looking down at the street. Long curls fall wildly down her back. She's wearing tight jeans, an ivory long-sleeve T-shirt, and little purple shoes. She's so beautiful, she leaves me stunned.

I close the door and she turns to face me. Her arms are folded across her chest and she's radiating anger. Everything in me immediately goes on alert.

"What's wrong?" I ask, walking toward her.

Time passes as she looks at me but doesn't say anything. I can see the mixture of emotions storming around in her eyes and I feel like she is reaching into me, looking to unfold all of my secrets. Knowing Leila like I do, I say nothing and just wait for her cue. Eventually, she holds up a credit card and glares at me with tears in her eyes.

She knows.

"Leila . . ."

"Don't you Leila me! You had no right!" She flips the credit card and it slices through the air toward me. Blocking it with my hand, it falls to the ground.

I always knew there was a possibility that she would find out, but I didn't expect her to be this angry over it. She was accepted to the school, and needed tuition money, end of story.

"I had every right!" When did life become so impersonal and stale that doing something nice for someone is against the norm? "I wanted to help you! I wanted to help make your dreams come true."

"But I wanted to do this on my own!"

I do understand this. Moving to New York was something that I, too, needed to do on my own. But what if the money for her never came through? She would have missed out on all of this, over something that could have been avoided, was avoided.

"Leila, you did do this on your own; it's really not a big deal!"

"Yes, it is! Where did you even get the money for this?"

"Don't worry about it. It's mine and I can spend it however I want."

"But I don't want you to spend it on me. I never asked for your help and I don't want your help; especially you, of all people!" She looks away from me, disinterested in my response.

The air freezes in my lungs and a sharp pain stabs me in the chest. *Especially you, of all people.* She can't mean that.

"What's that supposed to mean?"

She doesn't say anything and she still won't look at me.

"Why are you so mad at me?"

Her eyes snap back to mine, "Because, Beau . . . I waited for you!"

Waited for me? What is she talking about?

"When? When did you wait for me?"

The expression on her face switches to one of pain and then the walls slam down.

"It doesn't matter. Now I owe you, and you can be certain that I will pay you back every penny."

"It does matter. I want to know what you're talking about and I didn't do this so you would feel an obligation to repay me."

"Did you do it because you think you can sleep with me now? That you'll have some claim over me?"

I stumble back, shooting her a rather shocked glare. "What?!"

"I am not a whore."

I stiffen, shocked as yet another string of cold and ugly words fall from her mouth. I really shouldn't be. "What are you talking about? I have never done or said anything that should make you feel that way. And, trust me, if I wanted to sleep with you, there have been plenty of opportunities over the last couple of weeks that I could have—and you know it."

"That's funny; I seem to remember feeling that way when I woke up on the beach alone. You took exactly what you wanted from me and then left me there like what we did and who I was was nothing of importance to you."

"That's what you think happened? That's how you've felt all this time?"

"I *know* that's what happened. I was there."

I don't know what to say to this. Never did I consider that

217

she would think I had used her. She was the one who invited *me* to the beach.

Running my hand through my hair, I let out a deep sigh. "Leila, I don't know what to say. I'm sorry if you walked away that morning feeling that way. I can assure you, that night on the beach, what you gave me, means more to me than you will ever know."

She doesn't say anything. She just continues to glare at me.

Letting out a deep sigh, I walk closer to her. She stiffens and watches me warily.

"You weren't supposed to find out about the tuition money. I'm not sorry I paid it, though. I really just wanted to do something nice for you."

She grits her teeth and pulls her arms across her chest even tighter.

"Nice with a price doesn't sit well with me."

"There is no price! Are you even listening to me? You weren't supposed to find out!" I'm to the point of completely pulling my hair now in exasperation.

"It doesn't matter, Beau! I did find out and now I feel as if this entire experience for me has been tainted! It's not mine anymore. I didn't earn it on my own. I didn't get here because of me! I feel cheated of this and sad. Now I have to share it with you."

My mind sticks on the words she's yelling at me, and my heart sticks on the fact that we are never going to be any better than we are right now. This is it. The moment of truth.

"Nice with a price . . . wow. I didn't realize sharing something with me would be so bad. You know what? You're right. This is such a classic moment between the two of us. I don't know why it is that, after all these years, I still see you through rose-colored glasses. The truth is you've never been appreciative of or grateful for me. God, I could have saved myself years of torture if I had figured out sooner how much of a bitch you are."

I heard the slap before I felt it. Leila gasps and throws her hands over her mouth. Slowly, the fire and the burn set in, and I'm not talking about just my face. I can feel the heat radiating off of me as a swirl of emotions stampede through me.

She hit me.

When her hand struck my face, I didn't even flinch. I've been trained not to. Showing a reaction means more will come. Physically, I am frozen. Emotionally, I am breaking.

I suppose that a girl slapping a guy is somewhat a natural reaction after being called a bitch. After all, you see it in the movies and on TV all the time. However, knowing me like she does and the things that I've been through in my past, I can't believe that she just hit me; Leila, of all people.

"Beau . . ." Leila takes a step toward me. Fear shoots through me and I take a step back. My cheek and the side of my mouth are now pulsing from the impact.

I know this is an irrational feeling. Leila would never intentionally harm me, but it's as if that slap and watching her come closer have triggered flashback emotions.

I blink my eyes and a vision of him, my father, is standing before me. I can see the hunger to punish me in his eyes. He gets satisfaction knowing that he is hurting me. I blink again, and Leila is standing before me, in complete horror of what she's done. Tears are streaming down her face and she's shaking her head no.

Blink. Blink. The images flip back and forth and my heart rate takes off. I'm lost in this moment and I'm desperately trying to pull myself out of the imaginary scene and back into the real one.

Star light, star bright, first star I see tonight, I wish I may, I wish I might, have this wish I wish tonight.

"Beau . . ." Leila says my name again and she comes into focus.

My lips are pursed together and my nostrils flare as I try to catch my breath. My heart is pounding against my ribcage and it feels like everything is cracking. I have loved this girl almost my whole life and, now, in just one moment, she's become just like him.

My eyes are hard and fierce as they bore into her. "You win, Leila. You've wanted to be rid of me for so long; well, you just got your wish."

I continue to stare at her but my words have dried up. I'm shaking, my eyes have filled with tears, and a lump has formed in the back of my throat. I know the minute I walk away from her, the tears will fall. She just broke my heart.

"Please, Beau . . . I'm so sorry." She lets out in a sob and takes another step toward me. Tears are now pouring down her face and her arms wrap around her stomach.

"It doesn't matter, Leila. It never did." With that, I push past her, grab my bag and walk out the door, down the stairs, and into the snow.

Chapter Sixteen

LEILA

WHAT HAVE I done?

I can't believe that I hit him.

Should I go after him or should I stay here?

Numbly, I walk to the wall next to the door, lean back against it, and slide down to the floor.

Wanting to hide from this whole terrible situation, I pull my knees up and bury my face.

Silent, painful sobs rip through me as I'm consumed with guilt.

I hurt him and my heart breaks knowing this.

Not one single muscle even twitched when I made contact with his face. It wasn't a girly slap, either. I hit him. His eyes locked onto mine and I could see exactly what I had done to him.

In that exact moment, I watched a fog roll over the fear in his eyes. All of the emotion and life in him instantly shut off.

He was expecting more and he was ready to take it.

Pushing on the pain in my chest, I gasp, realizing that this is what he lived with every day. Witnessing this side of him, a side that only his family has seen, I can only imagine what this did to him. What I did to him.

Beau, of all people, should never have a hand raised at him and I know this better than anyone.

Lifting my head, I glance at the door. In my heart, I am willing it to open. I desperately want him to come back, even though I know he won't.

I hit him.

I hurt him.

Time passes and I don't move. The shadows from the setting sun slide slowly across the floor and I can't look away.

Out of the corner of my eye, I see something next to the base of one of the mannequins. I crawl over and instantly recognize Beau's brown leather journal, the one that I gave him all those years ago. It must have fallen out when he grabbed his bag to leave. Picking it up, I lightly thumb through it and see that at least three quarters of it is full. He's been writing in this for a long time. I know that I shouldn't open it, but I can't help myself.

Adventure #1

So, I'm supposed to use this journal that you gave me to write down all of my adventures. What a stupid idea. But in the spirit of things, here goes…

I've been lying on my stomach in this hospital bed for three weeks. After I woke up, I cried in fear for you because I was worried but then I was told you were okay and got to go home. Relief flooded through me because I did it. I protected you. I saved you. Then, I waited for you. I waited through endlessly long days and nights. At the end of each day before I fell asleep I cried. I cried for you. I cried because I missed you so much and I couldn't understand why you weren't coming. I needed you more than I have ever needed anything in my whole life. I just knew that the minute you walked through the door, you would be able to make this entire awful, painful situation so much better. You were always my bright light in a constantly dark world. I needed you to help pull me out of this darkness. But then a couple of days ago, I got your letter. Now, I cry every night because you broke my heart. Broke isn't even a strong enough word. You took a hammer and in its already-wounded state, you proceeded to beat on it and shatter it as if it never meant anything to you. There's really no other way to describe what you did to me. How could you, Leila? You were my person. My only person, and you left me. You left me here. Everything that I thought was true about you and about us instantly became a lie. Day after day, I pray to God that he will have mercy on me and end me. I want to die and I wish I wasn't such a coward, so I could do it myself. Everything in my life just sucks and it has for so long. There are so many things that I came so close to telling you over the years, but I didn't because I didn't want you to worry. You were my best friend. You were my days and my nights, but mostly you were the stars. My stars. How will I ever look at the stars again and not think of you? You were the reason I wanted to get out of bed every day and now you are gone. I love you and you left me. You left me with nothing and no real explanation. Didn't I at least deserve that? Apparently not. You have succeeded in making me truly feel like I am nothing to no one, and I just want to die.

I've stopped breathing.

What is this?

My fingers tighten around the journal and I read it again.

His words, his tears, the heartbreak . . . this is crushing my soul and I'm shaking.

I don't understand what I am reading. Why would he write this? It just doesn't make sense to me.

Adventure #2

They tell me I should be thankful that my arm was in a cast because the cast was non-flammable. That if it hadn't been, most likely I would have lost my arm. Would it have mattered? As it is I am covered in scars that don't appear to be healing. I was so excited when they told me I was leaving, I just wanted to go home and get in my bed, but instead I was moved to the burn rehabilitation wing where I am going to live for the next couple of months. Apparently, I am highly susceptible to infections. My dressings still need to be changed and they need to work on slowly incorporating physical therapy into my daily routine. I guess the scars will tighten the skin and make it hard for me to move. Maybe now I can give up tennis. At least while I'm here, this cast will finally come off. I never got to tell you about my arm. Dad broke it. When I got back from that last trip out to Bean Point with you, I went straight to my room because I was so mad and upset that you were leaving. I just wanted to be alone. He came in and told me he didn't care for my attitude—I should say he yelled it, not told. He hit me with my tennis racket until my upper arm cracked in half. That happened the night before the fire, when you were at Aunt Ella's for the family going-away dinner. Drew and Matt both stood in the doorway and cried as they watched him do it. I honestly

don't know which I think is worse; being on the receiving end or having to watch while someone you love is being made to suffer. Earlier that day was last time that I heard Matt talk. It's been over a month. Mom's the one who brought this journal to the hospital. Along with Matt, I can't say that I'm really talking to anyone either. She thinks the journal will help me to express my feelings. Such bullshit. She brought over that picture of us in front of Kelly's Kandy Shop too. She tried to leave it in my room, but I had her take it home. What's the point? Every day I wait for the mail to come. I am just hoping with everything that I am that there is something for me. But every day there never is. Mom shows up after work and disappointment floods in. So every night, before bed, I reread your letter. Was I really that unimportant to you that you can forget me so easily? I don't think I will ever be able to forget you, not as long as I live. Leila, everything hurts. My arm, my back, my body, my heart . . . I hate this life. I hate you not being in it. I will never understand why. We were together every day for six years.
What did I do wrong?

I don't know how to stop the tears that are pouring out of my eyes.

Closing the journal I clutch it to my chest. I can't read anymore. Holding it tightly, I hug it, as if I can somehow magically hug the past.

He's so broken. I broke him.

How did I not know any of this? I can only assume he's talking about the fire that I was in. He said he saved me. Why don't I even remember him being there? Why didn't anyone tell me? Why would his mom lie to me? No wonder he is the way he is with me. I did this. I ruined us.

For years, I wondered why he didn't show up to say

225

goodbye and, for years, he's wondered why I didn't love him enough. I hurt him in the most horrible way. It wasn't even face-to-face. It was through a letter. Charlie's right, I am a coward.

Scrambling up off the floor, I walk over to my center design table and pick up my phone. The other end of the line starts ringing and I am praying that she will pick up.

"Hey, sweetheart, how are you?"

"Mom," I sniffle out.

"Leila, what's wrong?" Concern is immediately etched in her voice.

"Tell me about the fire."

Silence.

"Mom, tell me about the fire!"

"I don't understand, Leila; you already know what happened."

"Mom, how did I get out of the fire?"

"Beau pulled you out. You know this."

That hammer that he mentioned swings and crashes into my chest. I sink to the floor next to the table.

"No, I didn't."

"How did you think you got out?"

"I just assumed it was a fireman. Why didn't anyone tell me?"

"Well, first off, I thought you knew and, second, I tried to talk to you about that night several times and every time you shut me down."

She's right; I did shut her down. I didn't want to talk about the boy I waited for, who didn't come and see me.

"Oh, Mom . . ." I can't help the tears or sobs as they pour into the phone. "Do you know what happened to Beau?"

"Yes, love. I do know what happened to him. I talked to

his mother several times over the months that followed. I thought you knew too."

"No, Mom, I didn't. I never saw him before we left. I thought he didn't care enough to say goodbye to me."

"Why on earth would you think that? That boy has loved you forever."

Deep down I know what she's saying is true. My stomach turns over and I feel like I'm going to be sick. So many pieces of the puzzle are falling into place.

"I am the worst person in the world. I have been so mean to him all these years."

"You know, I never understood why you stopped being friends with him after we moved. Your father and I always thought that the two of you were the once in a lifetime kind of friends. I'm not going to sugarcoat this for you and say that everything will turn out okay, but what I am going to tell you is that you need to explain yourself to him. I can only assume that, since you didn't know the details, he doesn't know either."

"I don't know how."

"You'll figure it out. Take care, my love, and good luck . . ." With that, she hangs up the phone.

The sun has set and the studio is now dark. I'm still on the floor and still trying to wrap my head around all of this. All I can see in my mind is Beau when he was fourteen years old, running into the fire to save me. He did save me, and not once have I ever told him thank you. No wonder he thinks I'm unappreciative, ungrateful, and a bitch.

Why he ever spoke to me again, I'll never know.

BEAU

IT'S BEEN TWENTY-FOUR hours since I walked away from Leila, from the one person who I was once again beginning to think could be my forever.

The last few weeks have been so good, too good. There's a tiny part of me that is completely disappointed in myself, because I allowed myself to become hopeful. Haven't I learned over the years? Her words and actions hurt. She's never given me the benefit of the doubt or cared about how these things affect me.

The loft is quiet as I lie on my bed and listen to the sounds of the street.

Nate and Coach both called this morning, wondering where I was and what was going on when I missed practice, but I just couldn't face them, or myself, for that matter.

After the beach, I had spent weeks trying to convince myself that it was time to move on from her, and all she had to do was wave one little tiny olive branch, no, make that a twig, and I fell right back in.

But the thing is that I really wanted to fall back in. These last couple of weeks, I've been happier than I have been in years.

My phone dings, alerting me that I have a text, and I pick it up off of my nightstand.

Drew – Dude! I don't know what the hell is going on with you and Leila but she's here with Ali and the girl is hysterical.
Beau – What do you mean?

Drew – Crying, Asshole.

She's crying?

Beau – Oh . . . how long has she been there?
Drew – At least thirty minutes. She's inconsolable. Keeps telling us she's sorry and she's muttering something about how she didn't know.
Beau – Didn't know what?
Drew – Beats me. Again, all she's said over and over is your name and she didn't know. This shit is upsetting Ali and I don't like it. Fix it.

Staring up at the ceiling over my bed, I don't understand why she would be saying she didn't know. We've already established that she now knows about the tuition money, so what doesn't she know? And what does all of this have to do with what just went down. Ugh . . . I wish that I didn't care, but I do. I hate knowing that she is this upset. Picking my phone back up, I take a deep breath and call Drew.

He answers on the first ring.

"Hey, put her on the phone."

"Alright." I can hear him walk through the condo, open a door, and then the sound of her crying hits me. Hits me right in the chest.

Leila is always so strong and easy-going. She's confident in herself and she never lets things upset her. I think in all the years that I have known her I have only seen her cry just a couple of times.

"Here, it's for you," Drew says. He must be handing her the phone. Uneven breathing lands on the other end of the phone line and I close my eyes.

"Leila . . ."

"Beau," she whispers through silent sobs. "I'm so sorry. I didn't know . . ."

"Listen, do you need me to come and get you or can you get into a cab and come to my place?"

"You want me to come over?"

Why does she sound so surprised by this? "Yes."

"Are you sure?"

"Leila, please don't cry. I'm sorry I left you at the studio, but I needed some time on my own. Come over here and let's talk this through . . . okay?"

She sniffs. "Okay."

Getting off the bed, I pick up yesterday's jeans from the floor and put them on, brush my teeth, and change into a fresh shirt. I forgo shaving, brushing my hair; the loft is a mess, but I just don't care enough to clean it or myself up.

Fifteen minutes later, there's a quiet knock on the door and I get up off the couch to walk over to open it up. Standing in the hallway is not the Leila that I left at the studio. That Leila was fired up and full of energy. But this Leila standing in front of me is clearly a broken girl. Her face is blotchy, her eyes are red and swollen, she looks like she hasn't slept in days, and her hair is wild and falling all around her face and shoulders. She's wringing her hands in front of her and her posture looks completely defeated. No matter what has happened between us, I hate seeing her like this.

Gently, I reach out and grab her elbow to pull her inside. Closing the door, the two of us stand there and stare at each other. Her eyes fill with tears and one by one they fall out and slide down her face.

"Please don't cry," I say, looking down at her.

Her chin quivers, she squeezes her eyes closed, covers her

230

face with her hands, and just breaks. Her crying like this hurts me so much that I can't help but reach out and wrap my arms around her. She folds herself into me and buries her face in my chest.

"Beau . . . I didn't know."

"Didn't know what?"

"About the fire." I go completely still. She can't possibly be talking about the fire that we were in.

"What fire?" She lets go of me and takes a step backward.

"Beau, please tell me what happened the night of the fire."

"You know what happened. You were there."

"Why does everyone keep saying that to me? No, I don't know. No one ever told me. I didn't even know you were there! This entire time I thought you never even showed up that night."

I gasp and take a step back from her. I don't know what to say because that means that everything that I thought about her for the last six years has been all wrong.

I feel like I have just been sucker-punched.

"Who did you think pulled you out of the fire?"

"A firefighter."

I'm shocked by this and confused. I want to ask her so many questions, but my brain has stopped functioning. I'm staring at her and she's watching my reaction to the bomb she just dropped.

"Your mom never mentioned anything?" I ask her.

"No. She thought I knew."

Walking away from her, I head into the living room, and she follows.

"Leila . . . I . . . how did you just figure all this out?" She reaches down into her bag that she had dropped on the floor

231

and pulls out my journal. I instantly reach over and snatch it out of her hand.

"How much of this did you read?" I'm furious and embarrassed at the same time. These are my darkest thoughts and hours. They are for me and no one else.

"Does it matter?"

"Yes! It matters to me. This is mine, and it's private."

I'm feeling so many emotions right now that I don't know which one to focus on. I'm angry at her for the things that she said yesterday and for hitting me. I'm angry that she read my journal, and I'm angry for the loss of six years with her. I'm sad because she hit me. I'm sad because if she read my journal then it most likely hurt her, too, and I'm sad because I was so heartbroken for so long and most possibly all of this could have been prevented. Six years gone, just like that . . . poof!

"Beau, please tell me what happened that night and what happened to you."

Looking into her beautiful blue eyes, I'm filled with remorse about how wrong I have been about her. I begin to tell her about the worst night of my life, one I've really never spoken of and one that I would just like to forget.

Somewhere in the back of my sleep-filled mind I hear the tiny beeping of the alarm on my watch. Grabbing it out from under my pillow, I turn it off and look to see that it's almost midnight. My heart feels achy in my chest because I know that tonight is going to be important for so many reasons. It's the last night that I'm going to see her. I need to tell her I love her, and I have to kiss her again at least one more time before she leaves.

She's leaving.

That ache in my chest tightens. I slip out of bed, slide on a pair of flip flops, and tiptoe to my window.

Before I went to bed, I left the window up, loosened the screen, and had Drew prop the ladder outside. With my arm in this cast and hurting something fierce, I didn't leave my room all day. He offered to help me out, instead of me trying to sneak down the hall to his room. I didn't want to risk them hearing me as I slip out.

Drew's bedroom window opens up to an upper sundeck. A while ago, he offered to switch rooms with me, but my mother said no. I think she knows that I sneak out, but she'll never tell.

Sticking my head out the window, I look around to make sure everything is as it should be. There's a light smoky smell lingering in the air, telling me there's been another fire.

Slowly, I swing one leg out the window and then the other. I can only hold on with one hand and I'm trying to move the broken arm as little as possible. It still hurts so much. Once I'm down the ladder and onto the back deck, I make my way over to the steps.

My emotions are torn because I'm so excited to see her, but I also know it will be the last time for a while. It's been almost two days since we were down on the beach. What am I going to do starting tomorrow?

Sprinting across the open backyard, I slip through the neighbor's fence and feel free. Every time I get away from our house, a sense of ease takes over. Pushing through the bushes, I run around to the front of the house, and come to a dead stop as I see Matt across the street.

Little Matt is standing directly in front of Leila's house. How did he get out here? Does he sleepwalk and I didn't know it? Jogging up next to him, he's staring at the house with eyes wide open, and he's shaking.

"Matt, what are you doing out here?" He doesn't respond to me, so I reach out and grab his shoulder. His eyes whip to mine and I smell fear pouring off of him. "Tell me what's wrong with you?"

"Fire," he whispers.

"I know; I can smell it." A tear rolls down Matt's face and he walks into me for a hug. Matt never hugs anybody, and the rate of alarm that I already feel from seeing him immediately increases.

"Hey, buddy, it's going to be alright, but you need to tell me what's going on." At that moment an explosion rocks from behind me and glass flies straight at us. Matt and I both duck down toward the ground. Looking over at the house, I realize Matt was telling me that Leila's house is on fire.

How did I not see this when I ran around the corner? Was it contained then? Is the fire primarily in the back? Maybe it's because the smoke blends in with the night sky.

That's when it hits me. Oh, my God, Leila is in the house.

"Matt, have you seen Leila?" I scream at him.

He shakes his head no.

"Shit." I push Matt away from me, scramble up off the ground, and run up the steps to the front door.

"Beau!" I can hear the panic in his voice.

"Leila is in that house! You need to find help and call 911!" He just stands there and doesn't move. I can't wait any longer.

"Go!" I yell at him one last time.

Grabbing the door knob to push it open, it sears my hand

and I drop it, never getting it turned. I can feel the heat as it is leaking out from the cracks of the door. Rearing back with all the force I can, I kick the door, and it gives flying open. Thick black smoke comes billowing out and I drop to the ground. The elbow of my broken arm hits the door frame and I scream out in pain. I'm temporarily paralyzed.

Somewhere in the house, there is another explosion. My heart is racing and pounding at the same time. It hurts to the point of feeling like I'm going to have a heart attack.

Crawling on my stomach, keeping as much pressure as I can off of my arm, I make my way to the living room. Our plan was to pitch a tent and pretend that we were camping. Sure enough, there it is.

"Leila!" I scream for her, but there's nothing in return except for the tears of the house as it creaks and moans at the destructive hands of the fire.

My eyes are burning, the heat is intolerable, but all I can think is—get to Leila. I know she is in here because, if she wasn't, she would've come to my window to tell me about the fire.

The orange flames of the monster have found their way into the room, crawled up the walls, and begun lapping at the ceiling. The smoke is so thick that I can barely see and I can't stop coughing.

The tent is sitting in the middle of the room. I continue crawling until I reach it, rip open the door, and see Leila lying there.

Relief and fear hit me at the same time.

"Leila!" I grab her leg and shake her, trying to wake her up. She doesn't move.

Oh, no, is she dead?

Tears are running down my face. I didn't even know that

I was crying. Maybe it's because of the smoke, but I doubt it.

Grabbing her arm, I drag her out of the tent and turn us towards the foyer to get out the front door.

All throughout the house, things are cracking, breaking, and exploding. Pieces of the ceiling have started falling and, along with the smoke, ash is flying through the air.

How has she not woken up from the smoke alone? Hasn't she smelled it? I wish that I could remember what they said in school about smoke inhalation. Is that what's wrong with her?

On my side, with my weight now fully on the arm with the cast, I use my feet to push us across the floor, dragging her with my free hand.

As we reach the foyer, I look up and see that the fire is completely surrounding the front door. The blaze is so bright I can't see what's on the other side. Realizing that there is no way I can drag us through the entrance with it like this, the horror of this moment grows worse.

Bending over, and wrapping my arm around her waist, with every bit of strength and adrenaline that I have, I haul her up against me. She's bent over at the waist like a ragdoll, but with my broken arm it's all I can do. Suddenly, the foyer seems to stretch—it's so long—and the distance to the front door gets further away. Knowing that it's now or never, I lean over her body and hug her to me as tight as I can. One step at a time, I carry us through the heat and out the door.

For a split second, relief surges through me as I take that first step out onto the front porch, but in that next second another explosion blasts from behind us, throwing my body forward. I try to regain balance, but I can't. In slow motion, I see the ground coming straight at us. As we hit, her head bounces and my body slams on top of hers. Something lands on my back and that's when I feel the pain.

I'm squirming and screaming but, whatever it is, it's holding me down. I'm trapped, sheer terror engulfs me, and I'm panicking to the point that I can't breathe. The smoke is violent and ripping into my lungs. My body is trying to cough but it just won't. I'm suffocating.

My eyes have clouded over and a blur of flames whips around us. Everything is bright and hot. The fire burns so immensely that it kind of feels cold and prickly, like I'm being stuck with pins and needles over and over again. I can feel the skin melting off of my back. This must be what it feels like in hell.

My head drops and hits Leila's. That's when I remember that she's lying underneath me. I'm trying my hardest to do what I can to keep Leila away from the flames. I need to protect her and save her but my body won't move. I have lost all sense of movement and nothing is happening.

The smoke from the monster has completely wrapped around us and it's trying to smother us.

My mind has shut off and mental numbness has taken over. Focusing on the one good thing that has ever happened to me, my tears drip off my face and onto hers.

Please don't let her die. Take me, not her.

I'm not sure how long we lay there, it could have been seconds or minutes, but as I pray for someone to save her, I see a flash before us and she is ripped out from underneath me. She's gone.

Please save her. I love her.

She is the last thing on my mind and in my heart as I take one final breath before succumbing to the darkness.

KATHRYN ★ ANDREWS

BEAU

I'M LOST IN my own personal hell as I retell this story. I almost forgot Leila was even here. I must have been on autopilot because I realize that, at some point, we've made our way over to the couch, and she's kicked her boots off. She's sitting in what I now refer to as her spot, with her legs curled up almost like she's in a ball, trying to protect herself from my words. The expression underneath her tears is one of pure horror, but then again, why wouldn't it be?

"I remember waking up in the hospital after the fire, lying on my stomach. Some machine was beeping and I could hear voices coming from outside my door. The lights in the room were so bright, and I tried to move my head but nothing was happening. I didn't know why I was there or what was going on. In the midst of my mini panic about my surroundings, that's when the smell hit me. I will never forget that smell. It haunts me," I whisper. "It was a mixture of hospital antiseptics, smoke, and burnt skin. That's when I remembered the fire."

Leila sniffs next to me and wipes her face on her arm. I don't have any Kleenex. It's not something I've ever thought to buy. I'm still getting used to the whole shopping and living independently thing. Mom would have bought the tissues. I look around and my eyes zero in on the paper towels I have in the kitchen. I go grab her one and then return to finish the story.

"Images and flashbacks of the fire started stirring through my mind," I tell her. "The beeping on the machine began to get louder and faster. I started crying. I was so afraid and worried about you. A nurse pushed through the door to my room and my mom was right behind her. She took one look at me and started crying too. I can remember thinking, *why is she crying?* I couldn't see what the nurse was doing. It didn't matter. I just kept my eyes on my mother. Pretty quickly after that my body started to relax. That nurse must have put something into the IV, but I remember whispering out your name and my mom telling me that you were fine and already back at Aunt Ella's." I smile softly at her. "I have never felt as much relief as I did in that moment, knowing you were safe."

Looking at Leila now, even after all these years, I would do it all over again. I saved her and I'm proud of that. There would be no question. I'd even take the scars again if it meant that she didn't. I can't imagine anything ever scarring her like that. She has the most beautiful, flawless ivory skin. It's always so soft and smells so good.

"I'm so sorry, Beau. I didn't know any of that. Why didn't anyone tell me?" She's looking at me and there's wonder in her eyes. She wipes her nose again.

"I don't know. All these years I thought you knew."

LEILA

I WATCH AS Beau walks into his room and into the closet. He's headed for the roof. He needed to walk away from me. I understand this. After everything that was just said, I want to walk away from me too.

My eyes scan Beau's loft. It looks different to me. He feels different to me. It's like when you think you know some-one but then realize that you really don't. Whatever percep-tions you had of them change, either for better or worse. I've been sitting here, listening to how he saved me, and I'm in awe.

Bits and pieces of his story replay in my mind. He was so brave and fearless to run in after me. The fire, the smoke, his broken arm, his dad . . . no one should have to experience the things in life that he has. All of a sudden, I feel like the worst person in the world.

Just thinking about Beau sitting up on the roof by himself, my stomach begins to ache. I don't want him to be by himself anymore. I don't ever want him to feel alone again. I want him to know that he has me in whatever capacity he wants me. Get-ting up off the couch, I grab the blanket, wrap it around me, and walk straight into his closet and up the stairs.

Pushing open the roof top door, I find him sitting in the middle of the couch. His head is lying on the back of it and his fingers are linked together and resting in his hair. His eyes are closed and he's wearing a look of intense concentration. I wish I knew what he was thinking.

The chill in the air from the cold front swirls around me

and I see that Beau has turned on the two outdoor heater lamps that are behind the couch.

I look up into the cloudy cold night and notice that there is a single star shining down on us. I wonder which one it is. I'm certain that Beau would know. The fact that it's there, though, in what is essentially a starless night, gives me hope; hope that I have been hanging on to for so long.

He hears me approach him and his eyes connect with mine. They glisten brightly, and I can't tell if it's from unshed tears or just the onslaught of emotions from the last twenty-four hours. Either way, they are beautiful, and tonight they are more whiskey than hazel.

Slowly he reaches out, grabs my arm, and pulls me between his legs. My heart squeezes and my tears return. Neither one of us says anything. Really, nothing more needs to be said tonight. Yes, there are still things that we need to talk about, and I'm sure that both of us still have many questions, but right now, in this moment—the quietness of the connection to each other is more important.

Beau slowly sits up and leans forward. Letting out a sigh, he lays his head on my stomach, wraps his hands around the back of my legs, and just holds on to me. It's such an affectionate move that the love I already feel for him swells even more.

He rolls his forehead and his face back and forth. The warmth of his breath seeps in through the fabric of my shirt, causing my stomach to tighten. My hands run up over his shoulders, neck, and my fingers tangle in his hair. His hair is so soft.

His hands drift up my legs, under my skirt, and his fingers slide under my underwear. He grips me and pulls me tighter to him.

I gasp at the unexpectedness of this but welcome his warm hands on me.

He leans back and watches me through hooded eyes as he slowly slides my underwear down my legs. I step out of them as they drop, and he pulls me toward him and sits back. Climbing onto his lap, I straddle his waist. Without even pausing, his hand wraps around my head and his mouth crashes onto mine.

Beau is taking everything that I have to give in this kiss and he is unapologetic about it. He is owning it, claiming it, claiming me, and he's kissing me like he's making up for years of lost kisses.

His hands are running all over my body; my back, my neck, my head, my thighs, my waist, my ribcage, and his thumbs pause as they brush over the outer swell of my breasts.

"God, I love the way you taste," he says against my lips.

Taking his face in my hands, leaving our mouths only inches apart, my eyes lock onto his. Both of us are breathing hard. I can feel how much I am affecting him and I can see the hunger in his eyes.

"I want you. I want all of you," I whisper out.

Can he read between the lines? Does he understand what I'm saying? I want all of him—every single bit. I want his body, his heart, his good days and bad. I want his fears and his dreams, and I desperately want him to be my future. He is my life. I've always wanted this.

Every day I think about him, and how different life would be if things had never changed between us. If there had never been a fire and if we had never moved, I'd like to think that we would have been together, always. I replay that conversation with his mother on the day that we moved, over and over in my head and now, looking back, I realize she lied to me. She's been lying to me, to us, for years and I don't know why.

Never breaking eye contact, Beau leans forward, reaches back, and pulls his wallet from his back pocket. My hands leave his face as I run them down his chest to the button on his jeans. Rising up on my knees, I pull down the zipper, and he shoves everything down.

I've never seen Beau naked. Well, actually he isn't completely naked, but I've never seen this part of him. The only other time we were intimate, he was on top and it was the middle of the night.

Nerves are racing through me at the size of him. The irrational part of me says there's no way this is going to fit, but I remind myself that it already has. I reach out to touch him and he sucks in a sharp breath of air through his teeth.

Beau rips open the package and rolls on the condom. Gently he takes my hips and guides me over him to position himself.

"Are you sure about this?" he asks, looking straight into my eyes.

I smile. This is the same question he asked me before. I love that he always cares enough to check in with my emotions, before anything happens or changes between us.

"I'm sure about you, yes." There really is no other way to answer the question, and the smile that lights up his face is breathtaking.

Slowly, I sit back down. He slides into me and, as I fully seat myself on him, neither one of us move.

My hand vibrates on his chest with the intense pounding of his heart. His breathing is getting faster and I watch, mesmerized, as he licks his bottom lip. Every muscle in me squeezes at being so close to him again, a place I never thought that I would be.

Beau groans and his fingers grip into my hips. "Leila, you

can't do that or this will be over before it starts."

"I'm sorry."

"Don't be. You are already so tight and you feel so good, when you squeeze it almost sends me over the edge."

"Okay . . ." I giggle.

"Now is not the time for giggling," he says, grinning at me.

"I know, but . . . this . . . us . . . together, it makes me so happy." I brush the hair off of his face and run my thumbs over his cheekbones. He is so beautiful.

"Me, too, Lei; me, too."

Slowly, he begins to move my hips forward, up, and down. He meets me in the middle of each thrust, and it feels so good.

The emotions he brings out in me are so close, so intimate, that I could stay this way forever. I bend and kiss him hungrily, and instantly feel his hand at my cheek, pulling me closer. His mouth and his tongue match the pace of our hips.

I am lost in him. I am lost in this moment, and I smile to myself, knowing that this is the second time we have come together under the night sky.

We rock against each other and the movement elicits a thousand sensations. I can't imagine that anything could feel any better. Beau tightens his grip on my hips, picks me up, and flips me over. I land on my back on the couch and he takes over.

I'm beyond turned on as he gathers my hands up in one of his and pins them over my head, the other begins exploring every part of my body before settling underneath me. His rhythm is hypnotic as he pushes further into me, forcing my legs to widen.

"Oh, God, Lei, do you even know what you do to me . . ."

he mumbles against my lips.

"Don't stop . . . I want to do everything with you."

He takes this as his cue, tucks his head into my neck, and loses himself in me. The rhythm, the force, the smell of him, this moment, all of it takes over. I feel like my skin is being warmed by the sun while snowflakes drop on it dozens at a time. Tingles are racing from one end of my body to the other. I feel light-headed and euphoric. He senses how my body is opening up and responding to him, and he quickly follows me to that state of complete bliss.

This was not at all like the night on the beach. We were cautious back then, careful, and sweet. Right now, it's like we're starved for each other, craving intense passion, and holding on tight.

"Stay the night with me," he says in a gravelly voice, his head still tucked into my hair. It's not a question. It's not a statement. It's a command. His breathing is still a little heavy but all of his muscles have loosened and the weight of him on me feels so good.

"Yes." There isn't anywhere I want to be more. The world could be ending and I would still be exactly where I want to be.

He pulls his head back and looks me in the eyes. "Really?"

I nod, taking in his appearance. His hair is completely sexed up, there's redness under the stubble on his cheeks, his mouth still looks so delicious, and his eyes are lighter—back to hazel. He's stunning, both inside and out, and I feel so lucky that it's me he's here with.

"Good, because I am not done with you and I want to do that over and over again."

The blush that is already on my skin, burns. He sees it and

his eyes drop back down to my mouth.

"You just gonna stare or are you gonna to kiss me?" I ask him.

Without hesitating, his lips land on mine. "Oh, I'm going to do a lot more than just kiss you," he mumbles, while biting my bottom lip. His hand that is holding mine above my head clamps down tight, his free hand comes up to my armpit, and he starts tickling.

Squealing and squirming, I somehow get us pushed off of the couch and on to the floor. Beau is laughing with me and it is such a beautiful sound. I hardly ever hear him laugh anymore.

"Payback's a bitch, Mr. Hale. Consider yourself warned."

His eyes are sparkling, clear, and happy. I love knowing that I am the one who made him this way.

Tucking some of my hair behind my ear, he says, "Game on, Ms. Starling; only, I hate to break it to you . . . I never lose."

Chapter Eighteen

BEAU

THE SUNSHINE STREAMING through the window and onto the ceiling is the first thing that I see when I open my eyes. Memories of last night flood through me and, now, here I am at the next fateful moment. Closing my eyes, I don't move a muscle. I just don't want to know. I'm afraid that reality is about to break the afterglow that's warming my heart.

I can't stop my mind, though; did she stay or did she go?

"What's going on over there in your beautiful head? Your whole body just went tense."

My heads whips to the left at the sound of her voice, and there she is. She's curled up on her side, facing me. Her hair is rumpled all over the pillow and those beautiful blue eyes are watching me.

My heart starts to ache in my chest. She is so stunningly gorgeous. Forgetting to breathe, I blink at her instead. I feel like the biggest weight has been lifted off of my shoulders. For years, all I have ever wanted was for her to stay. No moving away, no walking off, and no leaving me come morning.

Leila's eyebrows furrow and worry flashes in her eyes. She scoots a little closer and puts her hand on my cheek. I close my eyes and lean into the softness of her hand, then reach over and pull her under me. I need her close. I need to feel her warmth and I need to know that this is true.

"You stayed," I breathe out.

She pulls back to look in my eyes and I'm struck again by how bright and blue hers are. I hold her tighter, not wanting to have even an inch of space between us.

"What do you mean?" There's confusion on her face.

"You are always leaving me. You left me when you moved, you left me after the first twenty-four hour truce when Dad was arrested, you left me the morning after prom, you left me the morning after Drew proposed . . . you're always leaving. And that doesn't include all of the times that you have walked away from me."

She lets out a small gasp as her jaw drops a little. Her hand slips to my shoulder and her grip tightens. I can see so many different emotions swirling in her eyes as they shift back and forth, searching mine. Silence stretches between us and then she lets out a deep sigh. Closing her eyes, she shakes her head.

"Oh, my, how did things just get so messed up between us?" She looks back at me and there are tears shimmering in her eyes. "To me, how I saw things, you were the one always leaving me. You left and didn't say good bye to me when I moved to Atlanta, you left me standing on the beach when I moved back, you left me and walked away from me countless times over the years at school, and you left me on the beach the night after the going-away party. You left."

My lips pinch into a thin line and my heart rate starts to pick up. She's right. If I think about this from her perspective, it would seem that I was always the one to walk away from her.

She slides her hand down my arm, links her fingers with mine, and then brings our hands to her chest. She hugs my hand, holding it tight and close.

"Beau, you have hurt me so many times over the years. I always told myself that this would be the last time, but it never seemed to work out that way. After we moved back from Atlanta, I was so excited to see you. I knew that you had probably moved on and your life was completely different, but I missed you so much. On the beach, you scowled at me and turned away without saying anything. To me, I thought this was the second time, and I ran all the way to Bean Point and hid under the wooden walkway to cry. You ended up there with Drew, and I overheard you tell him that you hated me. You meant it, too. I felt so stupid. It was as if my entire childhood was a lie. I didn't understand how you could hate me. No matter what, I never could have hated you."

Letting out a deep sigh, I pull my hand from hers, wrap my hands around her face, and run my thumbs across her cheeks. Her little freckles are so light; you really don't even notice them unless you are looking for them. Her eyes drift shut and her eyelashes fall upon her cheeks. She looks so sad and this is from a memory that I caused unknowingly. There have been so many miscommunications over the years. It never occurred to me that she might have hurt just as much as I did.

"Leila . . . I'm so sorry you heard that. But knowing what you do now, can you understand how I was feeling? Those two and a half years were so hard for me. Losing you, dealing with my dad on a day to day basis, the pain, the rehabilitation and physical therapy, I wasn't the same person . . . I'm not the same person."

Her foot wraps around my calf, her hand moves to my hip, and she inches a little closer. Taking a deep breath, lavender registers, and it calms me. I love the way she smells.

"And I'm so sorry for what I said to you at the studio. I was angry and being irrational. I didn't mean it." The regret in her tone is evident.

"I'm sorry, too. I never should have called you a bitch. I was out of line, and I could never think that way of you. You do know that I really have had nothing to do with all of your success, right? You have done this all on your own. You were the one who got into the school; you were the one who was chosen for the Rising Designer award. You are the one who is making all of your dreams come true. Not me."

"I know that now. I'm so sorry that I hit you, Beau. I don't know what came over me. Please believe me when I say that I never want to hurt you." Tears instantly fill her eyes and roll down the side of her face.

My jaw locks at the memory of this and I feel my eyes narrow a little at her. "I'm not going to lie; you did hurt me. I never ever thought that you, of all people, would raise a hand at me."

"I'm so sorry." She lifts one hand to cover her face and her chin trembles.

"Lei, please don't cry. I really hate seeing you cry." I pull her hand away and wipe the tears. I know my next words are going to be harsh, but I need to say them, if only to make her realize how important they are. "I gotta say, though, do it again and we're done."

She turns into my chest and tucks her head under my

chin. Strawberry-blonde curls land on my face and inwardly I smile. She has gorgeous hair.

"I won't. I promise," she mumbles against my collarbone.

I let out a sigh.

My hand drifts to her back and I begin rubbing up and down. She's wearing one of my T-shirts and just a pair of underwear. I'm unnerved by our conversation, but I am still a red-blooded male, and Lei in my clothes is sexy as hell. My hand falls under the shirt and I continue the rubbing. Her skin is soft and smooth.

Her bare leg runs up over my leg and hooks over my hip.

"How did you even know that I got into Parson's?"

"It was completely random. One day at school, I was walking behind you and Chase in the hallway when I heard him mention Parson's."

"Hey, have you given a reply to Parson's yet?" Chase leans over and asks Leila, thinking no one else can hear them.

"No, I'm still waiting to hear back on that last scholarship that I applied for." Leila hugs her books to her chest.

"Are they the last one?" he asks.

"Yep." Her voice sounds sad. I wish I could see her face.

"What happens if you don't get it?"

"I don't know. I guess I'm not going to Parson's then."

"You've worked so hard. That would really suck."

"Tell me about it. It's all I've dreamed about for the last three years."

"Let me know, okay?" Chase bumps his shoulder with

hers.

"I will, but please don't say anything to anyone."

"You know I won't," he says, looking down at her. He gives her a smile and turns down the next hallway.

Leila's watching me closely as I tell her this memory. I grab her hip and hold her in place.

"I didn't even think twice about it. I walked out into the parking lot, Googled Parson's, and called the school. They didn't care where the money came from, so it was actually pretty easy to set up."

"But why? Why did you do this for me?"

"Because, despite what you thought, I never hated you. I've always wanted the best for you, and because I could," I shrugged. "I had the money and, well, I'm proud of what I spent it on . . . you."

"Thank you, Beau."

None of the anger that was pouring off of her two days ago is present now. There's gratitude in her eyes as they shine at me.

"You're welcome," I say, pushing some of her hair out of her face and behind her ears.

"So, where did you get all of that money?"

"Oh, when my grandfather died, Drew, Matt, and I each were given a trust that we were allowed access to at eighteen. It's how we bought the boat, too."

"The boat's yours?" she asks, astonished.

"Yeah, who's did you think it was?"

She shrugs her shoulders, "I guess I thought it was your dad's."

"Nope." Just the mention of him makes me feel edgy.

Looking into her beautiful face, I can see the wheels turning. She wants to talk more and her eyes are searching mine. They are searching for something, I just don't know what. Her eyes fixate on my shirt and my stomach drops as realization sets in.

"Can I see them?" she asks quietly.

"Can you see what?" I freeze, knowing what she's asking but hoping I'm wrong.

"The scars." Her eyes are big and innocent.

"No," I immediately blurt out. I don't even need to think about this one.

"Why not?" She pulls back to get a better look at me.

I shake my head at her in warning.

"You don't trust me." She tries to move away from me, but I grab her hip and hold her tighter. I don't want her to go.

"I do trust you, it's just . . . I don't show them to anyone." How do I make her understand? I don't want to hurt her feelings.

"No one?"

"Never. Since you've been back, have you ever seen me without a shirt on? Even that night on the beach, after the going-away party, I made sure that we kept part of our clothes on. I always wear a minimum of two shirts too. I don't even want people bumping up against me and feeling them. I pin your hands down. There's a reason for everything. The only two people outside of my family who have seen me without a shirt are Grant and Ali."

Devastation flashes in her eyes. I understand this; after all, the sex we had on the roof and last night here in bed, is the most intimate and trusting thing you can do with someone. She gave me that and I'm not giving her this.

"Please." Her eyes are pleading.

"No, Lei, I can't. I'm not ready. Maybe one day, but not today, okay?" I say a little softer to her.

"Okay."

Leaning down, I kiss the side of her mouth, her cheek, under her ear, and then down to her neck. She lets out a deep breath and relaxes into me. Her skin instantly warms and still smells so good. She can feel what this is doing to me. Her back arches up underneath me, she grabs the covers, pulls them over our heads, and all conversation stops.

LEILA

SOMETIME A LITTLE later in the morning, I feel him stirring, and I look over at him.

Beau is by far the most beautiful person I have ever seen. He makes my heart skip beats. He always has. With his eyes closed, he looks so much more like the boy that I knew years ago and I am so thankful to have known him then too. Although, I love that I have watched him grow into this amazing person.

Snuggling a little closer, I breathe in his warm sleepy skin.

"Are you hungry?" His voice is raspy and I find it extremely sexy.

Right on cue, my stomach growls and he chuckles.

"Well, there's my answer. How about an omelet?"

"You make omelets?"

"I make a lot of things. Like I said before, things were different after y'all left, and Matt needed me to be somewhat of a father figure, which I became, and I wouldn't change a thing. But I do feel like, in the process, I've changed and part of me does miss the old me."

"You *have* changed. We can all see it. I don't miss the old you or any version you thought you were . . . I've just missed you and all the pieces of you." Beau leans down and lightly places his lips on mine. My heart squeezes.

"Come on, beautiful. Get your cute ass out of bed and let me cook for you." He smiles at me as he throws back the covers.

"Okay, I'll meet you in there. I need to run to the bathroom. Can I use your toothbrush?"

"Of course." He grins.

Beau walks out of his bedroom and my eyes follow him. He's wearing a white T-shirt and a pair of boxer briefs. It's a really good look on him and I think about pinching myself to see if this is real.

Climbing out of bed, I walk into his bathroom and look around. It's bigger and nicer than the one that Charlie and I have. It has two sinks, and for a split second I let my mind drift to a place where one of them is mine. A girl can wish, can't she?

Staring at his shower, I decide to hop in. I am eager to get back out to him, but it's nice to be able to take a minute for myself. Being here, with him and all his things, still feels surreal. I need to soak it all in; right now I want to remember every detail. For years, I have thought about being with him, and now that I am, I would be lying if I said I wasn't nervous and waiting for the other shoe to drop.

Drying off in a big towel, I slip back into his T-shirt, brush my teeth and hair, and walk out to the kitchen.

He's standing at the stove, back to me, and I don't think I have ever witnessed anything as sexy as Beau Hale cooking for me in his boxer briefs and T-shirt. I squeeze my thighs together and let out a slow deep breath before moving closer.

"Did you know that the average person eats 173 eggs a year?" He glances in my direction and gives me a one-sided smile.

"No, I didn't," I say, hopping up to sit on the counter next to him.

"Yep, and 40 percent of all eggs are consumed in China."

"Really? That immediately makes me think of how any type of television show, documentary, movie, or whatever from China you always see chickens running around in the streets."

"Kind of gross don't you think?" he asks.

"Yes, it is."

Beau looks over at me for the first time since I entered the room and freezes for a moment. He grins and turns off the stove, stepping in between my legs. I smile seductively at him when I realize my presence has had an effect. His hands wrap around my butt and he pulls me forward so I am flush with him. He's letting me know the extent of how happy he is to see me. My arms loop around his neck and he smiles down at me. His hair is messy, his eyes are a bright hazel, and the stubble on his face looks so good. He's happy and he seems relaxed, carefree. It makes my heart smile.

"I like you being here in my home," he mumbles into my ear as he presses even closer.

His eyes lock with mine and butterflies take off. "I like being here with you too. But it doesn't matter where we are; I just want to be with you." Vulnerability flushes through me and my face warms. I know that we still have a long way to go, but in this moment none of that matters. I decide to take what I need and I pull his mouth to mine.

When Beau kisses me, he consumes me. It doesn't matter that I was the one to start it; he takes over and claims every second of it. It's as if my body knows him and immediately betrays me and panders to him.

"Mmm . . . minty." His lips move away from my mouth and make their way to my neck. The contact makes me tremble with need.

"Mmm . . . coffee," I retort as my hands slide from around his neck across his shoulders and to his upper back. I gasp and he freezes. Through the fabric of his T-shirt I can feel the bumps, dips, and unevenness of his skin.

Beau's breathing picks up and he starts to shake.

"Leila . . ." he whispers as he tries to pull away. My arms instinctively tighten around him. I don't want him to move.

"No, I'm sorry. I didn't mean to upset you or make you uncomfortable. I forgot. Please don't go. You refuse to show me and honestly I don't know what to expect. But, it is just me here—me—please don't go."

He takes a deep breath to calm his nerves; his eyes are wary, but I can see the trust in them, as well as the desire for me, swimming in the background. I wrap my legs around his waist and lean into him, trying to win him over. He lets out a sigh, takes another step back, and I release him, feeling a little rejected.

"Don't move." Again, this is not a request; it is a command. I watch as he backs away further, then winks and turns on his heel, disappearing from my view. Maybe he's not rejecting me.

It's only seconds before he strides into the kitchen with a wicked gleam in his eye and moves towards me like a panther stalking its prey. I sit, stunned, as he steps back in between my legs and flashes a condom at me. My heart rate speeds up with excitement, my hands immediately grip his hips, pulling him closer, and I watch as his eyes darken while locking onto mine. One of his hands tangle in my hair and he holds my head still so I can't look away. Slowly, he closes the distance between us completely and whispers against my lips.

"I need to lose myself in you, Lei, and when we get to the point where I take you on this counter . . . I'm not stopping."

I feel the blush that spreads rapidly from my head to the tips of my toes. Oh, my word, the ache that he's elicited has spread through me and I can't do anything except sit here and wait for him to make his next move.

His fingertips slide over my hips to the bottom of the T-shirt. He grips the edge and lifts it up and over my head.

I feel the coldness of the countertop bite into my hot, sensitive skin as he gently pushes me backward until I'm lying down. His hands slide over my breasts, across my stomach, and his fingers dip into the waistband of my underwear. Never breaking eye contact with me, he pulls it down. The fabric and his fingertips brush across my thighs, knees, and calves, leaving a trail of fire in their wake. My underwear drops to the floor and I am completely naked, bared to him. He smiles at me and I watch as the softness turns to pure craving as he leans over and kisses me in the middle of my chest.

As his warm lips trail down my body, the hair on his forehead falls forward, causing it to brush across my skin and make me shiver. It's soft and tickles as it chases after where his lips have just been. It's a complete sensory overload.

"You are so beautiful," he says as his lips move against

my skin. The heat from his breath gives me goose bumps and all I can do is moan out in response.

Before I can gather my wits about me, he sinks out of sight. I'm about to sit up and look for him when I feel his breath fan across my most sensitive parts. I freeze completely. Although I'm excited to let him do something new to me, I'm also slightly terrified.

I don't have time to voice my concerns as I feel his lips move up the inside of my thigh and over me. It's all I can do to stay flat on the countertop. I whisper his name and then marvel at the sound of my own voice. He's driving me to places I've never experienced and I can't keep still.

"Lei, I have no words. I'm loving every second of this." How do I reply to that?

"Beau . . . please . . . don't stop . . ."

I feel his smile between my legs and it pushes me over the edge. I couldn't control it even if I wanted to. Lights flash behind my eyes as a wave of heat rocks through my body and every nerve seems to dance in the exquisiteness of this feeling.

"Leila?"

"Yeah," I whisper. I seem to have melted into the counter as aftershocks crash against me.

"Hold on to the counter."

Hold on? I'm confused for a few seconds until I hear the condom packet tear and then he leans forward, pushing himself inside me. I slip backward. That explains his command. I grip the edge of the counter as he begins to move.

I hear him moan out my name and instinctively wrap my legs around him tighter, drawing him in deeper. *Oh my.*

"Lei, you feel amazing." His voice is rough and slightly strained.

I smile as I bite down on my bottom lip to stop the sounds

of pleasure and the words of endearment that are fighting to break free from my chest. I'm not ready to tell him how I feel about him yet, but when we are like this, everything wants to burst free.

"Beau . . . oh . . ." My back arches off the counter and he feels the changes taking place from the inside out.

"Let it go, Lei. I'll be right there with you."

His words are my undoing and seconds later, I feel his.

"I like you making breakfast for me." I smile up at him.

I'm rewarded with the most dazzling grin I've even seen. This moment couldn't be more perfect.

BEAU

AFTER BRUNCH, LEILA and I decide to curl up under a blanket on the couch and watch a movie. I can't help but continue to run through my mind, over and over again, the fact that she didn't know I was at the fire. That makes sense to me now, but what about the letter?

"Lei?" Her head is in my lap and all I can see is her profile. I tuck some of her hair behind her ear with one hand, while my other rubs her back and arm.

"Yeah?" She rolls back against me a little and glances up.

"So, I get that you didn't know I was at the fire, but what I still don't understand is why you wrote me that letter. Why didn't you try to talk to me?"

She stiffens, tilts her head to get a better look at me, her eyebrows furrow, and she thinks about her answer. "Because, what she said sounded so true."

She? I stop running my hand up and down her arm.

"What who said?"

"Your mom."

What? What is she talking about, my mom?

The hair on the back of my neck stands up. Somehow I know what she's about to tell me is not going to be good. In a way, I wish I could stop it, but I need to know and she needs to tell me.

"I'm not following you. Tell me what happened," I say to her.

Leila sits up to look at me, the blanket falls around her waist, and I pause the movie.

"After I was released from the hospital, my parents took me back to Aunt Ella's house. We ended up staying a few extra days because I had to see a pulmonologist for the smoke inhalation, and my father needed to settle things with the insurance company and the bank. I will never forget the coughing. My nose and mouth were caked with soot and I coughed for days. Every muscle was pulled, everything hurt, and I constantly had to use an inhaler. My throat hurt, my voice was hoarse, and the phlegm was awful. I waited for you to come see me."

She looks at me and her eyes show both sadness and regret.

"The day finally came when my parents were ready to leave, and I snuck away because I had to see you one more time. I was so hurt and devastated that you didn't come visit me, and I was heartbroken because I was leaving you. I will never forget walking up those steps to your front porch. If only I had known then how rapidly things were going to change."

Standing on the front porch looking up at Beau's house, I take a mental picture. Even though we didn't spend a lot of time here, when I think about him I want to remember all of the details of him.

Leaning forward, I knock on the door and wait. I'm so nervous that butterflies take off in my stomach. I'm confused as to why I'm nervous; it's just Beau, and I've spent almost every day with him for the last six years.

The door finally opens and Mrs. Hale frowns. She takes one step toward me and pulls the door almost closed behind her. She doesn't want me to see inside and the look on her face is one of annoyance. She's frowning at me.

"Hi, Mrs. Hale, is Beau home?" I ask her. She hears the hoarseness of my voice and her mean exterior falls for just a second and then slams back into place.

"No, he's not." She has always been so nice. I don't understand why she's being short with me and looking annoyed that I am here.

"Do you know when he will be home?"

"He's not coming home any time soon. He's off on a fishing trip with Grant."

My heart cracks and splits right down the middle. He never intended to say goodbye.

"Oh, well, we're leaving today and I just wanted to say goodbye." I look down at my hands and start twisting and pinching my fingers. I will not cry in front of her.

"I think he thought that you already left." My heart starts pounding and squeezing in my chest, and, as hard as I tried not to, the coughing starts. Bending over at the waist to clutch my ribcage, tears leak out, and she puts her hand on my shoulder. I can't look at her.

"No, we had to stay a few extra days because of the fire."

"Oh, that's right. I think I did hear something about that. It's a good thing you were already moving." She sounds so cold.

"Will you please tell him I stopped by and that I'll call him soon?"

"Now, Leila, I want you to stop and think about this; do you really think it's best to try to drag this out?"

"What do you mean?"

"Hasn't he spent enough time with you? He's fourteen years old. Don't you think he should be spending more time with boys his age?"

A cold sweat breaks out across the back of my neck. "I've never kept him or prevented him from spending time with other people."

"Yes, I know, dear . . . but you know how Beau is. He's a very responsible young man, and he's always felt responsible for you."

"It isn't like that. He's my friend."

"That may be, but I want you to think about all the other girls in your school. How many of them have a friend who is a boy who watches over them like he does you? Maybe your moving is good for both of you. You're at the age where you should be out shopping with girlfriends and he should be playing sports, or fishing with the guys. Think hard about this, Leila; when Beau is not with you, where is he? Who is he with? What is he doing?"

It's never occurred to me that I might be holding him back from doing something else, something that he might have rather done than hang out with me.

"Maybe you're right."

"Of course I am. If you want to leave your new phone number, I'm sure he'll call you soon."

"I don't know what it is."

"Oh, well . . . once you know what it is, you can always call here and I'll give it to him."

There is something about the way she says this that makes me believe she will never give him my phone number. A sudden panic fills me—this is it. He and I are over. I never saw this coming and I'm temporarily paralyzed from the pain.

Beau has always been the only friend that I have ever needed. When we weren't together, I would lie on the beach and read books. Sure, I have other friends who are girls who I occasionally do things with, but really I have always been happy with just having him. Thinking back over the years, I realize she's right. When he's not spending time with me, he's always out with Grant or Ryan. Was I causing him to divide his time? Was I making him have to choose?

"Okay." An unwanted tear slips down my face. "Goodbye, Mrs. Hale."

"Goodbye, Leila; best of luck to you."

Turning around, I walk down the steps and away from the home of the only person in this world that I considered mine. Beau was my best friend, he was the other half of me, and, although he didn't know it . . . I loved him.

With tears streaming down my face, I look back at her one more time. There are tears in her eyes, too, and she rubs her hand across her chest. Noticing a small movement, I look up and see Matt sitting in his bedroom window. He's watching me, and I find it odd that he looks so miserable and lonely. Lifting my hand, I give Mrs. Hale one more small wave. She doesn't return it, but walks back inside and closes the door.

Leila glances up as she finishes telling me about that conversation with my mother. After reliving that moment, her eyes are damp, her shoulders are hunched over, and I can see the sadness pouring off of her—she isn't making this up.

I don't understand. Nothing is making any sense to me. I can absolutely see my dad saying this to her, but why would my mother? She knew how close I was to Leila and what she meant to me.

The blood is thundering through my body and I can't sit on the couch anymore. Jumping to my feet, I get up and start pacing.

"So, let me get this straight; knowing how much I hated my father, and knowing the problems I was constantly having with both my parents, you decided to take something that she said as the truth? Why? Why Leila?" I stop right in front of her and cross my arms over my chest.

"I don't . . . I didn't think she was lying." Her eyes are locked onto mine and they are pleading for me to understand.

"You didn't think she was lying?" There's an edge to my voice and she watches me walk across the room to put some distance between us. Emotions are playing out across her face and the distance that is reflecting back at me through her eyes isn't just a physical one, but emotional as well. Right in this moment, things between us are changing . . . I can feel it and so can she.

"Did you stop to think at all? What about me?" I point to

my chest. "What about all of the things that I said to you over the years? Did you think I was lying? You knew me better than anyone!"

Leila narrows her eyes at me and gets up off the couch. She doesn't like the way I'm talking to her and she stands just a little bit taller to let me know she doesn't intend to back down. She's still wearing only my T-shirt and a pair of underwear, and with her hair wild all over the place, I can't help but notice how beautiful she is, even if I am pissed at her.

"Beau, she's your mom. Why would I not believe what she was saying to me? I knew that you weren't happy at home, but you never discussed it with me. I was fourteen years old, and at the time, what she said made sense to me. You had been spending more time with Grant and Ryan, and I thought maybe I was becoming just a responsibility to you," she says defensively, mirroring my stance and crossing her arms over her chest.

"I was spending more time with Grant and Ryan for several reasons. One, I didn't want to be at home. Bad shit was always happening at home. Two, we were both being forced to play more tennis. Grant wanted to be out fishing and I wanted to be with you. My mother knew that because I was constantly complaining."

"I didn't know that," she snaps at me.

"You didn't need to! I was with you every day and just about every night. That should have spoken volumes to you. If I had wanted to be somewhere else, with someone different, then I would have. You were never a responsibility or an obligation. You were mine, and I thought I was yours."

I see the last couple of words have a big impact on her. She lets out a sigh and the fire that was in her eyes switches to regret. She walks over to the window, looks down toward the street, and all of her beautiful wild curls fall down around her shoulders.

"You were . . . you are." Her voice is remorseful. Pulling down on the edge of the T-shirt in an attempt to make it longer, she looks at her feet. "I just wish we could go back . . ."

"Leila . . ." She looks over at me. "I could never go back to the person that I once was. I have gone through so much, and experienced so many things over the last couple of years that have ultimately changed me that there's just no way. And, honestly, I'm not even sure why you would want me to."

She lets out a sigh and takes a couple of steps toward me. Her eyes are glistening with tears and, along with my racing pulse, this makes my heart squeeze.

"Beau, please don't let this break what we've put back together," she whispers, shaking her head. "I'm sorry, I'm so sorry. I want to be with you; I've always wanted to be with you."

This is the first time that I can ever remember her saying that she wants me. It affects me so much that my heart stops racing and I'm shaking from head to toe. But, at the same time, my mind is completely wrapped around the fact that this just might break us. I'm so angry with her and at this entire situation. Why couldn't she have just come to me? Yes, I understand that she thinks I was on a fishing trip, but I wasn't. I was waiting for her in that damn hospital. If she had given me an opportunity to answer her letter, all of this could have been cleared up a long time ago.

Rubbing my hand over my face, I let out a deep sigh. "I want to believe you. I really do. I want to believe that what we have in here," I pat my chest, "what we've always had, is strong enough for us to hold a future, but I have many layers of trust issues with you, and right now I'm just not so sure. You believed her over me. All these years have gone by. How am I to know that, should something happen again, my words and actions won't matter?"

"I understand this, I do." She throws her arms out. "After having all of the details finally come to light yesterday, I realized that I am the reason we ended the way we did, but now you know too. Please, it's in the past. I want to move on. I want to move on with you. How long are you going to punish me for a decision that I made when I was fourteen years old?"

She starts fidgeting with her fingers and I start pacing again, back and forth in front of the windows.

"It isn't even just about when you were fourteen. What about when you came back and you were sixteen? What about when you were eighteen and you spent the night with me after my father was arrested? How about now, at twenty? You've had many opportunities to talk to me, to ask me!"

"Well, what about you? You could have done the same!" She's frustrated because she thinks I'm not considering what she's saying, and honestly, I'm so mad at her right now, I don't even care.

Walking to stand in front of her, she cowers a little. My hands are balled into fists and my jaw is locked tight. She can see just how angry I am as I glare down at her.

"You left me, Leila! I did not leave you. I did not leave you an irreversibly heartbreaking letter. I did not leave you with no way of contacting me. Up until that day at school in the photo lab, I thought you were right across the bridge. I didn't even know you were in Atlanta."

She blinks and the tears that were floating in her big blue eyes begin drop. She takes a step back away from me.

"Night after night, for years, hell, even now, I lie in bed and stare out the window at the stars—our stars—wondering what *I* did wrong. I've replayed that last day down at Bean Point over and over in my mind. The only thing I could ever come up with is that you were upset that I kissed you. You didn't seem upset at the time but maybe you changed your mind; that you didn't return the feelings and now somehow felt we couldn't be friends. I don't know! And then there were those last couple of months on the island before you moved here to the city, you didn't mind being affectionate with me then. I never could understand. All this time of wondering why . . ."

"You could have asked too." She pins me with a look to let me know that she thinks this should be a shared blame.

I pinch my lips together and try to rein in the anger, rage, frustration, heartache, loneliness, and disappointment of the last six years.

"We made plans that night. You knew how important it was to me to say goodbye to you, and do you want to know why? I needed to tell you how much I loved you before you left. I really wanted you to know that, no matter where you went, I was always going to be with you. God, I would have waited forever for you."

"You loved me?" Her eyes widen with what I think might be hope.

"Yes, I *did*." There's no mistaking my use of the past tense.

The color drains from her face and more tears slowly drip out. "Did," she whispers, pulling down on the T-shirt again.

"How could you not have known that?"

She looks away from me, doesn't answer, and that's when I decide . . . this did just break us. After all these years, doubts, her walking away, and all the unanswered questions, it finally hits me . . .

"In the end, Leila, now that the entire picture is so brilliantly painted and complete in front of me, I guess I think I deserve better than some girl who will just bail on me and never give me the benefit of the doubt. Three minutes for six and a half years. You let one three-minute conversation that you had with my mother on my front porch ruin us. You ruined me. No matter how many years go by, the fact remains that I never would have done that to you."

"But didn't you?" she asks, eyes bright and mixed with half challenge and half defeat. She still thinks I should have chased after her, that I should somehow own some of the responsibility in this.

"No, I didn't. I lay in a hospital bed for months and cried because the only girl I had ever planned on loving didn't love me in return."

"I'm sorry." Her lip quivers.

I can't watch her cry and see her tears anymore. I turn away. Walking over to the window, I look out at the street. The dusting of snow has melted, but it's overcast outside and still looks cold. Cold; that's a good description of how I'm feeling too.

"I need to be alone. You should go."

LEILA

STUMBLING OUT OF Beau's apartment, the walk of shame takes on a whole new meaning.

It's cold out but I don't feel it. I am in complete shock. Walking to the corner of the block, I lean against the building;

everything has become blurry, and I try to catch my breath.

I'm so hurt.

He's so hurt.

He's shut me out.

He's walked away from me, yet again.

How can he not see things from my point of view? I'm devastated that he doesn't, scared that he never will, and livid that he is pinning this all on me. How can he put this all on me? Can't he look in the mirror and see that he, too, is to blame?

Pushing off, I start walking. I don't see people, cars, or even streets. The numbness is so strong; I'm not even sure how I get home. Over and over in my mind, I just keep repeating, *this isn't happening. This isn't happening. This isn't happening.* The last eighteen hours flash through my mind. The way he was with me, how his hands held me, the things we did, the things he said, how could he just tell me to leave? This can't be happening.

Standing at the door to my apartment, it finally swings open, and Charlie is standing on the other side.

"I heard you trying to get your key in the door. What's wrong?"

Something inside of me snaps at the sight of him and I start crying.

"Oh, my God, Leila, what happened?" He pulls me into his arms and slams the door.

"Beau." It's all I can get out as I sob into his shoulder.

"I swear that guy pulls more emotions out of you than anything I have seen. What did he do this time? Because I'll kill him."

"I broke us," I stutter.

"What does that mean? How did you break it?"

273

"It means he asked me to leave." I pull away from him and glance toward the hallway. "I can't talk about it; I'm just going to go to my room, okay?"

"Okay, love," he says, frowning at me and wiping away a few tears. "If you need anything, just holler."

I nod my head, walk to my room, and close the door.

How could I have been so wrong about him over the years? Better yet, how could I have been so wrong about myself?

He's right, the Beau that I knew back then would never have let me leave without saying goodbye. I'm to blame for my decisions. Charlie's right, too; I am a coward.

Why did I listen to her? I did believe her over him. For years, he called me his best friend and, in off-handed little ways, he would tell me that he wasn't sure what he would do without me.

Climbing under my covers, I pull the blanket over my head, and let the tears fall. He told me I ruined him and I ruined us.

It's funny, because I'm not sure exactly what I'm crying for at the moment, but I can't stop. The numbness and shock are still lingering and I fear the repercussions that I am going to be assaulted with tomorrow when I wake up.

Three minutes for six and a half years.

Monday morning, the alarm goes off and for a split second I float into that space between being asleep and awake, and everything in life seems perfect, calm, and at peace. Then my eyes open and I see things differently. My life without Beau. Curling up in a ball, I squeeze my eyes shut and rub my chest as the pain and grief set in. I don't understand what's happening to me and I feel sick.

How I managed to get out of bed, get dressed, and get the café open, I'll never know. I'm moving on autopilot and not one person this morning asks me what's wrong. Every customer looks at my funnily and stays quiet. I'm glad, because there's no way I would be able to talk about this, him, or me. As the morning passes, what washes over me is so excruciating that after work I turn around and walk straight back home. The pain in my heart is unbearable and the weight that is pushing on me . . . I just need to lie down. What should I have done differently? What should I have said? I feel haunted by the disappointment that was radiating off of him, and in return I am disappointed with myself. The look on his face—that devastated look that I see every time I close my eyes—was of compete betrayal and it's all my fault.

We aren't over. We can't be. We just found our way back to each other. This has to be just another hiccup. I have to believe that this won't break us and that we're strong enough to overcome this. I have to hang on to hope, because if I don't, I will crumble. How do I get him back?

Lying in bed, I hug my cell phone to my chest, willing it to ring, beep, anything. At some point, I hear my door open, and Charlie peeks his head in. I close my eyes and pretend to be sleeping. I don't want to talk to him. I want to talk to Beau.

Three minutes for six and a half years of unanswered questions.

On Tuesday, I wake up and I'm just mad.

Stomping around my room, getting ready for work, I feel the blood boiling inside of me. Yes, I listened to his mom and, yes, according to Beau, I did write an irreversibly damaging letter, but what else have I really done wrong? I didn't ask why, but neither did he. If I was so important to him, or if we, as in he and I, were so important then why didn't he try to find me and ask me? I gave him all of me and he let me go. Bottom line, he's putting all of this on me, and that's not fair. He's broken my heart enough, too, over the years.

On my desk is the picture of us at prom. I walk over and lay it down. What's the point in keeping it up? He ended us. He made us something that will forever be in the past. He asked me to leave, but it's more than that; in his way, he threw me out.

I carry this anger with me throughout the day. Work keeps me busy and my mind preoccupied, and school flies by. No one questioned my absence yesterday and I'm glad because, if they had, I might just have gone off. I feel like a rocket that's about to explode.

Instead of heading into my studio, I go for a walk. I need to move, I need to process, and I need to cool off this feeling that is burning inside of me.

By the time I get home, it's dark out and Charlie has ordered us a pizza. I flop down on the couch, swipe a slice, and scarf it down. I try to remember the last time I ate, and then it comes to me; Beau's house, Sunday morning.

The image of sitting on his counter with him smiling at

me hits me like a sledgehammer. Immediately, all of the anger dissolves, and I glance toward my bedroom and feel panic because I laid the picture down, trying to hide us.

"What's going on in that head of yours?" Charlie hands me a beer and I drink half of it in one gulp.

"What do you mean?"

He raises his eyebrows at me.

Letting out a sigh, I turn to face him. "I don't know. I just don't know anything anymore."

"Are you going to tell me what happened?"

"No."

"Okay, but know that I'm watching you."

I give him a small smile that I have to force out, and I head off to my room.

Picking up the picture, I run my finger over him. He's so beautiful.

Tears fill my eyes again. I hate crying. I never cry.

Kicking off my shoes, I climb into bed with my phone and the picture. I'm so confused and I just don't know what is supposed to happen next.

Three minutes for six and a half years of unanswered questions and disappointments.

Wednesday, I'm already awake before the alarm goes off. I've been staring at the shadows on the ceiling, taking one breath at a time. Throughout the night, the anger completely dissolved and, in its place, sadness slowly seeped in. It hurts to breathe.

I completed my shift at the café, but instead of going to school, I went home. Sitting in my room, with complete silence, is my preferred activity. The blinds are drawn, and the blankets on my bed have seen better days, but I just don't have the energy or the motivation to make it better. Over and over in my mind, I replay Saturday night and Sunday morning. The last few weeks have been so wonderful and, now, I've lost it. Thinking about the things that he has said to me, the things that I did to him, the only answer that I can come up with is that he deserves better.

Better than me.

Remembering that I have a button-down shirt of his, from the last night we spent together on the beach, I pull it out of the bottom drawer of my dresser and slip it on. For the longest time, it used to smell like him; even though it doesn't anymore, I still rub it across my face.

My phone, the picture, his shirt; anything that I have to be closer to him, I cling to. I'm trying. These things are all I have left.

At six-thirty, Ali walks into my bedroom and turns on the light. It's so bright that a headache immediately sets in. She sees me wince and she turns it off.

"Charlie called me. What's going on with you and Beau?" I feel the bed dip as she sits down next to me.

"He doesn't want me." Saying this out loud causes a lump to form in my throat, and tears leak out of the corners of my eyes.

"Did he actually say this?" She pushes my hair off of my face. The tenderness in this makes my heart ache even more.

"In so many words; he said he deserves better, and he's right." The ache is now so strong I roll over onto my side and curl up.

"Well, I disagree with that statement," she says quietly.

"Ali, what am I going to do? I've loved him and only him for over twelve years." A small sob escapes.

"I don't know. But I think if you just give him some time, he'll come around; he always does."

"He asked me to leave."

"You know he internalizes everything and he needs to do it on his own. All three of them are like that. I think it goes back to their childhood and how much time they spent by themselves in their rooms."

"I don't know. He was so angry and so sad. The way he talked to me . . . it seemed so final."

"I'm sorry, Leila."

"Me, too."

Ali curls up next to me and lets me cry. She's always known that I care deeply for Beau and, although she doesn't know all of the details, she's always wanted us both to be happy. I wanted my happy to be with him, but it seems he does not reciprocate this.

Three minutes for six and a half years of unanswered questions, disappointments, and heartache.

It's Thursday. I've slipped into the darkness. Shock, denial, guilt, anger, pain; they all leave and in their place come loneliness, sadness, loss, and complete devastation. Nothing or no one could make me better, except for him. I feel crushed and depressed. How will I ever get over him? I didn't make it to many classes this week and, as the day turned into night, I knew there was no way I was going to make it to work tomorrow. I never call into work, so when I did, I had to assure my boss that I was fine and would be back next week. I just need a few days, but would a few days be enough? I don't want to see or talk to anyone.

Three minutes for six and a half years of unanswered questions, disappointments, heartache, and loneliness.

Days have passed and I haven't heard one word from him. I'm beginning to realize the magnitude of this, and I know in my heart that we are most likely over. I have no idea what I'm going to do now. I don't know life without him. I've hung on to the idea of him for so long and I have loved him even when he didn't know he was being loved. No one has ever loved him like I have, nor will they. For twelve long years, I have loved him so completely that, today, on top of all of the other emotions that I am feeling, I feel broken.

Six days ago, I walked out of his loft and I feel like I am suffocating. I am overwhelmed by this blanket of complete hopelessness. I don't know how to escape the physical pain that this is causing. It hurts to breathe. It hurts to just be.

No one can really understand how I feel. Charlie gets that I'm upset, he expects it, but at the café this morning, he tells me that it's time for me to return to the land of the living. The truth is that I feel like part of me has died, and with that went the life in me.

I feel so alone and I want to be alone at the same time. No one understands. In their minds, we have only been together for a couple of weeks, but that's not true. What I'm feeling covers years.

Getting off of my bed, I pull a suitcase out from underneath it. I walk into my closet and grab a handful of clothes, tossing them in. Grabbing a few things from the bathroom, I have all I need.

"Where are you going?" Charlie is standing in the doorway to my room as I collect a few last things, and he looks confused.

"Home," I say without really looking at him.

"Florida? But why?" He crosses his arms over his chest and scowls.

"I just need to go. I need to breathe. I don't feel like I can here, and I'm breaking. I won't be gone long, okay?"

He lets out a deep sigh and runs his hand through his hair. "I don't have much of a choice, do I? Do you want me to go with you?"

"No, I need to go on my own. I need to say goodbye."

"But isn't he here?"

"I don't know; I assume so. You don't understand. It isn't just him; it's everything." He's looking at me like I'm crazy, but I need to go. When I'm there, I feel like I am still with him, and here I am not. Even though I know I'm going to have to let him go, I need to do it surrounded by the things that made us, us: Bean Point, the sand, the sea oats, the bench, the candy shop, the coffee shop . . . the stars. The only time in my life I have ever felt truly happy was on Anna Maria Island, and that's all I can think about and where I need to go.

He walks over, gives me a big hug, and picks up my suitcase. "I'll walk you out."

Three minutes for six and a half years of unanswered questions, disappointments, heartache, loneliness, and a reali-

zation of unworthiness.

BEAU

THE FRONT DOOR opens and slams shut. Without even opening my eyes, I know it's Drew. He's the only one who has a key.

I hear him walk through the loft, open the blinds, grab a bottle of water out of the refrigerator, and then the covers are ripped off of me.

My eyes fly open and lock with his. "Dude, was all that really necessary? And what are you doing here?" I snap at him.

"You know why I'm here. Get up." He slams the water down on the nightstand next to the bed and walks over to the couch.

Throwing my arm over my eyes, I groan at the light.

"You're lucky that it's me who showed up here. Charlie is on a rampage and wants to kick your ass," he says as he sits down.

Charlie?

"What the hell for? What did I do to him?" Moving my arm, I stare up at the ceiling.

"You know exactly what you did."

"No, I don't." Sitting up, I gulp down some of the water.

"He says Leila hasn't eaten in a week, wouldn't come out of her room except to go to work, and she only went to school one day out of the last five."

I know I shouldn't find comfort in hearing him say that Leila is miserable, but I do. It's nice to know that I'm not the only one who is having a hard time processing all of this.

"That's not my fault." And technically it's not. She made her decisions. Those are all on her.

"Oh really?" he says sarcastically.

"You just don't get it."

"No, I don't, so why don't you tell me?" he says, watching me.

Climbing out of bed, I walk over to my desk and open the top drawer to retrieve the letter. I've memorized this letter. I hand it to him and watch as his eyes float over the lines. I see the confusion on his face as his eyes narrow, and his lips pinch down into a thin line.

I relive those exact emotions from the first time I read it, too.

It's been two weeks. I've been lying here in this hospital bed on my stomach and I am completely bored. I miss Leila something fierce, and right now there is no end in sight. These burns are taking forever to heal and no one will give me any answers about when I'll get to go home. This just sucks.

I'm realistic to think that Leila has probably already moved. Their plan had been to leave the day after the fire. Even if they were delayed a few days, too much time has passed. I don't know why she didn't come say goodbye to me. I know I'm hanging onto just threads here, but I'd like to give her the benefit of the doubt and think that maybe she didn't have anyone to drive her here. I suppose she could have called. There has to be a reason.

Mom walks into my room and very solemnly hands me a letter. I'm not sure why she looks like this, but whatever. I'm overjoyed when I see Leila's handwriting on the outside.

Finally!

I needed something from her and it's finally here. It's like a lifeline and instantly I feel better than I have in the last two weeks. I'm ecstatic, I'm smiling from ear to ear, and my hands are shaking.

Flipping the envelope over, I carefully open the flap. I don't want it to rip. Pulling out the letter, I can tell from the thinness that it's only one page. I'm slightly disappointed about this, but that quickly evaporates because I'm holding a letter from her.

Unfolding the paper, I scan the writing—there's not much here.

Dear Beau,

I had been hoping to get to say goodbye to you in person, but obviously that was never going to happen. We are getting ready to leave, but I couldn't go without telling you thanks. I know that spending so much time with me, a girl, probably wasn't the easiest for you, but I appreciate all the fun times that we had together. You are my childhood and because of you it is filled with great memories, so thank you.

I want you to know that I am realistic about how our friendship is going to play out. These things never last. Maybe one day we'll move back, or maybe we won't, but in the meantime I want you to know that it's okay to forget about me because that is what I'm going to do with you.

I had planned on giving you my new address, but I've changed my mind and now I think that it is best if I don't. It's just easier this way. I am no longer your responsibility. Consider yourself set free.

I wish the very best things in life for you.

You'll never know what you meant to me…

Your friend,

        Leila

What?

That's it?

I don't understand!

The excitement I had felt instantly turns to nervousness. My stomach starts to ache and my blood begins to thunder in my ears.

This is the letter that she leaves for me?

Upon seeing the envelope, I thought that it was a goodbye letter, but never did I think it was this type of goodbye. After all of these years and all of the time that we have spent together, I am just paralyzed with disbelief.

I flip the letter over and look at the back; there's nothing. I look inside the envelope, and again nothing. How can every word and every promise we made just be dismissed; completely dismissed as if they never even happened?

Panic floods through me and I can't breathe. My eyes flood with tears and one drops onto the letter.

"Sweetheart?" It's my mother. I didn't realize that she hadn't left the room, and that's when I hear the beeping on the heart rate machine pick up too.

"You need to leave!" I say without looking at her.

"What?" Confusion is in her voice. I know she doesn't understand and I just don't care. I don't want anyone to know, see, or hear what I am feeling right now.

"Leave me alone!" I yell. Squeezing my eyes closed, I picture Leila in my mind. My mom lets out a sigh as she opens the door, and it closes behind her.

Star light, star bright, first star I see tonight, I wish I may, I wish I might, have this wish I wish tonight.

Sobs burst out of me. I can't stop crying, and I don't even care. I'm staring down at the letter, reading it over and over as another tear falls and hit the paper. I fold it back up and put it in its envelope. Clutching it under my chest, I lay on it, realizing that most likely this is the last thing I will ever have from her.

I just don't understand. She has to know that I was burned in the fire pulling her out, saving her, and that every day I've done nothing but lay here and wait for her to come and visit me. Each day I have felt more and more anxious. What's ironic is that, somewhere, somehow, in the back of my heart, I knew she wasn't coming. How can she do this to me? She is my best friend and I am hers. Or should I say was?

She's going to forget about me.

I have loved her for every second of every minute of the past six years. She had to have known this. I just don't understand.

Was I not nice enough, sincere enough, or thoughtful enough?

Is she mad because I kissed her? Did I mess things up

with us by doing that?

I turn my head to lay it down on the pillow, and pain streaks across my back. The skin is still so weak and sensitive. These scars are going to be an endless reminder of her, the girl I loved who didn't love me back.

I feel like the world is laughing at me and testing me at the same time.

My father hates me, my mother doesn't love me enough to make my life better, Drew and I hardly ever talk anymore, I now have what are going to be the ugliest scars ever, and the one person I thought was mine, no matter what, just left me— she wants to forget about me.

I cover my face with my hand, the only hand that I can use, and cry. I cry for hours.

How could she just leave me like this? She was the one person I thought I would always be able to count on. I never in a million years thought that this would happen.

I don't want to be here anymore. This was the last straw. She broke me. I don't want to be in this room, in this town, on this earth. I have never been one to give much thought to suicide but, really, I just want to die. I don't want to live anymore. I have nothing to live for. I'm not wanted or really loved by anyone. What is the point of all this? Please, can't someone just put me out of my misery?

"What is this?" Drew asks, still looking over the page.

"It's the letter that Leila left for me when she moved to Atlanta. Mom gave it to me when I was in the hospital. I had already been there for two weeks, waiting for her to visit me."

Reliving the way that letter made me feel has me pacing around the loft like a caged animal. I've never shown the letter to or talked about it with anyone. But, then again, who was left for me? No one.

"Why would she write this to you, and why didn't you show me this before?" He holds it up and looks dead at me.

Stopping in front of him on the couch, I throw my hands out and give him an exasperated look.

"I didn't know why she wrote it, that is, up until last weekend and, as for not showing it to you, what was the point? You and I didn't share things. We didn't talk about our feelings. You never asked me anything about my life. It just wasn't what we did. *She* was all I had. I laid in that hospital bed waiting and waiting for her, and she never came! Then I got this," I say, pointing to the letter.

Drew runs his hand through his hair and glances back down at the letter. "You need to start from the beginning."

"The day before everything happened, we were down at the beach like always and she gave me this as a gift." I walk over to the desk, pick up the journal, and wave it at him.

He recognizes it and nods at me.

"I was so moved and so in love with her that I leaned over and kissed her. That was our first kiss. I don't know . . . I was both elated that she kissed me back and seriously pissed because she was moving away. That's why I was so angry when I got home. It wasn't fair. She was all I had. She was everything."

Drew continues to look at me and he frowns, knowing where this conversation is headed.

"I got home and just needed to be by myself. But no! He had to come into my room and beat the shit out of me, too.

You'll never understand what it was like for me. God, I didn't think that life could get any worse. Mom took me to the hospital; they wrapped up my arm and gave me some pain medication which knocked me out. I was supposed to call her that night, but I fell asleep and didn't. The next day, I was in and out of it. Mom took me to the orthopedist to have the cast put on and sometime late afternoon I started faking taking the medicine. My arm hurt so much, but I couldn't miss her. I had to see her. I hadn't talked to her and we had plans to camp out that last night in her house. The time finally arrived. I snuck out of the house and that's when I found her house on fire. You know the rest from here. The paramedics came and we were both taken to the hospital. I waited and waited."

"I knew you were waiting for her," he says, still frowning. "Did you ever ask her why she sent it?" He starts rubbing his chin, piecing it all together.

"First off, she didn't leave me a way to; there was no phone number and no address. Second, she made it clear that she didn't want me to contact her and, third, after everything that I had just gone through over the last couple of weeks, would you have? I mean, Dad was always telling us how no one would ever love us. I felt everything had come full circle."

"Back then . . . probably not. But now, most definitely. Go on . . ." He leans back into the couch, stretching his legs out and crossing them at the ankles.

Taking a deep breath, I walk to the window and look out. I don't want to see his reaction. "I paid for her to go to Parson's."

Drew gasps. "What! What do you mean you paid for her to go to Parson's? All of it?"

"Yep." Turning around to face him, I see that his eyes are huge and his jaw has dropped open.

"Why?"

"Because it was her dream and, despite everything, I still loved her. It was her dream and I wanted it to come true. You would've done the same for Ali, so don't look at me like that. Whatever, it's just money."

"I don't know what to say, little brother . . . ."

"Nothing to say. I didn't really intend for her to ever know, but she found out the other day from the school who her benefactor was and that's what started this entire shit storm."

The look on his face is one of shock and awe. He rubs his hand through his hair and watches me as I walk back to my desk.

"You know my journal," I pick it up and look at it. "I dropped it, she found it, and she read it. That's when she showed up at your house, saying she didn't know."

"Okay . . . go on."

"Turns out she didn't know anything at all about that night. When I had found her in the house, she was already passed out and no one ever told her exactly what happened. She didn't know that I was the one who found her and pulled her out. She didn't know that I was burned in the fire. She didn't know that I was in the hospital. She just thought that I didn't care enough anymore to say goodbye to her."

"How did she not know that? Why didn't anyone tell her?"

"That's the part I couldn't wrap my head around either. She just assumed it was a fireman, and everyone else assumed she knew. It never came up in conversation. So after she went back to Aunt Ella's, I never showed to say goodbye, and she thought I didn't care."

"See that's the part, after reading the letter, which I just don't understand. Why would she think that? She was your best friend."

"Mom told her I was glad that she was moving away, that I could finally spend some time with other boys my age, like Grant."

"What!" He gets to his feet and his eyes narrow. "She wouldn't do that."

"Apparently, she did! I don't know. The whole situation is so messed up. It *has* been for so long. And, honestly, I can't see Leila making all this up. That's not who she is."

He walks over to my desk and picks up the picture of Leila and me at prom. "You know that you are the only one for her. We can all see it, and have for years. She loves you."

"Well, then what was that shit you and Ali were trying to pull a couple of months ago with Camille? Both of you were pushing her my way."

He puts down the picture and looks at me. I'm angry and can feel heat spread up my neck. "Truth, she really does need friends, and Ali thought that if Leila saw the two of you together she might finally step up and say something."

"Are you kidding me? That's terrible! Did either of you think for one minute how it might make Camille feel?" Heat spreads into my cheeks. This entire conversation with Drew is putting me on edge.

"Trust me when I say you are not even a blip on her radar. That girl has so many things that are so much larger than what you and I have going on that it doesn't make a difference." He shoves his hands into his pockets.

"Well, Leila doesn't love me enough, or she would have come to me and demanded answers."

"The same could be said about you." He pins me with a know-it-all look.

This pisses me off and I start pacing back and forth.

"That's not fair. I didn't leave her. She left me! Don't you remember how bad it was for me? Even if I had wanted to, I was stuck in that hospital, then the rehabilitation center, and by the time I got out, I was so emotionally and physically depressed . . . I just didn't see the point!"

"Yes, I do remember what you were like in the months following the fire. I know better than anyone." He starts shaking his head. "I knew there was more to it than the burns. I wish you had talked to me. Maybe we could have figured out some of this a long time ago."

He walks over to the window to stand next to me. His eyes are sad. He blinks at the memory and then gives me a half smile, patting me on the shoulder.

"And, you're right; she did leave you. But if all this boils down to Mom lying to her—then both of you were lied to and the blame is equal. She was told one thing and, because of that, you were told another. Neither one of you sought out the truth; that's what you need to be thinking about. Reality is, both of you were fourteen. Fourteen. If this was to happen all over again tomorrow, don't you think you would handle things a little differently?"

"Whatever, it doesn't matter anymore."

"No, it doesn't. We've all made mistakes and we're all moving on from them. The question you should be asking yourself now that you know the truth is if you going to let all this mess go and finally get the girl, or if you're just going to walk away and forget about her."

"Drew..." I let out a deep breath, "you don't understand. She. Broke. My. Fucking. Heart!"

Needing to put some distance between us, I walk over to the couch and flop down.

"No, I don't understand, and I'm sorry for all of the shit

293

that you've had to go through! But I do know that you have loved that girl for years, despite all of this. So, man up; it's time."

He crosses his arms over his chest and pinches his lips together.

"Man, when you go big, bro, you go all out," I say smirking at him.

He lets out a sigh and drops his arms. "Yeah, I wish I had done it sooner. Leila's flight leaves in a half hour."

He immediately has my attention and I sit up straight. "What do you mean? Where is she going?"

"Home." He's watching my reaction.

My eyebrows furrow.

"Why?" Worry comes out in my tone, and Drew smiles.

"I don't know. Charlie called us right after she left, and that's when I decided it was time to come here and check on you."

Leila's not in the city. My stomach flips and my nerves instantly unsettle. Even when things aren't right between us, I still need her near. This makes me uncomfortable. She's too far from me.

Drew walks over to my desk, grabs a pen and a piece of paper, and jots something down.

"You need to decide. It's time to end all of this, one way or the other."

His expression softens as he pauses to look at me.

"You told me once that you were always going to be there for me. Well, the same goes for you. Don't forget that. Call me if you need anything." And then he's gone.

Getting up and walking over to the desk, I pick up the paper.

LaGuardia – Delta – 6:10 a.m. tomorrow.

LEILA

LAST NIGHT, MOM picked me up from the airport. She was surprised when I called her and told her I was coming home, but having some kind of inclination from when we talked last weekend, I was thankful that she didn't ask any questions. She opened her arms and gave me a much-needed hug. I cried, and she let me be. I think there were maybe five words spoken the entire hour-long ride home.

I can't stop crying.

I know that Charlie doesn't understand, but I was just sitting in my bedroom waiting, and I know I'm waiting for nothing. He isn't going to come for me. I listened to his mother and I doubted him, and ultimately us. He said it; I ruined us. It's because of me that I will never get to be with the one person I've loved forever.

All of this is my fault.

For years, even though I loved him, I've had this slight hatred toward him and this anger that never went away. He broke my heart and I lost faith in him; faith in this person I thought I knew so well. Six and a half years ago, I walked away feeling deceived and lied to. The bonds of trust that held us so tightly together were severed, and I blamed him.

I blamed him.

These words echo in my mind because, now, I know I have no one to blame but myself.

I've always tried to be a good person. To me, it's character that really defines someone. I've never been catty, I don't gossip, and I try to be kind to everyone. But what it still all boils down to is that I'm none of these things to the person who meant the most to me. For years, I've given him the cold shoulder and an attitude. I didn't turn my head when the term "Hale whores" was first mentioned in high school, and now I feel bad for all of the girls who were tagged with this too. That nickname implied that both Beau and Drew were less than honorable with those girls, and that wasn't the case at all. I've been so unkind to him.

I've deliberately tried to hurt him with my words, and no wonder he looked at me like he did the night I told him he could burn in hell. I don't think there is any other phrase that could have been more awful to say to him. He *did* burn, and I feel so ashamed.

I'm not the person I thought I was and, day after day, it gets harder to breathe. I'm so disappointed in myself and, now that the truth is all finally out, he must be so disappointed in me too.

I started us that day on the beach when we were eight, and I finished us the day he received the letter. Thinking about the heartache that I've felt over the years, I now know that what I felt couldn't have even compared to the pain and utter heartbreak that Beau felt.

He was sitting in the sand, working so diligently on his sand castle that he didn't even know I had approached and was watching. I don't know what it was about him. There were other kids on the beach I could have asked to play with, but something about him drew me in and led my feet in his direction. His skin was tan, his hair was messy, and he was frowning. It made me sad to see him sad. I wanted to make him happy—only I didn't; I ruined him.

It all hurts; everything. It hurts to breathe, it hurts to open my eyes, it hurts to move, and it hurts to think. I can't stop thinking about what happened to him and how I wasn't there for him; this person I claim to love. I need to stop thinking, to shut it off.

Over and over, in my mind I see the words from his journal . . .

I waited for you. I waited for days. At the end of each day, before I fell asleep, I cried. I cried for you. I cried because I missed you so much and I couldn't understand why you weren't coming. I needed you. And then I got your letter. Now, I cry every night because you broke my heart. How could you do this to me? You were my person. Day after day, I pray to God that He will have mercy on me and end me. I want to die, and I wish I wasn't such a coward and could do it myself.

His journal and thoughts of it continually cause me to freeze with complete horror. I did that to him. Me! I'm the only person to blame here. He needed me so badly, and I just deserted him and walked away.

I thought that by giving him the letter and setting him free I was being the bigger person, but I wasn't.

I let him down. I never asked for an explanation, and I never gave him the chance for one either. I understand why he didn't come after me. Had he sent me a letter like that, I probably wouldn't have either.

Needing fresh air, I know where my heart and my feet are going to take me, so I slip on some flip flops, grab my phone just in case he calls, and head out the door.

Not five minutes later, I feel the vibration before I hear the ring. My heart jumps with hope that it might be him, but it isn't.

"Hey, Charlie."

"Hey, beautiful. How's my girl?"

"You'll be happy to know that I'm out taking a walk."

"Well, that's good. Did your mom force you outside?"

"No." A small smile forms at his playfulness.

"Well, okay then, this is progress. Maybe you are moving into the acceptance phase."

"What?" I stop walking.

"You know . . . the healing, making peace with the loss." There's uncertainty in his voice. He's wondering if he's said something that he shouldn't—crossed a line, so to speak.

Hearing him say these things, I feel like I have been hit in the head with a two-by-four. I can't think of anything peaceful or healing about this situation and, in a way, he's made me mad. I don't even know what to say to him right now, and silence hangs between us.

"I just wanted to check on you, to make sure you're there and alright. You'll call me if you need me, right?" He knows he upset me.

Letting out a deep breath, I calm my anger; he really wasn't trying to hurt me. "Of course I will. Thanks, Charlie."

"You're welcome, love. Let's talk soon . . ." And with that, he hangs up.

It's interesting that he used the word 'phase'. On the plane ride down, it occurred to me that most likely I was floating through the phases of loss; that's what I've been experiencing. But the only problem with his logic here is that I don't accept anything, and there will be no making peace with Beau walking away from me.

I push forward and keep walking. It's slightly overcast outside, so the temperature is tolerable and isn't so bright that I have to squint. Walking past the shops, café, and houses, nothing has really changed and, strangely, this is soothing.

As my feet hit the sand of the trail, I don't know if it's being here, moving through the phases or that conversation with Charlie, but something inside of me has clicked. Slivers of light are beginning to appear in my darkness, and I have decided that I'm not giving up. I don't accept this at all. I've had an 'ah ha' moment and suddenly I see our relationship from a much broader view.

Coming to the end of the trail, I take in the beautiful sight before me. The water is so blue-green, the sand is so white, and there's our bench. Walking over to sit down, I run my hand across a few sea oats, they are swaying in the breeze, and in a way I feel like they are waving hello at me. My heart smiles for first time in a week. I may be sad and broken right now, but I am resilient. I know what I need to do, and I'm not going to give up.

BEAU

THE CAB DRIVER pulls up to the house. My mother's car is sitting in the driveway. Having to be at the airport so early this morning, and then sitting on the plane for three hours, anger is pulsing through me. She had to have known this day was going to come, and it is here. I want answers from her and I want them now.

Stepping out of the car, I am facing Ali's. Part of me doesn't want to turn around, but I know that I'm going to have to. Taking a deep breath as the cab drives away, I pick up my bag and turn to look at the house that holds so many bad memories. Suddenly, it doesn't seem so big and daunting. It used to be such an ugly home to me. Now, I can see some of the beauty in it.

Mom had the exterior painted and the shutters changed. The landscaping is more inviting and, in general, there is more color. It almost looks inviting, but, then again, I know the truth that lies beyond the walls. The most prominent thing in the yard, though, is the 'For Sale' sign. She hasn't mentioned this yet but, for Matt's sake, I can't help but think *Thank God*.

I walk into the house with a slight bit of trepidation, but remain focused on my purpose, and head straight into the kitchen. Mom is standing at the sink, and she turns at the noise. Shock registers on her face at the sight of me and, for a brief second, it lights up—and then if falls. I'm certain that my expression is not a friendly one. She knows why I am here.

"Beau . . .," she says with a sigh as she walks over to the oven and picks up the small hand towel that hangs over the handle, to dry her hands. She turns to look at me but doesn't say anything else.

"How could you?" I ask in a low tone. Seeing her look so composed, there's no question that she's guilty. She lied to Leila and she lied to me.

"I'm sorry." Her eyes fill with tears as she studies my face, but not once does she move; she stays completely still and poised.

"Years, Mom! Years! You had to have known that I loved her, and you watched me cry over losing her for years! Night after night, I would lie in bed and stare out the window, wondering what I did wrong. I didn't understand and all I wanted to know was, why? Why! Why did you do it?" I'm now yelling at her and I just don't care.

"Beau, you don't understand." She crosses her arms over her chest.

"No, I don't! So please explain it to me." I match her and cross mine as well. I will not be intimidated by a parent any longer. I used to be afraid of her, too, but not anymore. She's lost her hold over me and, knowing this, I feel a bit free. Just like Drew, I'm officially done with all of it.

She starts pacing around the kitchen like she is trying to come up with what she wants to say. Well, she's had years to think of this moment.

Every second that passes, my muscles grow tighter and my skin feels hotter. I'm so pissed off I've almost reached my boiling point. She's taking too long!

"Stop moving around and start talking!" She jumps at the volume of my voice. I might have felt bad about this at one time, but today I don't.

"Your father made me tell her that," she says so quietly that I almost don't hear her. Another tear rolls down her face but I'm not swayed. I'm also not surprised by her statement. Maybe I'll get more answers today than I came here for.

I continue to stare at her, the only movement being my eyes—blinking at her.

"Beau, you have to believe me when I say that I love Leila. I knew that she was your best friend and I knew that her leaving was going to be so hard on you, especially after the fire. When he told me that I had to get rid of her, and get rid of her for good, a huge part of me died for all of us: you, her, and me."

"Why?" At the mention of him, my hands ball into fists.

"He didn't think she was good enough. Her blue-collar family wasn't the type of family that he wanted us to associate with."

"So you lied to her and me. You've lied for years. You have had so many opportunities to tell me this, yet you never did; all of this time, and the fakeness that you've even exhibited around her over the last year and half… Why didn't you tell me?"

"You don't understand. Those years were not good for me, either. I'm trying to forget them. I don't want to talk about them."

"You don't want to talk about a lot of stuff. Tell me, did he have her father fired? Was it all a set-up?"

She gasps. "What makes you think that?"

"We all lived under the same roof! He wasn't discrete in anything that he did. Knowing him, he purposely used his bullying ways to get what he wanted, and he probably had something to do with all those fires, too. It's just too coincidental what happened to Leila's family. It all seems premeditated, and I'm surprised that no one else has put two and two together. Don't you find it interesting that when he went to jail, the fires stopped? There hasn't been one in a year and a half."

"Beau . . ." Her face is wary and her expression is guarded. She knows a lot more than what she's telling.

"I know you have answers. Why won't you give them to me? Why, Mom? Why did you go along with him? Why did you let him do this to us for years? Why didn't you ever tell me the truth? I need to know!"

"Why do you need to know? Can't we all just move on?"

"Because I need to know! And, no, I can't just move on! Don't you get it? He chose me to be his punching bag. He chose me to degrade the loudest, not only with his voice but his fists, too. He chose me to hate the most. Yes! I have to know why. What did I ever do that was so wrong? Why didn't you love me enough to protect me? All of this . . ." I sweep my hands out and around the room, "has shaped me into the person that I am today. Why did you force away the one good thing that was mine?"

"Because, Matt isn't your father's," she gasps, her hands fly up to her mouth, and her eyes are huge.

I'm speechless and confused. My mother just confessed to me that she had an affair. Not that I could blame her, given what she was married to. So many thoughts are firing through my head, but the one that sticks is that Matt is only my half-brother. Not that it makes a difference to me, but it probably will to him, and this causes my chest to tighten with worry for him.

Slowly, she lowers her hands and stands a little taller.

"I'm not going to tell you who his father is. Frankly, it isn't any of your business and, when I decide to tell Matt, he will be the first person to know. You will not say anything to him."

I can't argue with this and my heart aches at what Matt has gone through, when he could have been somewhere else, with someone else who could have loved him.

"Matt was born with anemia. He didn't have enough red blood cells to carry oxygen throughout the body, and needed a blood transfusion. I didn't know this. They had given me a sedative to help me sleep and asked your father for the blood. Well, you can imagine what happened next. He wasn't a match to Matt. Two weeks later, your grandfather died. Your father had worked for him for over ten years and he was certain that, if and when the time came, the business would be left to him . . . only it wasn't. He still kept his job and his income, but as you know your father, he was outraged. I, however, had slipped into a postpartum depression that was intensified with grief from the loss. Prior to his death, I had planned on leaving your father. He must have caught wind of this, so he had me sign some documents that were supposedly business-related— only they weren't. They were forms terminating my parental rights. I should have read them, but he was yelling at me to sign, so I did. If I divorced him or left, then the two of you be-longed to him, and as for Matt, well that's another story. I wouldn't have even been allowed visitation. I spoke to a lawyer about it once, but she said with the affair, the depression, and the signed documents, he could prove that I was unfit and I would most likely lose. After all, a signed document is a signed document. In the end, I chose not to say anything. I know that for several years, things were not good around here, but every night I went to bed thinking of you three, and that this time of your life really is short in the grand scheme of things, and it was almost over. I know I probably made the wrong decision, but what could I do? I couldn't leave you. What kind of life would you have had then? My fear was worrying more about the unknown of what was happening to you boys than the fear of being here. I love you, Beau. I know life hasn't been easy on you and I'm sorry. None of it was ever your fault. It was always mine."

After Dad went to jail, she apologized to us a few times, but that was it. She's very closed off and never truly lets her emotions show, so I often wondered if she really was sorry about what we went through or not. Even though I am an adult now, and living on my own, her saying that she loves me and that it wasn't my fault still affects me. My eyes well up with tears and I shake my head to try and clear them.

She walks out of the kitchen into the office, and then returns with a stack of papers. Laying them across the counter, she pulls out a pen, and hands it to me.

"What's this?" I ask, looking down at the pages.

"Your grandfather didn't want your father to have any part of the business. He never really liked him. In his will, he left the business to his family: me, you, Drew, and Matt. We each own twenty-five percent of it. If your grandfather had left it all to me, then your father could have divorced me and taken half of the business and all its net worth. This way guaranteed that he didn't have access to it. Don't get me wrong, your grandfather loved all three of you and would have done any-thing for you. All of these years, I have acted as your fiduciary and any money earned went into individual trust accounts. I've also decided to sell the company. As of January first, the busi-ness is sold. You, Drew, and I will each have access to the money immediately, and Matt will when he turns eighteen."

"Does Drew know about this?" I'm shocked by what she is telling me.

"No; I was actually planning on calling both of you to-morrow night."

Flipping through the document, I do see that it is a buy/sell agreement. I sign the papers and push them back across the counter to her. Looking up, I see that she's watching me closely.

"I'm sorry for your childhood, Beau. Believe it or not, every single bit of every second of it hurt me, too. But, hope-fully with what you have already received in your inheritance, and with this, as you begin your adulthood you'll be able to put this behind you, move on. I hope it's not too late for you to chase after every dream you've ever had. You, of all people, deserve the world."

There's only one thing I want to chase after, and there's only one dream I've ever had . . . and it's time to go get her.

My heart rate starts to pick up a little with excitement.

Giving her a small smile, I reach across the counter and squeeze her hand. She's never been too affectionate, and this takes her by surprise.

I grab the Jeep keys off the hook and, as I'm about the walk out the door, she calls my name.

"Beau." I turn around to face her. "At the time, I really didn't think that things would turn out this way. I thought you loved her enough to fight for her. I never thought that you would let her go."

"When you hear daily that you'll never be enough and that no one will ever want you it kind of sticks. What did you really expect?"

Her eyes are watery. "I'm sorry."

It is time to put all of this behind me, and I can't stand here and listen to any more. I need to go and there is only one place that I'm going, and that's to her.

BEAU

WALKING DOWN THE trail to Bean Point, something in the bottom of my heart tells me that she's going to be here. I didn't even stop by her parents' house. If she flew here, to the island, then she's at our spot on the beach. Leila has always been the type to suffer in silence and not talk about how she's feeling, which is why no one knew exactly what had happened when we were fourteen.

Reaching the top of the dunes, sure enough, I see her sitting by herself on our bench. No one is around today, leaving the beach and its surroundings completely undisturbed. She is so beautiful. I pause to take a mental picture of her in this moment; a moment where I'm going to lay it all out there. A moment that I hope is about to change and solidify everything for us.

In classic Leila style, she is wearing a pale blue sundress and her hair is blowing around her shoulders in the breeze.

What upsets me, though, is that her hands are folded into her lap and she's fidgeting with her fingers. Her shoulders are hunched over slightly, and she looks defeated and sad. I don't want her to be sad anymore. I want to make her happy. I want to see her smile . . . no, I need to see her smile.

As I close the distance between the two of us, she must hear me and looks up. Her eyes are red, watery, outlined with dark circles, and they grow huge. She looks exhausted.

"Am I dreaming right now?" she whispers as I sit down next to her. The look in her eyes is indescribable. If I ever had any questions about how she truly felt about me, they are immediately erased by the affection and awe that is shining in them.

A piece of her hair flips my way in the breeze, and lavender fills my senses. She smells so good. I tuck the hair behind her ear and take a second to soak her in. Why I waited so long to fix us, I will never know. There is no one else for me. There never will be.

"Here," I finally say. "I thought we could share like old times." I set a clear bag in her lap and pull out two bottles of soda from a small brown paper bag. She looks down at the bag filled with salt water taffy, grabs a hold of it tightly, and tears begin to drip down her face.

"Leila." Her eyes return to mine and my heart breaks and melts at the same time. "Please don't cry."

She looks back at the candy in her lap and sniffs.

Trying to think of something that will make her happy or lighten the mood, I say the first thing that pops into my head. "Did you know that, for most people, if you pinch the skin under your elbow as hard as you can, it won't hurt?"

Her eyes flip my way and a small smile graces her lips. I made her smile.

309

"So what are you doing out here?" I ask her as I reach over and cover her hands with one of mine.

She looks up at me through her eyelashes and her eyes scan my face. There's uncertainty in them but there's determination, too.

"Plotting out fifty different ways I plan on getting you back," she says, so matter-of-factly.

This makes me chuckle. I honestly didn't expect her to say that. "Oh yeah? So what have you got so far?"

She lets out a deep sigh but gives me a tiny smile. "For starters, I plan on sitting outside your door until you let me in. I don't even care how long it takes."

My smile grows a little bigger. "Kind of hard to do from here, don't you think?"

"Yeah, which is why I just finished booking my flight back." She pulls one of her hands out from under mine and flashes her phone at me. "It leaves tonight."

"Is that so?" Angling my body a little more toward her so our knees are touching, I flip her other hand over and lace my fingers through it.

"Yes. Come tomorrow morning, you would have found me on your doorstep." Her voice catches. She swallows, licks her bottom lip, and turns her head to look out over the water.

"I would have been happy to see you," I say quietly, watching her.

Her fingers squeeze mine and then another tear appears and rolls down her face.

"Lei, please, *please* don't cry." I tug on her hand so her eyes come back to mine.

"I can't help it. I'm just so sad," she whispers, dropping her head a little.

"I don't want you to be sad anymore." I run my thumb

across the back of her hand. Her hands are so soft.

She turns to look at me. "Beau . . . you don't understand; it's all I can think about. The things that happened to you and the part that I played, I'm stuck right now and I can't move past it. My heart hurts so much for what you went through. You are the one person in this world I never want to hurt, and I hurt you in the most horrible way."

More tears drop and, with my free hand, I reach up and wipe them away.

"It doesn't matter anymore; all of that happened a long time ago." I scoot a little closer to her. The closer I can get, the better.

"Yes, it does." She lets out a sigh. "It mattered a week ago when you asked me to leave, and I have to live knowing that this is entirely my fault. I read the first part of your journal. All of the things that happened to you, how you were feeling, I wasn't there for you . . ." She frowns and her chin quivers. "I'm so sorry."

"I'm sorry for how I left things between us last week. I was angry and confused. I think that maybe the sum of all of my emotions from the last six years finally caught up to me, and it wasn't one of my finer moments. I hurt you when I asked you to leave, and *I'm* sorry. I know this week hasn't been easy on you. It hasn't been easy on me either. I must have had a million different thoughts running around in my head, confusing me, but now all of that is gone and I'm certain about a few things." I shift again and gather both of her hands in mine. I need to touch her and I need to hold on to her. "The thing is, Lei, you didn't know at the time and that's not your fault. You can't blame yourself for all of this; I don't want that for either of us. We were both lied to and now it's over. It's in the past. The only thing that I ever wanted to know was why.

Why you left me. And I finally have all the answers. I can't live with what-ifs and I can't have regrets . . . and neither can you. If I had known then what these last six years were going to be like, but in the end, I would make it here, to this bench with you, I would make the same decisions every single time."

She's studying my face, searching for something, but I'm not sure what. Eventually she blinks and then swallows. "I hurt you," her voice is so grief-stricken it makes my chest ache.

"Yes, and I hurt you." She needs to know that she's not alone in this.

"It's not the same. I know deep down you deserve so much better, but . . . I can't, and," her eyes lock on to mine, "I won't let you go."

Hearing her say that she's not letting me go, gives me warmth that is soul deep. I've only ever wanted her to want me. This makes me so happy. I'm flying high.

"Yes, it is the same. And, just so we're clear, you do deserve me and I'm not letting you go either."

She inhales sharply and her eyes grow a little bigger.

Silence hangs between us. She's watching me and I'm watching her. Her big blue eyes sparkle and then she leans into me and tucks her head in my neck. I wrap my arms around her and just hold her. I want to hold her forever.

"So, last year, after my dad went to jail, Mom thought it would be a good idea for her, Matt, and me to go to family counseling." She pulls back to watch me talk. "This psychologist actually said a few things that stuck with me. She said that when children are abused emotionally, physically, or both, that a lot of the time they have relationship difficulties and trust issues. If you can't trust your parents, then who can you trust? And I think that maybe some of that slipped over into our relationship. For years, he told me that I wasn't worth anything and no one would ever want me, including him; especially him. I'd always felt that I wasn't good enough for you, so when you didn't come after the fire," I shrug my shoulders and let out a sigh, "I just gave into it."

She takes her hand and runs it over the side of my face and down my arm. "I'm so sorry, Beau. I never should have listened to her. I have always thought that you are the best person in my whole world and, in general, I don't think the world is good enough for you. You're kind, generous, thoughtful, loyal, and so loving." The sadness seeps back into her as she collects her thoughts. "I broke us and I'm afraid. You just mentioned trust, and once the trust in a relationship is broken, it can never be repaired."

Leaning forward just a little and placing my elbows on my thighs, I look directly at her. I want to be eye to eye, not looking down at her. I need to see into those beautiful crystal clear eyes of hers.

"Oh, Leila, you didn't break us, and I do trust you. You know better than anyone that there are very few people I trust, but those I do, it's because they would never have the heart to lie to me. You didn't lie to me. We both listened to people whose hearts were never in the right place. We should've known that. Excluding what my mom said to you and your letter, our problem over the last couple of years was a fear of communication, not trust. I believe in you and not for one second would I ever hesitate sharing my deepest feelings and fears with you. In fact, I have. Even through all this mess, you were the one I wanted and you are the only one I've ever opened myself up to. Trust for me is someone who is honest, reliable, gracious, and good. You are all of these things to me."

"Beau . . ." her eyes get watery and the tension in them eases slightly.

"Leila, I don't want to feel broken anymore. You've always been the one to put me back together, but I should have been the one to put us back together. In the end, it all comes down to insecurities. You should have had more faith in me and I should have had more faith in you. After removing the heartbreak of that letter and the fear that you were leaving me, I should have known that something must have happened, and I should've tried harder to contact you. You were my best friend and I didn't treat you like it. You deserved better."

Letting out a sigh that seems to push her forward, Leila lays her forehead against mine.

"I never should have listened to your mother," she whispers, shaking her head. "Looking back, there's no way you would have left without trying to say goodbye to me and, had you caught wind that I had been in a fire, I know you would have come for me. I made a mistake by shutting down and closing off the 'you' part of my life. If I had talked to anyone else, I would have known. You were my best friend and I didn't treat you like it. You deserved better."

My fingers tangle in her hair as I breathe her in. Her eyes have slipped shut and she's chewing on her bottom lip.

For years, I wanted her to take responsibility for hurting me, but now that she has, I just want to take it all away. I don't want her to feel guilty and sad. She said that she wants me, but I can tell that she's still nervous I might walk away. Looking around and seeing that the beach is still completely empty, there's only one thing that I can think of to show her exactly how much I trust her, and it's time.

LEILA

"I WANT TO show you something." He looks at me hesitantly and then moves to the edge of the bench. Never breaking eye contact with me, he takes a deep breath and then reaches up over his head to his back, and pulls his T-shirt up and off. For just a split second I see the fear of rejection in his eyes, and then it is gone. Knowing how difficult this is for him, I refrain from showing him any kind of emotion.

I'm frozen, watching him. I haven't seen Beau without a shirt on in over six years, and even though he is wearing pants, to me right now, he is completely naked. His chest and stomach are pale in comparison to his arms and face. It's easy to see that he never takes his shirt off. Gently, he takes my hand in his and places my palm flat over his heart. I can feel it pounding in his chest. It's beating frantically and this causes me to move my eyes from his chest to his eyes. His eyes are wary but I can see he is certain that he wants to do this.

My hand trembles under his. His skin is warm and I can't help but to lean into him again and lay my head on his shoulder. His free arm wraps around me to pull me closer, and my other arm moves around him to hug him tighter.

My hand rests on his back and over part of the scar. He tenses and so do I; neither one of us moves.

A breeze blows by, ruffling the hair on his forehead and the sea oats make a swooshing sound in the wind. I lift my head, and his eyes lock onto mine. He's watching my reaction to the changes in his skin very closely. I raise my head a little higher and place my forehead against his. Slowly, I move my hand from his chest, under his arm, and around to his back.

Without even seeing the scars, I can feel how prominent they are. No wonder he is so self-conscious about them. Gently, with my hand flat, I rub up and down his back, soothing him like one would a child. My fingers slip in and over the contours of his skin. Some areas are smoother than others, and my eyes drift shut as I take in the feel of finally having him, just him, in my arms.

"No one touches me." His voice is quiet and shaky. "No one has touched me since the day they cleared me from rehabilitation.

"Do you want me to let go?"

"No, Leila, I never want you to let me go." He tilts his head and his lips brush and settle against mine. It is such a tender kiss from him that my heart squeezes.

Calmly and affectionately, I continue to slide my hands up and down his back. He's shaking and his breathing is hard.

"I want to show you," he says to me as he leans back.

"Only if you're sure; I don't ever want to make you uncomfortable."

He doesn't say anything in return. He pulls my arms from around him and slowly turns around. I smother and swallow down the gasp that I want to let out. My eyes blur with tears and, cautiously, I lift my hand and lay it on him.

His hands grip his thighs as I gently begin to trace the outline of the Summer Triangle. Yes, the scar is there, and it breaks my heart because I know it's there because of me, but it's not what has left me speechless. He's tattooed our stars on his back.

"You need to understand," he says. "When I see you, I see beautiful. I see calm. My heart smiles. No matter what we have been through, just the thought of you brings me peace.

Yes, the scars are there and they are permanent but, Leila, so are you. On bad days when I turn around and see what has become the ugliest part of me, I don't see the scars, I see the stars. I see you instead. I had these stars tattooed on before you even moved back to the island. You are my North Star and with you I always feel grounded and like I am being led home."

I don't know how to respond to what he just said to me and my mind has gone blank. He's right; the scars are there, but I don't see them either. I only see the stars.

"They're beautiful," I say to him, while running my fingers over them again. I desperately want to kiss each one, but I know that would cross a line with him today. He's already taken such a monumental step toward me that I would hate to push him more out of his comfort zone than he already is.

He turns back around and wraps his hands around my head. "You are beautiful."

"I'm sorry, Beau." And I am. I'm so sorry for all that he has had to go through and for all that I missed out on. I wish that I had been there for him, just like these stars. A lump forms in my throat.

He looks at me questioningly and uses his thumbs to wipe away fallen tears.

"Tell me how to take this away from you. I don't want you to feel sorry anymore. I want us to move past this."

"I'm trying, I am."

"Leila, I forgave you, I forgave myself. I need you to do the same."

I know I need to forgive myself, but it's hard when you love someone as much as I love him and feel responsible. But, I'm better and stronger today than I was yesterday, and I will fight for him always, because he's worth it.

"Do you want to be with me?" he whispers, looking over my shoulder and not at me.

"I am with you. Haven't you figured that out yet? There has never been anyone else, only you, and I plan on keeping it that way."

His eyes come back to mine and I look deep into his beautiful hazel eyes. They are clear. Clear of pain, clear of anger, and clear from all confusion. I used to look in them and see uncertainty. Now, with all his walls down and all his questions answered, all I see is complete adoration.

"You're right. I should have figured that out sooner." He takes a deep breath and his thumbs swipe again across my cheeks. "I love you. I have loved you my whole life. There has not been one minute or second when I didn't love you."

I tilt my head a little in his hands. His fingertips apply pressure and I feel it all the way down into my stomach. If I could stop breathing to freeze time, I would. I have waited so long to hear those three little words from this beautiful soul sitting next to me that, in many ways, my life just changed.

"And I love you. I've loved you for so long."

His eyes soften and the pace of his breathing increases. A small smile graces his lips and I return one, knowing that I just made him happy. I want to make him happy forever.

Closing the distance between us, my mouth meets his, and today feels like the first day of my life. This kiss isn't desperate or filled with years of longing; it's filled with forgiveness and understanding. I feel hopeful. I feel proud that he chose me, and I feel loved—so loved.

Beau lays his face next to mine, cheek to cheek. I love the closeness to him. He lets out a sigh, but this one is of relief, not resignation. I wrap my arms around him again, and he tenses underneath me.

"Sorry, just not used to it yet." He lets out a shaky breath.

"It's okay." I pull back to look at him. He picks up his shirt to put it back on. Carefully, I take it from him and slide it over his head. He slips his arms through and shakes it down into place.

"Thanks." Instantly he's more comfortable—less tense— and he smiles at me.

"Want to go for a walk?" I ask.

"I'd love to go for a walk with you." He stands up, puts a few pieces of taffy in his front pocket, and then shoves one soda into his back pocket. "Ready to go?" he reaches for my hand.

Sliding my hand in his, our fingers lace together, we walk over the dunes and down to the water's edge.

"So which one do you think we should buy?" He looks down at me and smiles.

"Which one what?"

"Of those houses over there." He points to the beachfront homes that look out over Bean Point.

I start laughing. It feels so good to laugh. One hour ago, I felt like my life was hanging on by a thread and, now, I'm here with the one person I love more than anything and he's talking about buying us a house.

"I don't care which house, as long as I'm with you."

Beau stops walking, bends down, and picks me up around the waist. Our bodies are flush together and my arms slide around his neck.

"It makes me so happy to hear that," he mumbles against my lips, kissing me. I love when he kisses me. There's never a question about where I belong in those moments. He takes control and reminds me that I'm his, and he's mine.

He drops me to my feet and we start walking again, "So,

yeah, back to that house discussion . . . I wasn't kidding."

"We can't afford one of those houses." I look at him like he's crazy and he returns it with a smug one of his own.

"Turns out we can. You and I have a lot to talk about." He wraps one of his arms over my shoulders and pulls me tight up next to him.

"It's a good thing I love to hear you talk," I say, looking up at him.

He smiles down at me and his eyes light up as he thinks of something. "Lei, did you know . . ."

I start laughing, cutting him off, and he laughs with me.

"You know eventually you are going to run out of those fun facts."

"Never!" he smirks at me. "I've got a lifetime of them saved up for you."

"Promise?" I ask him.

"Promise." His eyes lock with mine and he bends down to give me a soft, sweet kiss. Beau doesn't really do sweet, so this kiss is a promise, and in his own way he's just sealed the deal.

Reaching into his pocket he pulls us out each a piece of taffy, and hands mine to me. As I pop it into my mouth, I look around at the beach, our beach. The clouds have lifted and the sun is out. It shines across the water and lights up the sand. I'm so happy and content in this moment, I can't help but smile.

I think of all the shooting stars and all the wishing that I have done, and at last my wish has come true. For twelve years I've loved this boy. I've finally told him and he's finally mine.

BEAU

"OKAY, OPEN IT!" she says, shoving a small package my way and bouncing up and down on her toes. Her crystal blue eyes are smiling at me and she's grinning from ear to ear.

It's been three weeks since we came back from the beach. Leila spends most of her time here and I love every second of it.

Looking her over from head to toe, she's wearing a long sweater with tight black leggings. Her hair is down and curls are flying everywhere. She's gorgeous and my heart squeezes.

Leila invited our friends over for a TBT, Tuesday before Thanksgiving, happy hour. In keeping with our friend Grant's tradition, last year Ali hosted and this year we are. Trying to stay out of her way, I've been sitting on the couch watching Nate's brother, Reid. He plays professional football for Jacksonville and he's really good. Drew, Charlie, and I have all enjoyed following him this season. I pause the game on the TV and smile at her. She's so happy it's infectious.

"You bought me a present?" I look at her questioningly.

"Yep, and I really hope that you like it." She plops down

next to me.

"Are you sure you don't want to save it for Christmas?" I ask, glancing back and forth between her and the package.

"Nope, I want you to have it now." She bounces up and down a little bit. She's so excited—it's so cute.

"Okay." Carefully, I pull off the paper and run my fingers across the soft black leather. "You bought me another journal?" I ask, looking at her.

"Yes. I think it's time to pack away the other one. I'm hoping that, together, we can fill this one with new adventures, happy ones." She reaches over and rubs her hand on my leg. I love it when she touches me.

The look on my face must be one of astonishment. She's right; it is time to pack away the other one, but she also knows that I need to write out my thoughts, the good ones and the bad. My current journal holds so many awful memories that I try on a daily basis to forget, and often just seeing it causes many of them to come flooding back.

This journal will be about us, the way it should have been.

"Thank you. I love it." Just like that day so long ago, on the bench, I lean over, place my lips on hers, and give her a sweet small kiss. I purposefully make this kiss feel just like our first one after she gave me the brown journal.

She giggles and I pounce, knocking her backward and underneath me on the couch.

"Hey, this isn't what happened!" She squirms. I know she's also thinking of that day.

"Yes it is." I say smiling down at her. "This is exactly what was happening in my mind that day on the beach."

"In your mind . . ." she giggles again. Pulling my mouth down to hers, she breathes out, "What am I going to do with you?"

I can think of a few things that she can do with me, and all of them involve our clothes being on the floor.

As her soft lips move with mine, I know that I'll never get tired of kissing or tasting her. If I had my way, I would kiss her as much as possible, every day, all day. And it's this thought that tells me it's time.

"Move in with me," I mumble against her mouth.

She pulls away, leaving us just inches apart. A small smile forms on her lips and her eyes sparkle with excitement. "What? It's only been a couple of weeks."

I brush a few pieces of hair off of her face and run my thumb across the freckles on her cheekbone. "No, it hasn't. We've been together for twelve years. Maybe, at times, it was a little untraditional, but I have wanted you every second of every day and I don't want to waste any more time. I want to have dinner with you every night and learn what your favorite foods are. I want pick out Christmas trees and light sparklers on the roof. I want to learn about wine with you. I want to wake up every morning to the smell of the coffee pot going off and look over and see you. I want my every moment to include you."

Her eyes are glistening. She reaches up and wraps her hands around my face. "How can I say no to that?" she whispers.

"I'm hoping you won't."

Not giving her a chance to respond, I close the distance between us and run my tongue across her bottom lip. She tastes like candy and I love candy. Sliding one hand under her backside, I press her into me. She giggles. She feels the effect that she's having on me.

"You do realize that our friends will be here shortly, right?"

"Yep," I say, nuzzling my head into her neck.

Her fingers find the bottom of my shirt. She pulls it up and over my head.

"Well, then, you'd better make this quick," she says to me.

Looking down at her, I grin. She has no idea that, when it comes to her, I can be *really* quick.

Leaning back on my knees, I slip my hands up under her sweater and grab a hold of the leggings and her underwear. I'm determined to get them both off in one move. She laughs as I struggle to pull them down. Damn things are so strong and stretchy.

Once they are finally on the floor, my hands run up and down her smooth legs. She has the most gorgeous legs.

The air between us shifts, and all playfulness is quickly gone. I kiss the inside of her thigh and climb back on top of her, while taking my time to feel every curve.

Her hands find their way to my belt. Never breaking eye contact with me, she pulls it free from the buckle, pops the button on my jeans, and slides down the zipper. Her thumbs hook into the waistband and she pushes them down off my hips. One foot comes up and continues the removal; next thing I know, my jeans and boxer briefs are down around my knees.

Her hand wraps around me. I groan at the contact and she pulls me closer to where she wants me. I'm ready for her and, as I slide into her, both of us let out a sigh of pleasure.

"I love you," she says, wrapping her arms around me, hugging me tight.

At this moment, I realize that I no longer flinch when she touches me. I'm not sure when I stopped, but the significance of this to me is huge. I meant it when I said I trusted her and this just adds another layer to that trust. Contentment washes over me as I sink even further into her and into her arms.

"I love you, too. More than you will ever know."

"Beau, did you know that a pig's orgasm can last up to thirty minutes? Can you even imagine?!" Nate says, grinning.

"Oh, my God, I cannot believe you just said that out loud." Camille frowns at him in complete distaste.

The rest of us break out in laughter.

A light breeze blows over us and the twinkle lights that Matt and I had hung sway.

The weather for the happy hour turned out to be quite nice. Yes, it is briskly cold, but once we turned on the heater lamps, the roof turned out to be the perfect spot. We were lucky tonight to have a semi-clear sky and, together, laughing, the seven of us watched the sun set over the West Village.

Leila bought us a fire pit, and as I toss another log on to it, I look over and across our circle of friends at Nate.

"Why am I not surprised that you would drop a fact like that?" I say, shaking my head at him.

"Just keeping it real, man," he smirks at me and winks at Camille.

"Speaking of keeping it real, let's go around and say one fact about ourselves that people don't know," Leila suggests. "And I'll go first."

She looks over at me and smiles. My eyebrows shoot up. I'm curious.

"Next weekend, I'm moving in with Beau." Her eyes lock on to mine and they are sparkling.

My breath catches in my throat. I just asked her, and even though I didn't give her a chance to respond, I thought that she might need a little time to think about it. I guess not and I'm so happy I could burst. We're sitting next to each other on the couch and, with everyone staring at us, all I can do is link our fingers together and squeeze her hand.

"Thank God! It's about time," says Charlie. "At least this way, I can find a roommate who actually lives with me."

"Hey, now, it hasn't been that bad." Leila breaks eye contact with me and fires back.

"Come on! When you aren't with him, you are either talking to him or about him . . . and quite frankly," he looks in my direction, "no offense, Beau," and then back to Leila, "that shit is girly and I can't handle it."

Everyone busts out laughing. Coming from Charlie, I know it must be bad.

"Okay, my turn," he says, waving his hands in excitement. "I just accepted a job at Interior Design Magazine."

"Really! That's so great, I didn't even know you had applied." Leila is beaming at him. "You've wanted this ever since I met you!"

"I know, I can't believe it's happening. It's not a big job but it's my foot in the door."

"I'm so proud of you." Leila gets up off the couch and gives him a hug.

"Congratulations, man." We all raise our drinks to him and he smiles.

"Beau, your turn," Leila says sitting back down.

I pause and smile at Leila. She gives me the biggest smile back and nods her head. She thinks that now is a good time too. I look over at Drew; his eyebrows furrow out of curiosity. "I've dropped out of Columbia, and I entered the pro-tour."

Drew visibly relaxes and everyone looks at him to see his response. "I think that's a great idea," he says.

I smile at him and a moment of silence passes between us. I didn't need his approval to do this, but knowing that he supports me makes me so happy.

The others are staring at us, but they should know by now, this is our thing. He knows what I'm saying, without having to vocalize it, and vice versa.

"Hasn't that always been your dream?" Ali asks.

My eyes shift left to her. "I wasn't sure. I needed to come here, be by myself, and make these decisions. For so long I hated tennis because it was his chosen sport for me. And although I've always known I was really good at it, I wasn't sure what it meant to me. I needed to be out from under his influence. Does that make sense?"

"Of course it does, and I think that most people would probably feel that way," Camille chimes in.

She's been pretty quiet most of the evening and we all look at her. She sinks back into her chair, not liking the attention.

"I just think it's nice that you are getting to decide what's best for you." She shrugs her shoulders and gives me a small smile.

"Well, I think that just sucks." Nate scowls.

"Oh shut it, Nate. You know you're happy for him." Leila returns his scowl, but squeezes my hand. I love that she supports me like she does. "Quit pouting, it's your turn."

"Nothing too much on my end. Reid is coming home once the season's over. I'm looking forward to seeing him. It'll be good to spend some time with him."

"Really! Do you think I can meet him?" Charlie's excitement just shot through the roof.

"Sure, but, man, tone down the fan-girling."

Everyone laughs again.

"I promise," Charlie says, grinning from ear to ear.

Nate just shakes his head at him.

"Alright, I'm up," Drew looks at Ali and then he looks at me. I chuckle because this is very déjà vu to a few minutes ago. "As of the first of the year, I'll begin Olympic training, and in eighteen months, enter my first trials."

There are some murmurs around the group, but it all drowns out as my eyes widen. "You're really going to go for it." I'm surprised by this and not, at the same time. I'm so proud of him.

He nods his head and smiles. "Seems so."

Both of us stand up at the same time and embrace each other.

"I'm proud of you." I pat him on the back.

He pulls back, "And I'm proud of you." He pats me on the shoulder. He knows me so well.

Sitting back down next to Leila, I see that she has tears in her eyes.

"What's wrong?" Concern instantly fills me. I still hate it when she cries.

"Nothing, that was just really nice," she says.

I look at Ali, and she has tears, too.

"Whatever, enough of that, you two," I say, taking a sip of my beer.

Ali smiles at me and then shifts forward on her seat. "Well, I was just cast as lead principal in our spring production of Sleeping Beauty."

"Yes, and she deserves every bit of it," Camille says shining with pride at her.

"Congratulations, Ali! We can't wait to come and watch

it." Leila grins.

"It could have been yours," Ali says quietly, looking at Camille.

"No, it couldn't have." Camille frowns and lets out a big sigh. "Here goes nothing . . . I'm getting married in February"

"What?" Ali yells at her. "You're engaged? Why didn't you tell me?"

"When did this happen?" Leila's frowning.

Tension builds in the air between Camille, Ali, and Leila. I can't say I blame Ali and Leila; as much time as these three girls spend together, surely getting married should have come up by now.

"Before I moved to New York, and I don't know why I didn't tell you. Honestly, I really don't want to talk about it, but I wanted to ask if you all would come for me."

I remember her saying something about this guy the night I walked her home. She wasn't happy then and she doesn't look happy now. I feel bad for this girl.

"Of course we'll come," Ali says without hesitating. She gets out of her seat, looks over at Leila, and then back to Camille. "Let's go inside for a bit."

Camille smiles and the three of them head back into the house.

"Well, that's enough sharing for me today. I need another beer after that," Nate says.

"No kidding," Charlie replies.

Drew reaches into the cooler next to him and tosses each of us a fresh beer, leaving me for last.

"So, you're gonna go pro," he says, smiling at me.

"And you're headed to the Olympics." I smile back.

A moment of silence passes between the four of us. No one says anything. Drew's eyes are locked onto mine and all the smiling leaves his face. He tilts his head slightly to the side and looks at me earnestly. "I think it's time, don't you?"

I know there is so much more behind this statement than just sports. I can see it is his eyes and feel it pouring out of his heart.

It's time to forgive them all. It's time to let go. It's time to move on. And it's time to own our own futures. It's time.

Letting out a deep sigh, in many ways it feels like a final release. A release that's saying goodbye to a life that I've feared and hated, and goodbye to a life that I am no longer going to allow to consume me. I look up at the stars and then back to him.

"Yes, I do think it's time."

Everyone ended up leaving around eleven. Except for Charlie, the rest of us understand the dedication required to continue dance and sports on a higher level. Practices and rehearsals always start super early and go on for hours. A good night's sleep isn't required but it is highly encouraged, and after all these years of experience, necessary.

Instead of heading inside, Leila and I decided to hang out on the couch under a fleece blanket and let the last of the logs on the fire pit burn down. The night is so beautiful and calm, now that it's just the two of us. I can hear hypnotic melodies floating through the air from the jazz bar across the street.

I'm so content in this moment, and I feel completely at peace.

Since Leila and I have been back together, she has spent

most nights with me. The nightmares haven't come as often, but when they do, she cries. I hate it when she cries. So, I went back to see the psychologist. He said that dreams and nightmares are associated with anxiety and trauma, both of which have and are still affecting me. He also said that nightmares can be interpreted many different ways, but that the way he saw mine, after listening to the details of my past, is it's not that I'm being made to choose between Leila and Matt, it's that I'm afraid I'm going to lose one or both of them.

I've always felt this sense of responsibility to Matt, and even though I am just his brother, our relationship has always been so much more. And as for Leila, with how I felt about her always leaving me, he says that fear of abandonment is a huge part of it. We want to hang on to those that we love and when we fear losing them for one reason or another, our subconscious grasps on to that and sometimes it's hard to escape it.

Every day, I feel like she and I are growing closer. It makes sense what he's saying, because the more confident I feel in us, the less she appears in my dreams. I'm not afraid of losing her anymore. Instead, for the first time ever, I feel hopeful and eager about the future.

Shortly after we got back from Anna Maria Island, I sat down with my coach and we talked about me deferring out of Columbia. Although he's sad to see me go, he said it's where I should be, not competing on a college level. I was also surprised to hear him say that amongst other professionals, I have been labeled as 'the one to watch'. I'm excited about what this opportunity has the potential to bring, not to only me, but to Leila and me both.

Looking down, her head is in my lap, and she's fallen asleep. I brush some of her hair out of her face and just admire her. She has the most beautiful face and heart, and I'm so lucky that she's mine.

Daily, I think about the fire. I think about how quickly that one night, that one thing, that small tiny ten-minute window caused a domino effect in my life that changed everything I thought. But I guess that's life. Things are always going to be thrown our way and it's how we handle and deal with these changes that shapes and defines not only our future, but our character as well.

Everyone has something that they have to deal with. Just thinking about Leila's and my circle of friends and family, life hasn't been easy. Each of us has had challenges that we've had to overcome: abuse, abandonment, illness, death, divorce, disappointment, stereotyping, judgment, and loss. The struggles are there and some are still being dealt with, but we are all strong and, in the end, we know we will prevail. We have to. That's survival, right? Or should I say . . . that's life.

Looking back, I do realize now just how young Leila and I really were. We were fourteen and we were too young to understand that we should have had faith over fear. Faith in each other, faith in ourselves, and faith to know that, in the end, everything always works out the way it is supposed to.

Drew's right; if the fire had happened yesterday, nothing could have kept me from finding her. I meant it on the beach when I said I've forgiven the fourteen-year-old me for giving up so quickly, because I know I never will again. She's worth fighting for.

Laying my head on the back of the couch, I look up into the night sky. In the past, I would have taken a glance and seen that there weren't any stars, but looking now, I know I was wrong. Past the haze that the lights of the city give off, if you focus on the darkness, one by one, little specks of light begin to peek through. And then, before you know it, an endless number of flickering silver dots appear, once again leaving me in awe of their beauty.

I'm not surprised that I never saw the stars before; maybe subconsciously I had blocked them out. Life with the stars meant a life with Leila. Without her, I felt lost, alone, and generally like I was navigating through the dark. But with her by my side, everything is a little bit lighter. She will always be my North Star and with her I know I can find my way anywhere.

Reaching into the pocket inside my coat, I pull out the new journal that Leila bought for me. I'm so used to carrying one on me that, before our friends arrived, I replaced the old one with the new one. It's so clean, fresh and pure. The pages are ivory and untouched. The possibilities of where our adventures will take us are endless.

Placing the journal on the armrest of the couch, I pull out a pen. Flipping to the first page, I run my hand across it. It's so smooth and blank. As the tip of the pen hits the page, I can't help the tears that well up in my eyes. I'm so happy because I know that this journal will be exactly what it is supposed to be.

The Adventures of Us
Adventure #1

I've often thought about the day that I met you when we were eight years old. I know we were just kids and the likelihood of this happening is slim to none, but I truly believe in love at first sight. That's what it was for me. I have loved you every day that I have known you, since we were eight years old. At this point, I should just say I've loved you my whole life, because that's what it feels like.
Three times now you have dropped into my life and all three times, it's as if I am being struck by lightning all over again.

This feeling doesn't get less intense either, it only gets stronger. The first time was when I met you, the second was when you returned to the island, and the third was that fateful morning in the coffee shop.

It's after midnight, which means tomorrow is Thanksgiving.

So, lying under the stars here at our home (yes, I am so excited to say 'our' home), I thought I'd start off by telling you what I'm thankful for.

I'm thankful for sandcastles. They're what brought you to me.

I'm thankful for useless facts. They've always made you smile and I love to see you smile.

I'm thankful for the stars. You'll be happy to know, that yes, I do believe in wishing on shooting stars. As much as the stars have always been a reminder of you, what I didn't have, they've also been a comfort. I knew that wherever you were, when you looked up at the night sky, we would be looking at the same thing and you'd most likely think of me.

I'm thankful for the beach. It gave us hours and hours of time together. My best memories with you have happened on the beach. Even this last one, when it brought us back together.

I'm thankful for time. It's something I felt I didn't have before, but now I do. We may not know just yet what the future holds for us, but I know we'll be holding on to each other as we take our time to figure it out.

I'm thankful for you. You brighten my world and allow me to love. I have so much love that I want to give to you. You do deserve it and I think that for our next adventure, I'm going to come up with twenty-five different ways to say 'I love you,' because I do.

But what I am most thankful for and the thing that I'm most certain about is with you by my side, no matter what life throws at us, or where we end up . . .

I will never ever again have another starless night.

MATT

STANDING, FACING THE Gulf's horizon, my feet sink into the sand as the water washes onto the shore and then recedes. The sun glows orange and the heat from the rays penetrate my skin. Year after year and day after day, I continually find myself in this exact spot, watching the sun as it dips into the water and disappears. Watching, that's what I do. It's become what I'm best at.

Drew and Beau are my two older brothers. Drew is eight years older than me and Beau is seven.

When I was seven years old, I watched Beau almost burn to death in a fire.

When I was twelve years old, I watched Drew fall in love, and be loved in return.

When I was thirteen years old, I watched Beau finally get the girl of his dreams.

When I was fourteen years old, I watched Drew get married.

When I was fifteen years old, I watched Beau win his first professional tournament, The U.S. Open.

When I was sixteen years old, I watched Drew win two gold medals in the Olympics.

When I was seventeen years old, I watched Beau marry the love of his life.

When I eighteen years old, Beau moved back to the island.

When I was nineteen years old, my niece Quinn was born.

When I turned twenty, I finally asked myself, what happens to me? The answer is nothing.

I'm now twenty-one. I've watched as other people's lives have grown, evolved, and changed. But not mine. Mine is exactly the same.

I've never really been included and I've never felt like I truly belonged. But, then again, how could I? I've seen and heard too many things. Lies and secrets. They keep me locked to myself. They're the real reason I stand on the edge of the horizon and I watch from afar.

Even if I wanted to forget, I know that I never could. Every morning when I step out the front door, I'm met with the heat from the sun's rays and I pause to allow my skin to burn. It's a constant reminder of a life that I didn't ask for, but was thrust upon me.

The orange glow, the heat, the burn . . . it's never-ending. No matter what I do or where I go, the sun will be there making everything . . . unforgettable.

From the Author

Thank you for reading *Starless Nights*, book two in the Hale Brothers Series. If you enjoyed this book, please consider leaving a spoiler free review.

Listen to the Playlist for *Starless Nights*
(http://open.spotify.com/user/12146142241/playlist/2IoMplxY
MCRNtkhlyV5zYQ)

OTHER BOOKS IN
The Hale Brothers Series

Drops of Rain
(Book 1)

Starless Nights
(Book 2)

Unforgettable Sun
(Book 3)

Acknowledgments

TO MY HUSBAND, most people know that I am a huge fan of the 'Happily Ever After' and this is all because of you. Every day, I wake up and feel so blessed and happy. You are my perfect person and you make me believe that anything is possible. Thank you for giving me the key. I love you.

To my sweet boys, I love you. Thank you for encouraging me to write my books and follow my dreams. I am the luckiest mom in the world to have the two of you. Although, we'd better be careful, with the endless amounts of peanut-butter and jelly sandwiches you eat while I'm typing away, you just might turn into one. Thank you for being on this journey with me, and as the three of us grow creatively, I can't wait to see what you both write next.

Elle Brooks, my book bestie, we've done it again! I am so proud of us. Every day this journey gets more and more exciting. Just think, in less than a year we've published two books and had a girls' weekend! I'm hoping to get to see you again sometime soon. This book isn't complete without a toast, so cheers to us with our pink Moet Champagne!
http://ellebrooksauthor.wix.com/blog

To my dear friend, Megan C., I don't even know where to begin. Day by day, over the last several months, you have been by my side, line by line for *Starless Nights*. When we first talked about you BETA reading for me, never in my wildest dreams did I imagine that I would find someone as wonderful as you. The amount of time, effort, and care that you put into helping me make this story what it is today, I am speechless and so grateful. You have challenged me to show more, give more, and feel more, I only hope in the end you are as proud of this book as I am. Thank you so much, Megan.

Vanessa, from PREMA, behind every great manuscript is a great editor. I can't thank you enough for the personal involvement and personal touches that you gave to me and to this story. It has meant so much to build a relationship with you that's not only professional, but personal. I've enjoyed our many *many* conversations and I hope that you have too. Thank you for being such an advocate of *Starless Nights*.

Kim H., thank you for proofreading Starless Nights to make it as clean as possible. I appreciate how quickly and efficiently you worked on this manuscript. I feel so much better knowing that your touch of perfection has fingered through, page by page. Thank you... xo

Michelle H., Sejal A., Jenn H, Cindy T., Heather Y., and Donna S., thank you so much ladies for your willingness to BETA read *Starless Nights* in its roughest form to offer me ideas, suggestions, and improvements. Your continued support, which came to me at different times throughout this process, means more to me than you will ever know. I love each of you. Thank you again.

Elexis D., Irma J., Rachel N., and Jennifer S., I don't have a street team, but if I imagined that I did, the four of you would lead the way. Thank you so much for continually sharing my teasers and links to the book community. I'm touched that each of you loved *Drops of Rain* so much that you think the world should know about it. Thank you for your friendship. I can't wait to get to know each of you more.

Michelle B., thank you so much for offering to be my final set of eyes as *Starless Nights* got ready to meet the world. I appreciate how excited you have been for me and that you wanted to be a part of this experience. Much love to you... xoxo

Ari, from Cover it Designs, I love the cover for *Starless Nights* and I love how you have worked your magic into making the series have the same look, like they belong together. That was my hope and vision and you have made it a reality. Thank you. I look forward to working with you more in the future and I can't wait to see what you come up with next!

Julie, from JT Formatting, thank you for being my formatter and for creating the inside look of both *Drops of Rain* and *Starless Nights*. Every time I open one of the paperbacks, I think of you and smile. I love knowing that each manuscript I hand over will come back looking perfect and professional. Thank you for what you do . . .

To the book bloggers . . . Thank you! The book community on a daily basis humbles me. I am awed by the kindness and support that I have been given by so many. I have loved getting to meet, talk, and interact with truly some of the most wonderful people. I know it's because of all of you that *Drops of Rain* has been so successful. Thank you from the bottom of my heart. I can't wait to hear what each of you think of *Starless Nights*. Don't be shy . . . I'll be looking and waiting for your messages. :)

And finally . . . to the readers: Thank you, Thank you, Thank you! If it wasn't for you, this book never would have been written. *Drops of Rain* was intended as a stand-alone, and then the interest in Beau took off. I hope you have loved read-

ing *Starless Nights* as much as I loved writing it. May you never stop wishing on stars . . . Take care . . . Kathryn xoxo

About the Author

OVER TEN YEARS ago my husband and I were driving from Chicago to Tampa and somewhere in Kentucky I remember seeing a billboard that was all black with five white words, "I do, therefore I am!" I'm certain that it was a Nike ad, but for me I found this to be completely profound.

Take running, for example. Most will say that a runner is someone who runs five days a week and runs at under a ten-minute-mile pace. Well, I can tell you that I never run five days a week and on my best days my pace is an eleven-minute mile. I have run quite a few half marathons and one full marathon. No matter what anyone says . . . I run, therefore I am a runner.

I've taken this same thought and applied it to so many areas of my life: cooking, gardening, quilting, and yes . . . writing.

I may not be culinary-trained, but I love to cook, and my family and friends love to eat my food. I cook, therefore I am a chef!

My thumb is not black. I love to grow herbs, tomatoes,

roses, and lavender. I garden, therefore I am a gardener!

I love beautiful fabrics and I can follow a pattern. My triangles may not line up perfectly . . . but who cares, my quilts are still beautiful when they are finished. I quilt, therefore I am a quilter.

I have been writing my entire life. It is my husband who finally said, "Who cares if people like your books or not? If you enjoy writing them and you love your stories...then write them." He has always been my biggest fan and he was right. Being a writer has always been my dream and what I said I wanted to be when I grew up.

So, I've told you who I am and what I love to do . . . now I'm going to tell you the why.

I have two boys who are three years apart. My husband and I want to instill in them adventure, courage, and passion. We don't expect them to be perfect at things, we just want them to try and do. It's not about winning the race; it's about showing up in the first place. We don't want them to be discouraged by society stereotypes; we want them to embrace who they are and what they love. After all, we only get one life.

In the end, they won't care how many books I actually sell . . . all that matters to them is that I said I was going to do it, I did it, and I have loved every minute of it.

Find something that you love and tell yourself, "I do, therefore I am."

Ways to Connect

www.kandrewsauthor.com
https://www.facebook.com/kathryn.andrews.1428
https://twitter.com/kandrewsauthor

OTHER BOOKS IN
The Hale Brothers Series

Drops of Rain
(Book 1)

https://www.goodreads.com/book/show/22046210-drops-of-rain

Unforgettable Sun
(Book 3)

https://www.goodreads.com/book/show/22607887-unforgettable-sun

40003804R00214

Made in the USA
Charleston, SC
21 March 2015